OFF THE LEADER BOARD—PERMANENTLY

"How was he killed?" asked Morris.

"Strangled . . . wi' a wire, I'm certain. An' the toornament only begun!"

"The man insulted the Old Course. He insulted Scotland. Kings and Queens have died for less," Morris said.

"Aye," agreed Tait. "But I dinna ken the killin', e'en of a boorish mon."

"No," agreed Morris. "Half of America would like to strangle him. The other half buys and sells him, joyfully. You have to say the bastard could play the game of golf."

They turned toward a small clutch of figures deep among the rows of timeworn gravestones, and moved toward the body. . . .

Also by John Logue

Murder on the Links

THE FEATHERY TOUCH OF DEATH

At the British Open

John Logue

A Dell Book

Published by
Dell Publishing
a division of
Bantam Doubleday Dell Publishing Group, Inc.
1540 Broadway
New York, New York 10036

ISBN: 0-440-22063-7

Printed in the United States of America

Published simultaneously in Canada

January 1997

10 9 8 7 6 5 4 3 2 1

RAD

To Polly and Hanchey
and the Auburn Logues,
wherever they are

Go fetch to me a pint o' wine,
An' fill it in a silver tassie,
That I may drink, before I go,
A service to my bonnie lassie.
—Robert Burns

THE FEATHERY TOUCH OF DEATH

• CHAPTER ONE •

Julia Sullivan paused on the tall steps of the St. Andrews Golf Hotel. Her light brown hair trembled in the damp breeze off the North Sea far below her. It felt exactly like July, if July came in November. She crossed the street ominously named The Scores and leaned over the old wall, which had its beginning in the year 1200, to marvel at the bathers far below, skittering across the wide beach to splash in the icy water. Down to her right, to the east of the medieval city, low waves crashed against the ruins of The Castle, with its surviving Bottle Dungeon into which victims were lowered by rope to their dark fate.

It was in front of The Castle in 1545 that Protestant reformer George Wishart was burned alive at the stake, while Cardinal Beaton sat and watched in ecclesiastic approval. Two months later, the same cardinal fell into the hands of John Knox and his angry band. And when French troops stormed The Castle a year later, they found the remains of the cardinal floating in a salt solution in the dungeon. Mary, Queen of Scots, had been born in this city, only to have her oft-married head separated from her shoulders here at age forty-four.

Leaning over the ancient city wall, Sullivan could see Martyrs' Monument, rising up above the Old Course with height enough to list all the citizens who had died here in the *comforting* cause of religion.

Sullivan knew that St. Andrews had taken its name from the quiet apostle Andrew, brother of Simon Peter. The Roman governor of Patrae sentenced Andrew to be crucified, his having converted the governor's own wife to Christianity. Andrew's bones were removed to Constantinople and then to Amalfi in 1208. But as recorded by Scottish monks in the Aberdeen Breviary, St. Regulus, or St. Rule, removed "three finger bones, an arm bone, and a kneecap" of the apostle Andrew to "the western limits of the world," which became the shrine and the city of St. Andrews.

The great fourteenth century Cathedral at St. Andrews was stripped of its altars and images in 1559, during the Reformation, and now only its marvelous ruins survived, rising up like an enormous outdoor sculpture, including the intact Tower of St. Rule. The stones from the walls of the cathedral were consumed to build much of the delightful city of St. Andrews, with its third oldest university in Great Britain.

Sullivan didn't know if she was shivering at the sight of the bathers far below or the thought of the religious wars that had raged over the ancient city and all of Scotland. She turned to the west and started down the steep hill toward the true, delicious terrors of St. Andrews: the *continuing wars of golf,* which had been fought within the city limits far back into the mist of the twelfth century. She could see the formidable stone clubhouse of the Royal and Ancient Golf Club, built in 1854. It rose above the Old Course, with a large bay window looking out over the first tee from the Big Room, with a balcony above that on which you expected the captain of the R&A, like the pope, to emerge and bless the multitudes along the green golfing links that swept into the very heart of the city.

Sullivan knew where she would find John Morris, sitting as if he had been there since the Old Course came gradually into being over the centuries. She walked past Martyrs' Monument to the intersection of Golf Place and Golf Links, where the high, temporary bleachers obscured the 18th green in the center of the city. She passed Old Tom Morris's Golf Shop, still in business since the mid-nineteenth century. Now she eased clear of the bleachers until she spotted him, just off the 18th fairway, large enough to make two Scotsmen, resting on his portable seat, one leg draped over the low white rail that defined the Old Course. Just down from Morris was Granny Clark's Wynd, a narrow paved roadway that crossed the 1st and 18th fairways: when there was no tournament being played, sightseers afoot and in automobiles drifted through the playing grounds as they had for hundreds of years; there was even a donkey parade every July. Old Scotsmen were appalled that a traffic light had recently been installed to prevent passing pedestrians from the threat of golf balls driven off the 1st and 18th tees; the old guard would prefer they take their chances as had their fathers and grandfathers before them.

Sullivan paused to see the great Jack Nicklaus walking to his mighty practice drive, which he had flown within twenty yards of the Valley of Sin, which swirled dangerously up to the 18th green. She eased behind John Morris and slipped both of her hands over his eyes.

"Och!" Morris said, in his appropriated accent. "Scottish lassies niver leavin' a mon alone."

"*Niver* my anatomy," Sullivan said, leaning over and kissing him full on the lips, almost toppling the bulk of him off his narrow perch.

"What will the Royal and Ancient members think?" Morris said, both of his feet now on the ground and his breath back in his throat.

"I know those boys," said Sullivan. "They may be royal, but some of them are not so ancient."

Nicklaus had run a chip shot up the Valley of Sin to within two feet of the 18th hole, to the quiet applause of appreciative Scots, sitting and standing in stern judgment. Now Nicklaus was shaking his head and pointing his finger at Morris and Sullivan, as if he'd caught them misbehaving in the open air of Scotland, to the embarrassment of all Americans.

"You're just jealous!" shouted Morris.

Nicklaus only shook his head again and grinned, and turned to his practice putt on the old green on which, eight years ago, he had won the 1970 British Open when Doug Sanders, with the good-time heart and the abbreviated swing, missed a three-foot putt on the 72nd hole to throw the championship into a play-off, which he had no hope of winning against the greatness of Nicklaus.

"So, where did you leave your plane?" asked Morris, not letting go of her arms until she was sitting on the white railing opposite him. He dreaded to think of her flying her Learjet across the Atlantic, even with a copilot, who was probably sleeping beside her as he often did.

"In Edinburgh," Sullivan said. "I rented us a small Ford. But I hid my eyes driving across the terrible bridge over the Firth of Forth. You know how I hate heights."

"Except at forty thousand feet," said Morris, who was always amazed at the contradiction of love and fear in Julia Sullivan. Only in her plane did she love heights. She closed her eyes on the steep escalators in the London Underground. He could thank his old drinking and singing pal, Monty Sullivan, for dying in the terrible car crash and leaving her downtown Denver, along with his U.S. Open and Masters golf titles and money for the bloody airplane.

She read his thoughts, as she so often did. " 'Yes, lad, I lie easy,/I lie as lads would choose;/I cheer a dead man's sweetheart,/Never ask me whose,' " quoted Sullivan with a funny-sad absence of guilt for them both . . . and their living affection for the dead Monty Sullivan.

"Did you find our old room at the hotel?" asked Morris, careful to keep his voice under control.

"Yes. They said they had to ring the room to get you down for breakfast. What? Out with the boys, were you?"

"Best not to ask," Morris said, his head now back to only half-again its regular size. How could he have known so many old champions would be toasting one another and telling lies in the Chariots of Fire, a bare block from his hotel? In the wee hours, it was the longest block he'd walked in his life, and all uphill.

"Well, I feel like a punter," said Sullivan. "Who should I put our hard-inherited money on this year, Yank?"

Morris pointed toward the carefully layered blond hair of Jack Nicklaus, who was walking off the huge 18th green. "Whoever can beat that man will win everything."

"We'd be getting short odds on Jack. But then, the idea is to win the bet," she said, knowing she had a fabulous knack for it.

" 'Nae wind, nae golf,' " quoted a stolid, aristocratic man stepping up behind Morris. He tipped his soft cap toward Sullivan, who stood and kissed him on the cheek, which turned quite red in the chilly air off the North Sea.

Morris propped himself up on his good right leg with his cane and shook the hand of Mr. A.W.B. Tait, captain of the Royal and Ancient Golf Club, himself out among the citizens of St. Andrews, worrying over the Open championship, which had been played successfully since 1860, and first came to St. Andrews in 1873. Tait, with his rugged face denying his steel-gray hair and his seventy years, stood as if bracing himself for some unknown calamity. "Noo, the Old Course does na' 'ave her winds aboot her, Morris," he said, "an' thair's watering to softin 'er." This was the first year that a fairway watering system had been introduced to St. Andrews, taking some of the luck of the hard bounce out of the game, to the consternation of many old Scots.

"But the Old Lady is still wicked," said Morris. "Don't fear they'll disgrace her. Not when the Open title is to be decided and there isn't air enough to breathe in all of Scotland." Morris assured Captain Tait that he did have a press pass, though his twenty-five years with the Associated Press were behind him. Now he was working off a modest contract to capture the Grand Slam of golf in one book, a job that only Herbert Warren Wind, the grand writer for *The New Yorker,* might achieve. But the work would keep him out of too many pubs and next to the game he loved. In truth, it had kept him in a pub into the wee hours, but who was splitting hairs?

" 'Ave ye seen the Open program?" asked Tait, cutting his eyes toward Sullivan.

"I have one in the room for her," Morris said. He was keeping the feature he had written as a surprise. Tait understood and touched his cap and disappeared among the citizens of Scotland; nodding to this one and speaking to that one, golf more surely their lives than the high titles they carried or the menial jobs they held, every man a commoner under the strict articles of the game.

Sullivan nudged Morris to his feet just as he had sat back down. Coming toward them was Old Alec MacLaine, smiling to see them, already touching his old wool cap, which had faded into time with his old wool sweater, with no rain or sleet of Scotland able to penetrate either. In the mist that was now falling off the North Sea, Old Alec was sure to smell as if the wool were still on the sheep. He had caddied the Old Course for fifty-nine years, since he was a boy of thirteen. He'd carried the bags and furnished the local knowledge for all the greats: Cyril Tolley and his storied nemesis and Oxford classmate, Roger Wethered. Oh yes, Hagen and Sarazen. The immortal Bobby Jones. ("Nae gowfer e'er came up to Jones.") Old Alec could count the ripples in Swilcan Burn under the Old Stone Bridge up the 18th fairway or the grains of sand in Hell Bunker. He'd caddied for Henry Cotton and Denny Shute. And the modern greats: Bobby Locke, of the magical putter, and Gary Player and Peter Thomason ("Wis'ist lad to strike a ba' at St. Andrews"). But now the leading professionals brought their own caddies from the four corners of the earth. And Old Alec would catch the bag of some formative young professional or the rare amateur who cracked the field at the Open. Still, on any golfing day, the old man could swing two bags over his shoulders and walk eighteen holes, pausing only to pinch the filters off his cigarettes and pull the smoke, undiluted, into his lungs, with never a show of fatigue.

Morris had written about Old Alec and knew that as a volunteer in WWII, at age thirty-nine, he had made savage, killing, hit-and-run raids on occupied Europe, until he took a bullet in the lungs on the ill-fated raid at Dieppe, his own commandos bleeding and dying with the Royal Regiment of Canada. He was mobbed back to civilian life in St. Andrews to recover and had never left the city since. *Honor* was the one word Old Alec knew could equal *golf.* He would not carry for any American or Englishman or Japanese who rolled his ball over in the fairway or nudged it out of the gorse; no Scotsman, unjailed, would consider such an act.

Catching up to Old Alec, and tugging on his sweater, was a young woman with the fairest complexion Morris had ever seen. The old man ran his huge hand through her short red hair as if she were still a small girl. "Did ye e'er see so comely a lass?'' asked Old Alec, remembering his granddaughter, Sharon, to Sullivan and Morris, who had known her as a skinny little girl chasing after her grandfather, whom she called ''Pa-Pa.'' Sharon blushed as red as her hair. Morris also remembered that her father had died young and that she and her mother, Anne Kirkcaldy, lived next door to Old Alec, who lived alone on Pilmour Links Road, just beyond the Old Course. Morris had given him a lift home more than once when he caddied for Monty Sullivan the year he nearly won the Open. Old Alec's home was a low, seventeenth-century stone house with an old stone barn attached, from the days when sheep grazed among the golfers over the links of St. Andrews.

''I'm up to university next year,'' Sharon said, pleased that the two Americans remembered her.

''What will you study?'' asked Morris.

''I'm thinkin' mathi'matics.''

''Oo, she's the heid for it, Morris, like Pith'uh'gor'us 'isself,'' said Old Alec.

Sullivan could not resist touching her bright red hair and envying its soft, natural wave, short as it was.

''Who are you caddying for?'' asked Morris.

''Yoor guid yuung Yank, Lowrey,'' Old Alec said, not too old to be impressed by a rookie professional. ''Two roonds an' he's na' in the ruif an' niver a bogey.'' He shook his old head at such practice rounds over the Old Course, which had destroyed the confidence of centuries of golfers who first came to it.

''Could he win?'' asked Morris, who was familiar with the young Southerner's rise on the professional tour.

''Aye. But dinna forgit Mr. Nicklaus.''

''I think not,'' Morris said.

Sullivan promised Sharon a ride in her plane and, perhaps, an afternoon in London before leaving St. Andrews. The young woman's fair face blazed with excitement.

Morris couldn't have been more pleased that Old Alec had caught a strong bag for the first time in many Opens. He and Sullivan eased their way to the press tent, which Sullivan crashed with an old press pass pinned to her blouse, her custom at all of the Grand Slam tournaments. They came on Tom Rowe, who continued the tradition of "gentleman golf writer" at *The Times* of London, a standard set for forty-six years by the late Bernard Darwin, grandson of Charles himself and a great student of Dickens and Trollope. It was Darwin who described for all time the feckless career of a sportswriter: ". . . a job into which men drift, since no properly constituted parent would agree to his son starting his career in that way. Having tried something else which bores them, they take to this thing which is lightly esteemed by the outside world, but which satisfies them in some possibly childish but certainly romantic feeling."

"Ah, romance," Morris said aloud, to Julia Sullivan's raised eyebrow.

Tom Rowe, a rail-thin man with a cowlick in his brown hair, interrupted his conversation with defending U.S. Open champion Hubert Green, of Birmingham, to hug Sullivan, while carefully ignoring Morris.

Green had just played the first practice round of his life over the Old Course. Asked about the luck of the hard bounce on the Scottish links, Green said, "If you don't like it, don't come." As for the enormous double greens on fourteen of the holes, he laughed, "Those aren't greens. They are enormous house plots. I'd like to own one." Green did not pretend to yet know where all the bunkers lurked on the course, and he had been startled to play with the wind in his face going out, then to have it quiet playing "round the loop," only to find it blowing in his face again on the way home. Green had finished among the top five players in the Open three times in the last four years, and was low scorer in 1977, behind the priceless, head-to-head battle of Watson and Nicklaus at Troon, won, of course, by Watson, with Tom's final round 65 to Jack's 66.

Tom Rowe liked Green's chances at St. Andrews and told him so as he left to work on his putting.

Finally turning to Morris, Rowe said, "Sullivan, I'm proud you're here. I hope you can get this man out of the pubs at a decent hour."

"It was my *friends* who wouldn't let me go home," insisted Morris. "You know the British press . . . a rowdy lot. Who do you favor, forgetting Mr. Nicklaus?"

"Then I suppose we could forget the American Revolution," said Rowe. "I am not trying to promote Lee Trevino as favorite," he said, using the exact words he was to write for tomorrow, as if rehearsing his own copy. "He's been delayed in that play-off in America, hasn't seen the course. But the man has won the Open twice."

"If he's fit, Trevino's accuracy and touch around the greens suit the Old Course," agreed Morris. "What do you think of Barry Vinson?"

"A splendid golfer. And end of commentary," Rowe said. "I have a deadline, old man, but you wouldn't know about that with your fat book contract . . . that gives you years to type a sentence." He tipped his notepad to Sullivan.

"I think our boy Vinson has as many friends among the press in Scotland as he has in America," said Morris. "You could put them all in the hole your finger leaves in a glass of water."

"He's sexy," Sullivan said, to annoy him.

"You'll have to get in line," said Morris. "In fact, look who's taking the mike."

At the front of the press tent, Barry Vinson stood up

to his full 6′2″, 185 pounds, with his thick blond hair awry on his head, looking as angry as the man under it. Vinson was a two-time PGA champion, a Masters champion, and had won the British Open at Royal Birkdale in England. He seemed on fire with anger.

"This tournament has become a *royal* pain in the ass," Vinson said to the startled silence, many of the writers just now looking up from their typewriters and word processors to see who was talking. "And the *ancients* who are running it have nothing more to do than put a microscope to the grooves of my golf clubs," said Vinson. "Are they measuring the grooves in Christy O'Connor's clubs? Who knows how deep the fucking grooves are in his fucking golf clubs?"

Vinson would be quoted, vulgarity for vulgarity, in the London tabloids. Morris smiled to think how Tom Rowe would manage to quote him in the ever-proper *Times*. It would make a wonderful opening paragraph in his own gentlemanly book.

Vinson was just getting his second wind. "If they don't want a former British Open champion in the field, I'll get on a goddamned airplane and go home."

"Frightfully sound idea," came a voice at the front of the tent, provoking a burst of laughter that infuriated Vinson even further.

"Oh, no," Vinson said. "I can get around this third-rate Old Course with a goddamned broomstick." He later agreed to be photographed for the tabloids addressing his ball with a broomstick, to the unspoken outrage of members of the Royal and Ancient Golf Club and the citizens of Scotland, and to the embarrassment of the other American golfers, who did not hesitate to speak their minds, as did Tom Watson, saying: "The Old Course and the British Open were the heart and soul of the game before any of us ever picked up a club, and they will continue to be long after we are gone from the scene. It is a privilege to put a tee in the ground at St. Andrews."

Small wonder that Watson was one of the best-loved American golfers in Scotland since Bobby Jones himself. Ironically, a few years later, Watson had to discard his own irons because *their* grooves were measured to be too deeply cut. Watson, of course, picked out another set without a whimper.

Writers fell on the story as if it had come from the gods, saving them from tedious quotes on the eve of the championship. Several called for the "Ugly American" to be cast out of the tournament for his "insulting and vulgar remarks." Local citizens, a few caddies among them, suggested in the pubs that the old Bottle Dungeon be put to use again in the castle. Members of the Royal and Ancient took the more effective action: they *ignored* Barry Vinson, as if he had not yet come into existence, refusing to make even one comment on his outburst.

Morris decided to wait on the edge of the controversy until the next day, when he figured Vinson himself would be sick of it . . . not to mention his agents in America and Europe, who had to be frantic at the massive reaction to his remarks.

Sullivan, snooping around their hotel, told Morris, "The hot scamp is that Vinson is not renewing his contract with British Easywear. That he is dumping them for more money in the States. But this uproar could upset his plans."

"I imagine Easywear will be happy to unravel the contract for him," Morris said.

Morris looked up Sir Arthur Maxwell, whom he had long known and enjoyed. In the late 1940s, Arthur's father had expanded his then modest sports fashion line to America, where it found a willing audience among the country club set. Morris himself was wearing one of their old sweaters, whose label he delighted in showing to Arthur.

"My God, Morris, small wonder we are struggling," Maxwell said. "How can we make a profit if a man doesn't buy a new sweater *every twenty years*?" He laughed, but did not disguise his own true dilemma. "Unfortunate remarks by young Vinson, who will live to regret them," said Maxwell. "Our line under his name does extremely well in America and around the world." Maxwell winced to admit it. "Not an attractive man, but he looks exceedingly fine in his clothes. My father warned me of him. Death is an unsatisfactory state in every respect, Morris, especially when you were very right and cannot stand up to say so."

Maxwell laughed again at himself. At age forty, he would have looked very smart in an ad for his own sportswear, with his solid physique and small, becoming mustache. Morris knew Maxwell had been heavyweight boxing champion of Cambridge, and he hadn't gained a pound under his wide shoulders.

"What'll you do?" asked Morris. He added, "Don't worry about my stuff, I'm writing a book that won't be out for years . . . if ever."

"I'll hope the very bastard wins the Open," admitted Maxwell. "And that the American company will fear to sign him. So that I can re-sign him to a new contract. That's an embarrassing admission. But my company is in profound trouble, Morris. The sharks circle this small island hoping to swallow us up . . . and perhaps they will."

"I'm sorry," Morris said. "You make a damn good sweater. And I promise to buy a new one."

"Oh, don't go that far, old man," cautioned Maxwell, his smile not concealing the true pain in his face.

Morris feared for Maxwell's company, but not for the man, not with the set of his jaw. Young Vinson had better temper his language when he dealt with Sir Arthur Maxwell.

Morris watched to see which Jaguar Barry Vinson was driving, and waited near it in the car park after his Wednesday practice round. Ironically, the young Floridian was alone, as if the twenty-four-hour media virus had burned itself out, which, of course, it had not . . . and never would.

"You got a minute?" asked Morris. He had known the young man since he was an ill-tempered junior player of great promise, and had seen him win his two PGA titles and his Masters championship. Morris had watched for some sliver of generosity in Vinson, but had never seen it. How a golfer treated his caddy was a great barometer of his character, and Vinson alienated a new caddy about once a month.

"Shit, get in line, fellow," Vinson said to Morris. He had a maddening way of calling everybody *fellow*.

Morris ignored it. "You can never unsay it, Barry. You know that."

Vinson, his car keys in his hand, thought about it. "You're right. But they won't forget me, *fellow*."

"No," admitted Morris. But memory could make a cruel revenge, he thought. "In truth, does the golf course suit you?"

"Yes," admitted Vinson. "You know I grew up putting goddamn Bermuda grass greens. I hate the fucking slick greens at the U.S. Open, cut and rolled by idiots. The only way I won in Augusta was to overpower the par fives. I could two-putt 'em and still make birdies, and just lag the putts on the other stupid greens. Only two par fives out here, *fellow,* but I can strangle 'em. The greens roll all over the goddamn place, but they're not so slick I can't get a feel for 'em. If I can just keep from making ten at the goddamn stupid Road Hole, I will win this tournament. Shit, I've been playing my new irons for two months. Just thought I'd throw a little life into this goddamned past-tense country. And you can write it, *fellow.*" He put the key in the door of his courtesy Jaguar.

Morris had had an island-ful of young Mr. Vinson. "Barry, you ever read a story: 'A Good Man Is Hard to Find,' by Flannery O'Connor?"

"Who the fuck is she?"

"She wrote . . . She quoted a misfit killer: 'She would have been a good woman . . . if it had been somebody there to kill her every minute of her life.' Lucky Flannery O'Connor never met you, *fellow.*"

Vinson left the key in the door and turned his frustration on John Morris.

Morris took a half step forward, until he was nearly against him, propped his cane on the Jaguar, and looked *down* at the 6′2″ young man and shamelessly hoped he would say *fellow* one more time.

Vinson stood for only half a minute, thought better of it, turned, opened the door to the Jaguar, and cranked it, abused the engine, and muscled it out of the car park.

The Royal and Ancient Golf Club members stuck to their guns not to be quoted on the subject of Barry Vinson—though Morris learned they had filed a formal complaint with the PGA of America, which had no control over the British Open. It might, however, censure one of its members for behavior detrimental to the game of golf. And perhaps they would.

Morris had also deliberately waited to seek out one Gerald Balfour-Melville Dougall, a member of the rules committee of the Royal and Ancient. And a man who loved the sight of his own name in print. Dougall would know why the grooves in Vinson's irons came to be measured. Morris suspected the rich, burly Scotsman ached to give his opinion on the matter. He was not wrong. He caught up with Dougall on Wednesday, the day before the Open began; he was walking down the No. 2 fairway, checking on a particular spot of ground under repair.

Dougall was a large, powerfully built man, who affected a full beard and played golf to a stern four-handicap, his game more a thing of power than control. He was better known for the shrewdness of his bets than his mastery of golf.

A.W.B. Tait had told Morris, privately, that all of Dougall's wealth and shrewdness had not bought him the captaincy of the Royal and Ancient Golf Club. He said he himself had warned Dougall that only a man "with an honest love of the game" would hold that office. Tait said that he held "some faint hope" the man might change his attitude. Tait also told him how Dougall came about his illustrious middle name. It seemed his father claimed a kinship to Leslie Balfour Melville, a great golfer of the nineteenth century and a much-loved figure at St. Andrews, and that his father bestowed the one-time British Amateur champion's name on his only son, who gloried in it.

Tait said members of the Royal and Ancient tolerated Dougall, and his father before him, for the memory of his grandfather, who had been captain of the R&A and much respected at St. Andrews—for his love of golf more than for his financial empire, which had been passed along to his grandson.

Dougall recognized Morris from Opens past, when he wrote for the Associated Press, with its overwhelming access to America's media. The Scotsman had but a faint native accent, having been shipped off to public schools in England since he was eight years old. He had a powerful grip, but his large hand fit easily inside of Morris's.

Morris wasted no time on pleasantries. "I'm under contract for a book on golf's Grand Slam tournaments," he said to Dougall. "It won't be out for two or three years. I thought you might want to have your say about the grooves in Mr. Vinson's irons . . . and his response to the action by the Royal and Ancient."

"Na' to be shared with the daily press?" said Dougall, putting one hand to his beard as if reaching for a certain wisdom.

"No," Morris said.

"Vinson meant ta cheat th' game," said Dougall. "He knew o' the grooves. I've collected many clubs, but na' a dishonest one. He's a cheat and a bloody rude bastard. Put tha' in your book."

"Did you personally measure the grooves?" asked Morris.

"Aye." Dougall was pleased to say so.

"Did you check the clubs of any other golfers?"

Dougall, reluctantly, shook his head no.

"What made you suspect Vinson's?" asked Morris.

Now Dougall was not at all comfortable, tugging at his beard, buying a little time. "Tip from one o' the lads," he finally said.

"Sure. A caddy fired by Mr. Vinson," Morris said.

"It's na' my place to say." Dougall's teeth showed jaggedly through his dark beard.

"Do you agree with the Royal and Ancient's policy of 'no reply' to Vinson's behavior?"

"Na'. I'd kick him oot of Scotland and 'is damned clubs with him," said Dougall.

Morris had all he needed from the burly Scotsman. It took him most of the afternoon to run down Vinson's ex-caddy, an American college kid, Paul Mason, from Atlanta. He'd dropped out of Georgia Tech for a quarter to carry Vinson's bag, more as a lark than a scheme to make money.

"What did your parents think about your decision?" asked Morris, having identified himself and his project.

"They were underwhelmed," Mason said. He was a rather thin, but obviously strong, young man with an appealing grin and a thick, dark head of hair that he kept rather short.

"What happened with Vinson?" asked Morris.

"It hasn't been easy," Mason said. "I caddied for him in three tournaments in the States. The man can play golf. But he can be a pain. Even when things go well—you read a putt correctly and he sinks it—he takes it for granted. If you walk quickly, he complains you're hurrying him. If you try to time your steps with his, he says, 'You're dragging ass again.' You can't win. I knew his reputation. I thought I could make it for a summer. See something of the world. Watch him play. Improve my own understanding of the game. I'm just a stroke or two away from making the Georgia Tech team. I can hit the golf ball. It's my short game that kills me. I have to say, I've learned a lot. But you wanted to know what happened here?"

The young man realized he had been rattling on and was embarrassed.

Morris nodded.

"It's a bit embarrassing. I was having a beer with some fellow caddies and a couple of locals . . . at the Bull and Bear pub."

It was a pub near the Old Course that Morris and Sullivan had frequented at British Opens since their first pilgrimage to St. Andrews.

"And I met a young girl," Mason said. He, himself, was not too old to blush. "And who comes in the pub but Vinson, and he starts hitting on the girl. Maybe just to annoy me. I don't know."

"What did the girl think?" asked Morris.

"Truthfully? She seemed rather impressed. Oh, he's known in St. Andrews."

"What happened?"

"I told Vinson we were having a private conversation. And he tipped a beer in my lap," said Mason, his face full of remembered anger. "He did it on purpose. I challenged him about it. He said to bug off. I lost it. I stood up and told him I was going to whip his ass. He's a big guy. But I know my way around a boxing ring. I think I could've done it."

Morris had the idea that he might've, at that. "And?"

"He fired me. Right that instant. It got pretty nasty. I told him he was a disgrace to the game of golf."

"What did he say?"

"He laughed."

"And you told the R&A about the illegal grooves in his irons," suggested Morris.

"I did *not,*" Mason said. "After the blowup . . . he left the pub. I was seething. And somewhat worried, though I did have a plane ticket home. I was agreeing with the lads in the pub, that Barry Vinson was a prick. And I said to them that I had noticed the grooves in his irons seemed to have been filed deeper since the last tournament. That I wouldn't put it past him. That I had intended to ask him about it. One of the guys in the pub must have said something to the R&A. I did *not.*"

Morris believed him. "How will you pay your expenses home?"

"I called my mom," admitted Mason. "She's wiring me some money. My dad is still hot that I'm not working for him this summer. But he'll get over it. I'm going to stay and see the Open. I may never have another chance."

"What happened to the girl?" asked Morris, not hiding his curiosity.

"She disappeared," Mason said.

"Too bad," Morris said.

"Yes," Mason admitted. "She's a 'bonnie lass.' But St. Andrews is not Atlanta. I'll find her again."

Morris didn't doubt it. If Sullivan were here, she would be taking notes and finding the girl before dark, especially since dark didn't come here until about 10:30 in the evening. Golfers would still be teeing off tomorrow, the first day of the Open, at 4:30 P.M. There was that advantage in summer to being so near to the Arctic circle, but you paid for it when the great dark of winter came down.

"Tell me, how is Vinson playing?" asked Morris.

"He's hitting everything stiff to the flag," said Mason. "The man is a machine . . . if a nasty one. I wouldn't bet against him."

Morris pushed open the door to their tiny hotel sitting room. Sullivan was stretched out on the couch, catching BBC on the telly. "What did you mean, John Morris, when you said, 'Ah, romance' to Tom Rowe?" Julia Sullivan was a person who never forgot *anything,* often to Morris's regret.

He quoted Bernard Darwin's description of a young man's descent into sportswriting.

"I remember Mr. Darwin," Sullivan said, sitting up to give him a hug. "An old man, always in a tie and a vest and a soft cap, with the end of a cigar exactly in the middle of his mouth. He must have been eighty years old, Morris, and still writing so brilliantly for the *Times.* And what have you learned that's brilliant?"

He told her of his confrontation with Barry Vinson and the other fallout from the great "grooves scandal," including a description of the fired caddy, Georgia Tech, and the mysterious girl-who-got-away in the the Bull and Bear. Sullivan wrote a note to herself to find the girl.

Morris said, "Probably Mr. Vinson will score a fat 80 in the opening round, and all I'll have to use is one sentence in this impossible book I'll never finish. Who did you put your 'hard-inherited' money on to win the Open?"

"That's my secret," Sullivan said.

"Speaking of secrets . . ." Morris went to the tiny closet in their tiny bedroom and pulled out the program for this year's Open. He turned to page 29. "I forgot to show you this. . . ."

Sullivan took the thick program carefully, as if it came from Tiffany's. There, on page 29, was the wonderful photograph of Monty Sullivan, the year he was runner-up in the Open, standing behind a mike with four-time champion Bobby Locke. Monty had swept off his cap and thrown it at the feet of that year's winner and five-time Open champion, Peter Thomason. Monty and Locke had taken the mike from Thomason, who stood, startled, behind them as they sang an old Scottish ballad by Robbie Burns to a soon-weeping crowd: *And fare thee weel, my only love/And fare thee weel a while!/And I will come again, my love,/tho' it were ten thousand mile.*

The byline on the story recalling that year's Open: "John Morris."

Sullivan made no attempt to hide her tears. She might have been standing again in the weeping crowd, as she had stood that day. How could any of them have known that Robbie Burns's ballad would not come true. That Monty would be dead before the year was out. She read the story through twice. And hugged Morris again. She punched him on his massive shoulder. "Young man. Let's go down and have an early Wednesday-night dinner. And then . . . I haven't been properly welcomed to Scotland."

• CHAPTER TWO •

The sun broke through the cold shroud that had engulfed St. Andrews for two days. Play was to begin Thursday, July 13, 1978, in the British Open . . . which in all of Great Britain was known only as *the Open*.

As he waited for a table and breakfast, Jack Nicklaus, who did not tee off until the afternoon, was saying of the Old Course: "I love it. I think it's fabulous . . . a course which has nothing phony about it."

Tom Rowe of the *Times* and Morris and Sullivan were standing near enough to Nicklaus to overhear him. Rowe whispered to Morris, "The Old Course *is* fabulous. I think it gives Jack an advantage over the field to think so."

It had been like youth revisited, seeing Nicklaus, now thirty-eight, practice all week in the company of Jimmy Dickenson, the old, Yorkshire-born caddy whom he had coaxed from retirement to carry his bag and help read his putts, as he had done in Jack's Open victory at St. Andrews in 1970. Now sitting at breakfast with Nicklaus was Jack Grout, his boyhood mentor, who was helping him strengthen the grip of his left hand on the club, to recover distance Nicklaus felt he had lost from his tee shots.

"If he hits it any farther, we'll have to lengthen Scotland,'' said Rowe. Conversation turned to the other contenders.

Tom Watson, who had already won two Opens, had been unable to get a sense of the Old Course until his fourth and last practice round. Now he felt better about his understanding of the course, saying that it required a strategy ''similar to Augusta National,'' home of The Masters. Lee Trevino's back was stiff from his long plane ride from America. Gary Player had won three times in the States, including The Masters, but at age forty-two had suffered from exhaustion at the U.S. Open, and, oddly, he'd never played well on the Old Course. Johnny Miller had finished sixth in the U.S. Open and was looking for the magic that somehow had escaped him at age thirty-one. The great Spanish player Seve Ballesteros was spraying the ball off the tee and felt lower than an earthworm about his own chances.

Bookmakers had set the odds: Nicklaus and Watson, 6–1. Trevino and Hubert Green, 14–1. Ballesteros, Player, and Tom Weiskopf, 16–1. Miller and Hale Irwin, 20–1. Ben Crenshaw, Raymond Floyd, and Andy Bean, 25–1. Young Nick Faldo, at 33–1, was given the best chance to win of anyone from Great Britain.

The Old Course in the new sunlight, still without its protective winds in the early morning, seemed to lie there vulnerable, even in its uniqueness. Morris and Sullivan had walked every step of it many times until they knew it for the sly and beautiful and wicked being that it was. Morris had lain in the dark of the early morning and walked the Old Course in his imagination:

The par-4 No. 1 hole offers a benign start, with a fairway as wide as a cricket pitch and only Swilcan Burn, just deep enough to drown an ill-struck ball, guarding the green. From this moment forward and back again to the clubhouse, a golfer would be hard-pressed to find one level spot wide enough to lie down in.

Narrow is the way on the par-4 No. 2, between Cheape's Bunker on the left and a great sea of heather and gorse, with its millions of stickers, rolling up the right side all the way to No. 7.

The earth explodes with bunkers down the same right side of the par 4 No. 3, and evil Cartgate Bunker guards the left side of the green.

You would have to be buried standing up on the heaving, pitching earth of 463-yard, par-4 No. 4, with its Student's Bunker and an earthen ridge concealing the huge green.

Avoid the platoon of seven straight-faced bunkers down the right side of par-5 No. 5, and clear the high ridge with its twin bunkers in front of the massive green, and you might putt for eagle 3.

Avoid the gorse, heather, and ravines in front of the No. 6 tee, and aim your drive toward the hangars at the RAF Station at Leuchars, by all means avoiding the two Coffin bunkers 200 yards out, all this to a par of 4.

What's this? A valley of *near-level ground* as the par-4 7th hole crosses the 11th hole (with players down No. 11 having the right-of-way). Both holes share the same enormous green; avoid the gorse on the right and Cockle Bunker guarding the green and you are home free.

The 7th hole begins what is known as the Loop, with Nos. 7, 8, and 9 hooking sharply around to the right, toward the clubhouse, and Nos. 10, 11, and 12 looping back, giving the Old Course from above the look of a great fishhook. Coming back, the 10th, 11th, and 12th holes share gigantic double greens with the 8th, 7th, and 6th holes going out. Morris knew that rare was the great round of golf shot at St. Andrews in which the six holes of the Loop were not turned well under par, with a legitimate chance for six 3s being scored.

As if with a gesture of remorse, the Old Course offers

its first par 3, short and simple, at No. 8, heading toward the River Eden. Jock Hutchinson holed out in one shot there to win the 1921 Open.

Only 356 yards to the par-4 No. 9; men have been known to drive so near the green as to putt their second shots. Tony Jacklin scored a 2 to turn in 29 strokes in winning the 1969 Open.

Now the golfer is homeward bound. Par-4 No. 10 is named after the beloved Bobby Jones; it's short, with a slightly raised green, and anything over par is a disaster.

The world of golf knows no greater par 3 than No. 11; the green sits 172 yards away, sloping sharply upward, looking down on the River Eden; anything short falls into fearsome Strath Bunker or Hill Bunker, where you are likely to play backward to escape. Gene Sarazen failed to defend his Open title in 1933 when he took three strokes to blast from Hill Bunker. The tee shot at No. 11 is sometimes made into a forty-mile-an-hour gale, calling for the longest club in your bag.

The par-4 12th hole is short, but mined with small bunkers that Bernard Darwin once described as only wide enough "for an angry man and his niblick."

From No. 13 to No. 17 the Old Course turns savage. Heather and gorse make a cloud of doom down the right side of No. 13, which plays at 425 yards. The Coffin bunkers are back in play and the infamous Cat's Trap and Walkinshaw bunkers are about 260 yards out. Play short or over the Coffins but not into the Cat's Trap, and still waiting is the Lion's Mouth pot bunker in front of the green.

No. 14 is more difficult. Bobby Locke has made 8 here and Peter Thomason 7, and they hold nine Open titles between them. There's an out-of-bounds down the right side of the 567-yard par 5. Your aim is the tall spire at the far right of the town of St. Andrews, escaping the Beardies bunkers on the left and a greystone wall on the right, landing your ball safely in Elysian Fields. Even the great golfers must play left of Hell Bunker, which is long enough and deep enough in which to lay a four-story building on its side, and is backed up by Grave and Ginger Beer bunkers. There is a great frontal bank to the 14th green, making it difficult to hold and putt.

Get your breath on the par-4 No. 15, unless the tee shot is into the wind—then you may need two wooden clubs.

The 382-yard, par-4 No. 16 is played along the defunct railroad track that runs from the right side of the tee to the green, marking out-of-bounds every step of the way. The landing ground is barely fifteen yards wide between the three bunkers—called the Principal's Nose—and the former railway line. The 15th green is raised, with tricky hollows to the front and back.

The Road Hole. No. 17. A par 4 of 461 yards. The most terrifyingly difficult hole in championship golf. The Old Course Hotel has built an open trellis fence, which protrudes into the golf course at the same height and angle of the old railway shed that once stood there, requiring a blind tee shot to be struck directly over it, from out-of-bounds to in-bounds.

Running along and behind the 17th green is a road, backed by a stone wall. The green itself was never built to accept a shot from 200 yards, and is wrapped around and pitches precariously down into Road Hole Bunker. Many is the championship golfer who has not only pitched but putted into Road Hole Bunker. Doug Sanders should have won himself the 1970 Open with an heroic explosion shot from the bunker, followed by a two-foot putt for par 4.

The intelligent approach shot to No. 17 is short of the green and bunker and road, followed by a pitch and, in the best of worlds, a one-putt. Bobby Jones made a fortunate escape in 1930 from an errant second shot on No.

17, in his famous sudden-death match with Cyril Tolley, to keep his Grand Slam hopes alive in the British Amateur. Afterward, Jones said of his victory over nineteen holes: "I felt the same exultation and desperate urgency I should expect to feel in a battle with a broadsword or a cudgel." Take both to the 17th tee at St. Andrews.

Peacefully home. The Old Course offers the wide acreage of the No. 1 and No. 18 fairways up to the 18th green, which is surrounded by the town of St. Andrews, many of whose citizens would be looking out the windows of the old gray buildings down the last fairway. The small green golf shop, with its pointed, shingle roof and white sign . . . W. McAndrew . . . sits on the grassy slope above the 18th green. Only the shallow Valley of Sin, leading up to the 18th green, poses a serious problem, especially when the pin is placed just above it.

And then there is the burden of a certain immortality that goes to the winner of the British Open and makes the free air of Scotland all but impossible to breathe in the third week of July.

And so, play began in the 107th Open.

Morris and Sullivan crossed the Old Stone Bridge over Swilcan Burn, Morris poling his bad left leg with his cane. They took up a position behind the first green among the friendly Scots, most of them smaller and easy to see over, bundled in their wool sweaters and caps despite the unnaturally warm morning.

"It couldn't be Scotland . . ." Sullivan said, "all this sun and no wind."

"The afternoon players should be so lucky," Morris said. "Who do you want to follow?"

"The Old Course. That's what I came to see," said Sullivan.

The course itself was hidden, as it had been for five hundred years, dipping and rising and pitching and disappearing into mounds of gorse and fields of heather, with hardly a level place for a man to stand over his ball, if he could find it. Oddly out of place, over the pitching and yawing landscape, were the tall, portable television towers that reached into the air like thin, prehistoric beasts of prey. Jack Nicklaus had been the first golfer, local or international, to assimilate the towers, along with the spires of the old town, as targets for his tee shots, which were otherwise struck without visible reference to the landscape. No wiser golfer than Nicklaus ever teed up a ball, thought Morris.

Trevino, looking even more twitchy than usual and playing without benefit of a single practice round, swung his low fade onto the first green. He was playing with the two left-handers, Bob Charles and Peter Dawson. Trevino drew a mild laugh, making as if to address his own putt left-handed. Then he missed it right-handed. It wasn't to be his day or his tournament.

Morris didn't need his binoculars to identify the tall young man wearing Scotch-plaid trousers, who sent his approach shot as high in the air as a mortar shell, spinning the ball back to a makable putt. Tom Weiskopf, ever serious, putted the ball into the hole for a birdie 3 and lifted it out with only a hint of a smile. Morris remembered that eight years before, a younger, more impetuous Weiskopf had failed to break 70 in four rounds at the Old Course and had gone home to tell his wife, "The Old Lady is not worth another trip." It was good to see that he had grown in his game and in his judgment since winning the British Open at Troon in 1973.

"I think I'm ready to have a look at the rest of the Old Course," Sullivan said.

"The hell you are. You want to follow those Scotch-plaid trousers," Morris said.

"There's that," she admitted, already on her way over to the No. 2 tee.

Weiskopf, with his upright stance and long, powerful arc, put his enormous drive into the gorse and reached the second green one shot late. Morris could see him struggling not to light his well-known short fuse of a temper. In fact, he stood over his twelve-foot putt and sent it home with a level stroke to save par in the manner of his fellow Ohio State graduate, Nicklaus, whose great shadow he was destined to live under.

At no hole on the front side did Weiskopf require a second shot longer than a five-iron, and that only at the second hole. He dropped putts of twenty and thirty-five feet and made the turn in 31 strokes.

"You're with *me* . . . not *him,*" Morris whispered to Sullivan, who did not take her eyes off the tall and appealing Weiskopf as he swept a tee shot into the sky like an earth-bound meteor. His wedge within three feet of the 10th hole would have brought a smile to the face of Bobby Jones, the man whose name the hole carried. A birdie followed the wedge as spring the winter.

"What did you say your name was?" asked Sullivan, while saluting Tom Weiskopf in the British manner, with her palm outward.

"*Morris.* You know . . . the man who pays the rent on your hotel room."

"Oh, that man," Sullivan said.

Seagulls dipped in from the Firth of Tay as if part of the Open tradition, several of them landing and bobbing along the ground like low spectators.

"Let's leave the 11th to young Mr. Weiskopf and catch up with the field back at the 17th," Morris said. "I've had all the male sex appeal I can stand. I'm ready for some carnage at the Road Hole."

"You don't have the glands for it, Morris," allowed Sullivan, taking his large arm and leading the way back up the Old Course to the 17th tee.

They caught up with Isao Aoki, the Japanese artist

with a pitching wedge, who was having the round of his life on the first day of the Open. He stood on the 17th tee, a full six feet tall—an unusual height for a Japanese—and four under par, a grand score for any nationality.

It was his misfortune that it was not 1821, and the 17th hole playing to an orthodox, straightaway par 4. When the railroad—now unhappily extinct—came to St. Andrews later in the nineteenth century, loading sheds were built so that they angled *into* the 17th fairway, to such a height as to make the drive an absolutely blind shot from the tee box. As mentioned, the Old Course Hotel had taken the place of the sheds, and in the spirit of tradition had erected an open-trellis fence of the same angle and profile, keeping the tee shot quite blind.

Aoki could not see the 461 yards of fairway threaded between the out-of-bounds stone wall and the high grass of the rough. Nor could he see the distant green that poured itself, as a living whirlpool, around and down into the Road Hole Bunker, while spilling overly ambitious shots onto the road behind and perhaps against the greystone wall itself. The par-4 hole played to a 4.5-stroke average, and held much deadlier arithmetic than that for golfers whose boldness exceeded their ability.

Aoki finally settled over his ball and struck his drive over the trellised fence, but too cautiously away from the stone wall and through the narrow fairway and into the rough. Even his most aggressive second shot would never carry the distant green. Morris watched through his binoculars as Aoki played wisely to his own strength, laying up within a full wedge of the green and playing that shot safely away from the Road Hole Bunker, thirty feet to the right of the flag. Quite remarkably, he rolled the putt into the hole for a par of 4, which was to give him nearly a full-stroke advantage on the field on the 17th hole, on that day.

Sullivan swiped his glasses to see Aoki play a terrible tee shot on No. 18, missing a landing area as wide as the Firth of Tay, and then blundering onto the green in three strokes, but, undismayed, rolling in a twenty-foot putt for a second straight remarkable par 4. Aoki left the green in a hurry, as if the gods of the Rising Sun might change their minds and take back both scores. His 68 would stand as one of the day's two best opening scores on the Old Course.

Aoki said later in the press tent that he "had to study the Old Course so much to avoid so many bunkers that I got a headache."

Scotch-plaid trousers could be seen in Morris's binoculars long before young Tom Weiskopf could be identified by the intense look on his face. Walter Hagen might have struck the wedge he buried into the 16th green, eight feet from the flag. His putt drifted away from the hole for no observable reason—as Weiskopf himself drifted from the major titles of golf that might have been his. Still, at that moment he led the British Open at five under par, having lost a stroke with a failed approach at the par-5 15th, after his layup shot came to rest in an old divot in the heart of the fairway.

Sullivan stood so near young Tom that she might have reached out and touched him on the 17th tee. Morris was ready to restrain her from doing just that. Twice Weiskopf took his stance over his ball and twice he backed away. First the players on the nearby 16th green distracted him. Then spectators scrambling for position along the 17th fairway upset him. Now Weiskopf took his stance and seemed to rush his shot, as if to avoid further distraction, and sent it hooking madly onto the distant second fairway.

All was not lost; Bobby Jones had often played the hole from there on purpose. Morris could only shake his head as Weiskopf's attempt at a fade on his second shot failed and left his ball in the wild heather, with no chance of reaching the green with his *third* shot. By the time Tom holed his putt for a double-bogey 6, he was one shot out of the lead, and that was how he finished the 18th hole, at 69.

"I lost my concentration," he said afterward in the press tent. Asked if he suffered a headache from studying the course, as had Aoki, Weiskopf quipped: "Orientals are into these things. . . . I'm not an intellectual. . . . I get headaches from double-bogeys." But he was still very much in the hunt.

"Why are we standing here? Why do we love the sight of disaster?" asked Sullivan, touching her toe to the 17th tee.

"Oh, it's very much like observing someone else's failed love affair," Morris said. "We get all the juicy sounds and sights and none of the pain."

"Whose affair?" asked Sullivan, her curiosity peaked.

"Gentlemen never tell."

Sullivan punched him solidly. "John Morris, you've never been a gentleman a day in your life."

It pained them both to see Arnold Palmer, four-under-par and his name at the top of the Open scoreboard like old times reborn, send his drive crashing over the stone wall and against the five-story Jigger Inn for a *triple-bogey 7* on the 17th hole. Still, he finished at 71, a bare three strokes behind Aoki and with three rounds to catch him.

Morris and Sullivan eased over to the Bull and Bear pub along Golf Links Road for a bit of lager and shepherd's pie.

"Who do we catch this afternoon?" asked Sullivan.

"Watson and Nicklaus," Morris said. "But they won't have it easy. The wind is up. The Old Course will claim its victims."

"Will I get to see our boy, Barry Vinson?"

"You can see him, Sullivan, but you can't have him."

That afternoon, with the wind drying out the greens and adding the element of uncertainty to every club selection, Watson fell among the victims, driving twice over the wall at No. 14 and falling into Hell Bunker to boot, but escaping the wrath of the day with a 73, his tournament chances intact, his powerful game capable of lowering that score by ten strokes.

Nicklaus himself blew a short putt on the 14th but stood on the 17th tee, two under par and no quality of mercy in his eyes. He struck his tee shot over the trellis wall and directly down the fairway, as if out-of-bounds did not fall within his purview. He struck a one-iron, as no other living golfer could, onto the front of the 17th green. But he missed another short putt to bogey the hole and finish, like his old rival Palmer, with a 71. "You should play the 17th as a par four and a half . . . if you have any sense," Nicklaus said afterward, undisturbed by his bogey there. Asked about Aoki's fine 68, Nicklaus said, quite cold-bloodedly: "I don't know how Aoki will play in the wind."

Sullivan, to irritate Morris, said, "Here *he* comes. You have to say he looks good in his slacks."

Barry Vinson stepped onto the 17th tee as if it had been built in the previous century only for him. He did not test the winds. He did not speak to the young kid who was carrying his bag and had arrested terror in his eyes. He pulled out his driver and struck the ball as unswervingly as had Nicklaus, directly down the 17th fairway. Morris watched him putt from the fringe of the green and get down in a rare par 4. Sullivan pried away his glasses to see Vinson birdie No. 18 with a short putt to tie Aoki at 68 and share the first day's lead.

"Take that, Scotland," Sullivan said, still looking through Morris's glasses.

"He isn't the first leader of the Open to make an ass of himself," Morris said. "But he may be the first to make a profession of it."

Sullivan cracked up in spite of herself. "You are just trying out your one-liners on me. Save 'em for the book. Remember, I get a free copy."

"Oh, no! Oh, hell no! And tonight's drinks are on you. I got the shepherd's pie."

She leaned on him, walking along the 18th fairway, a large anchor in a high wind.

There was a talented crowd at the top of the leader board. Ballesteros of Spain and Raymond Floyd of the U.S. shot 69s, as did Jack Newton of Australia. Ben Crenshaw of the U.S., Simon Owen of New Zealand, Michael Miller and Carl Mason of Britain, and Tsuneyuki Nakajima of Japan stood at level 70. All of which amused Tom Rowe: a Japanese, a Spaniard, a New Zealander, an Australian, and various Americans at one time or another during the day leading the *British* Open. Thirteen players, including Palmer and Nicklaus, were locked at 71, among them the brilliant young English golfer Nick Faldo.

Morris was pleased to see that the young American, Lowrey, with Old Alec on his bag, had managed a competitive 72 in his first round at St. Andrews.

Morris pushed Sullivan's money across the bar at the Bull and Bear, careful to include a fat tip, looking fruitlessly for the pub owner, Issette, who was no doubt in the tiny back room trying to balance the books that had been shaky for two hundred years.

"Is the Royal and Ancient shocked to have Barry Vinson sharing the lead?" asked Morris.

"Oh, they hate it," said Rowe, having filed his story

to the *Times,* "but they won't say a word. They are praying the gorse will consume him, body and soul."

"What did he say about the course?" asked Sullivan.

"He said it reminded him of other *municipal* courses he had played as a boy . . . when he couldn't afford to belong to a *proper club.*"

"How did Captain Tait respond to that?" asked Morris.

"With a stiff whisky," Rowe said.

"A man shouldn't tempt the gods," Morris said. "But Vinson has the talent to win the tournament, if the winds don't dry out the greens until he can't cope with their speed. He doesn't love ice-slick greens, though he won at Augusta by overwhelming the par fives."

"Thank the same gods the Old Course only has two of those," Rowe said. "I best go see if the boys in London got every other paragraph of my immortal work."

So ended the first day of the Open. It was 10:45 P.M. and only now was the sun finding its rest in the Highlands.

• CHAPTER THREE •

The dark twisted itself into sound, tearing and tearing into the room until Morris was awake.

"Are you there, old chap?" asked the very proper British voice of Tom Rowe.

"No. There's . . . a strange woman . . . in . . . this bed . . . holding the phone to my ear," groaned Morris, refusing to open his eyes.

"And I hoped Sullivan had decent company," Rowe said. "Let her sleep. But you might want to drag your considerable self up to the cathedral ruins."

"Whatever for?" Morris had his eyes open, looking at his watch, which showed an obscene six o'clock in the morning.

Rowe said, "A countryman of yours is lying up there . . . extremely dead."

"Who?" Morris said, entirely awake and sitting up. No need to worry about waking Julia Sullivan, who always slept the sleep of the innocent, showing that she could fool even the night gods.

"Who else? Barry Vinson."

The phone went dead in Morris's ear.

Morris stumbled around in the near-dark, finding fresh clothes in the still-strange hotel room. He made an instant decision to leave the rental Ford with Sullivan. It was a short walk east to the cathedral ruins and the parking place in front of the hotel was more precious than a score of three on the Road Hole.

"Who wouldn't want to kill Barry Vinson?" Morris said aloud, as if he had a companion in the early morning mist off the North Sea. He passed the Castle ruins, below him on St. Andrews Bay, and turned one block south, hurrying by the War Memorial to the abbey wall enclosing the cathedral grounds. Beyond the stone wall Morris could see the surviving twin spires of the north transept of the church and St. Rule's Tower, which pierced the dawn like an earth-bound arrow.

Waiting at the gate in the wall was the rail-thin form of Tom Rowe, his cowlick blowing in the early breeze.

"Afraid you might have trouble getting past the local bobbies," Rowe said.

Morris lifted his old Associated Press pass.

"That should get you by."

"What happened?" asked Morris.

"A pair of lovers stumbled on the dead bloke among the graves," Rowe said. "Captain Tait of the Royal and Ancient called me after the police woke him. He dreads the terrible publicity to come. As well he might."

"What was Vinson doing here? How was he killed?" Morris might have been questioning himself.

"Worthy questions I can't answer," Rowe said. "You can ask an old friend of yours inside the wall. But no answers are going to salve the wounds of the Royal and Ancient . . . losing the coleader of the Open after the first round, however much a bastard he had made of himself."

"What friend of mine do you mean?" asked Morris.

Rowe stepped toward the entrance to the cathedral grounds without answering.

The young officer inside the gate had been instructed to let "the man from the *Times*" pass, and he reluctantly allowed Morris inside with him. They could see Captain

A.W.B. Tait of the Royal and Ancient Golf Club standing in the early light as if at parade rest on some military assignment from his youth. His steel-gray hair shone around his rugged face. He nodded at Rowe and seemed genuinely relieved to see Morris.

"Ye'er lookin' on the divil's work, an' 'ere a' the cathedral," Tait said.

"How was he killed?" asked Morris.

"Strangled . . . wi' a wire, I'm certain. Why . . . d'ye think? An' the toornament only begun?"

"The man insulted the Old Course. He insulted Scotland. Kings and Queens have died for less," Morris said.

"Aye," agreed Tait. "But I dinna ken the killin', e'en of a boorish mon."

"No," agreed Morris. "Half of America would like to strangle him. The other half buys and sells him, joyfully. You have to say the bastard could play the game of golf."

"Where is his body?" asked Rowe.

Tait turned to lead them toward a small clutch of figures deep among the rows of time-worn gravestones. As they moved toward the body Tait spoke of the terrible public consequences to St. Andrews and the Open . . . of having a coleader killed in the city, on the very cathedral grounds. No such outrage had occurred since Willie Park won the championship over Old Tom Morris in the first Open in 1860. Tait, despite his indignation, expressed no false sentiment for Barry Vinson and his dark fate.

Now Morris could make out the tallest figure standing over the body, a man even taller and thinner than Tom Rowe.

"John Morris," Rowe said, in a needless introduction, "you know Inspector James Emerson, from New Scotland Yard. It's his bad fortune to be on holiday here for the Open, and Captain Tait's good fortune to have him here."

"Good Lord, James." Morris shook his long, thin hand. "I haven't seen you since Turnberry."

The inspector, himself a fine golfer, always took annual leave to follow the British Open. He had been at Turnberry to see Tom Watson outlast Jack Nicklaus for the Open championship in the most stirring head-to-head final round of golf ever played in Great Britain. He and Morris had met a full ten years before that, when Roberto de Vicenzo had finished ahead of Nicklaus to win the British Open at Hoylake in England.

Emerson gripped Morris's large hand, as if for reassurance. "Wretched piece of work here, Morris," he said. "It puts me in mind of the tragedy at your own Open in Atlanta."

In 1977 Emerson had come to America for the U.S. Open, the year after the infamous murders at the U.S. Open in Atlanta. The inspector had nearly died from the oppressive heat in Tulsa, Oklahoma, while Hubert Green won the U.S. Open title at Southern Hills. Each night the inspector had offered a new set of questions to Morris and Sullivan about their roles in solving the murders of leading American golfers the year before in Atlanta. And here, two years later, was a Yank golfer lying dead in his country's own Open championship.

"Did you know the man?" asked the inspector.

"I knew him well enough to despise him," Morris said. He told of his encounter with Vinson the day before the tournament began, including his own parting quote to Vinson, from Flannery O'Connor, implying the golfer would be a good man *if it had been somebody there to kill him every minute of his life.* Morris said, "A particularly unfortunate quotation, considering what has happened to him."

Neither Tom Rowe nor Inspector Emerson concealed

their smiles, though the inspector's quickly vanished under the weight of his concern.

"Then he was as unpleasant a chap as he sounded in his public statements," Emerson said.

"He enjoyed being a bastard," agreed Morris. "As you know, from seeing him win the Open at Troon, he could play golf."

"How could so unlovely a man have so lovely a game?" asked Rowe. Then he quickly answered his question. "He isn't the first crude man to play championship golf."

"Oh, no," Morris said. "But you'd be hard-pressed to name a cruder one."

"Does he have a close friend on the tour?" asked Emerson. "Someone who would know of his private life?"

"I couldn't name one," Morris said. "His American agent is Mark Bradley, something of a newcomer, a young hustler. I haven't seen him, but I imagine he is here. You might try the Old Course Hotel first. I know that was where Vinson himself was staying. By the way, Vinson, before the tournament even started, fired his American caddy, a kid from Georgia Tech, who was carrying his bag for a summer's lark."

"What's his name?" asked the inspector.

"Paul Mason," said Morris. "I understand he's staying in a local hotel. I don't know which one. Mason did say he would hang around for the tournament. His family wired him money. And he had a plane ticket home."

"I assume Vinson firing his caddy was not a rare thing," Emerson said.

"Oh, no," said Morris. "He went through three or four a year." Morris did not say the kid was fired in a flap over an unknown local girl. He'd let Mason speak for himself.

"I assume you want to see the body," Emerson said. "It's no thing of beauty."

Morris and Rowe were cautioned where they might stand. They leaned over the uncovered form of Barry Vinson, lying full-length beside a tombstone, whose lettering had worn entirely away with time and rain and wind. Vinson lay on his back, his eyes open, his mouth fixed in a grotesque scream, the horror of which Morris could only imagine. There was a thin, bloody circle perfectly drawn around his neck, but no rope or wire or implement of execution. Vinson's hands were claws, turned toward his own throat, as if to gouge away the noose that was closing off his life.

"Godamighty," said Morris.

"I expect He shut His eyes at the sight," said Rowe.

"Oh, there have been bloodier doings at this cathedral and at the castle down there," Inspector Emerson said, turning his eyes toward the bay-front.

"Have you ever seen so terrible a face?" said Morris.

"In truth, I have not," Emerson said. He shined his torch directly into Vinson's open mouth. Perhaps there was a flicker of a reflection.

Morris felt in no way ill; he might have been looking into a particularly gruesome piece of ground under repair.

"I believe something is stuck in his throat," the inspector said. "I can even feel it." He pressed two fingers against the throat, just under the jaw of the dead Barry Vinson, who had never looked worse in his casual clothes.

"Who found him?" Morris asked.

"Young lovers . . . who came to the cathedral grounds after one A.M. . . . on a dare . . . to stay until dawn," said Emerson. "They stumbled on the body, nearly fell over it, around 4 A.M. They'd taken cold and were going home, dare or no dare. Stumbling over him gave them quite a turn, as you might imagine. The lad struck a match not six inches from *this face*. The girl was still hysterical when I talked with her an hour ago. They insist they came into the churchyard with only a bedroll, well after midnight . . . on this foolish dare. They had no torch. They saw nothing, heard nothing. I can only believe them. They would never have stayed on the grounds, had they seen or heard *this*."

"Unless they were too terrified to move," Morris said.

"Na' lik'ly they 'eard from 'im," Tait said, nodding at the body.

"Why do you say that?" asked the inspector.

"Na' wi' the wire aroond 'is neck," Tait said.

"You are certain it was a wire?"

"Aye. I haff seen the likes in the war."

"Tell me," the inspector said.

"In th' dark at Normandy . . . German lads died like this an' na' a sound 'eard." Tait said there was one peculiar thing about the red, circular line around the victim's neck. He pointed out, using the inspector's torch, the several converging gashes at the *front* of the throat. He said they meant the killer did not slip behind Vinson and garrote him—as Rangers were taught to kill in World War II—but that Vinson, who was a stout young man, must have known the killer to allow him to stand face-to-face, near enough to garrote him from the *front* . . . causing the several creases by the wire at the front of his throat.

Tait said that when the forensic team turned Vinson over they would find one round, seamless gash digging into the back of his neck. Another thing about the bloody circle bothered Tait; he didn't believe it gouged deeply enough into Vinson's neck to kill him. Wounds he had seen—Morris was sure he meant *wounds he had made*—were buried far deeper into the neck.

Morris could see Inspector Emerson was impressed with Tait's interpretation of the wound and with the war experiences that informed his opinion.

"I'm not sure but that the object stuck in his throat didn't kill him," said the inspector. "I have no doubt he died of asphyxiation."

Tait nodded his agreement.

"The killer was no small man, or woman," Morris said, indicating with his finger how the wire had cut into Vinson's neck at a consistent angle, and had not been drawn down precipitously at the throat, as would have been necessary for a killer shorter than the 6′2″ victim. "Unless the killer stepped up on the loose marble slab here on the plot. . . . I assume he was killed right here?"

"Oh, yes," Inspector Emerson said, pointing the torch toward the torn-up ground, where Vinson's feet had dug at the grass and soft earth. The inspector turned toward Rowe. "If you would report in the *Times* that he was murdered, but not *how* he was murdered . . . it would be of great benefit to our investigation."

Rowe nodded, but said, "That information won't keep still for long, old man."

"No," agreed the inspector. "But give us what time it will. I'll release the news of his death locally, in a couple of hours."

"Och, the press wi' throw a' 'avering fit," said Tait, who left, reluctantly, to prepare to round them up, writers and broadcasters.

"Morris, I know you've given up daily journalism," said the inspector, "but may I call on your long knowledge of golf and golfers, and your experience with murder in Atlanta? I'm afraid the job offers very poor compensation."

Morris said that he would help in any way possible without getting in the way.

A rather old man staggered over the uncertain ground of the graveyard toward the corpse. The inspector introduced him as Dr. Calvin Stewart, head of the local forensic team. He was a man of sounds and grumbles and no words; as soon as photographs were taken he set about his dark science with the body.

Waiting at some distance, Morris remembered to tell the inspector: "I understand Vinson was ending his contract with British Easywear."

"Sir Arthur Maxwell's firm," Emerson said.

"Yes. A splendid man," Morris said. "I spoke with him yesterday. Word was, Vinson was signing with an American sportswear firm . . . for more money, of course. But then there was the huge flap about the grooves in his irons and his vulgar remarks about the Royal and Ancient Golf Club and the Old Course. Sir Maxwell was hoping the American firm might get cold feet over signing Vinson, and he would sign again with Easywear, which is in trouble and needs him, as much as it might despise him."

"I'll speak to Sir Maxwell," the inspector said, making a note on his notepad.

Emerson then introduced Morris and Rowe to Detective Chief Inspector Hawkins, a short, thick man with a dark mustache who had come walking among the gravestones; he had driven up from Edinburgh with a team of three detectives, who were awaiting assignments at the police station. Emerson said that New Scotland Yard was flying two other experienced detectives from London to help with the case, which was sure to rain down an international furor by mid-morning. Inspector Hawkins obviously had little use for the press and soon turned his back on the two of them and moved nearer to Dr. Stewart, who was finishing with his hands-on examination.

Tom Rowe left to call in his story for the early edition of the *Times*. Morris accepted a short ride with Inspector

Emerson to the police station on North Street, one block behind his own hotel. The inspector had been given a wide room on the first floor from which to direct his investigation. Without being asked, a tiny woman brought two cups of tea. Morris had never been more thankful for a hot swallow of the national drink.

"The *manner* of his death frightens me, Morris," Emerson said. "If he'd been stabbed, or even shot on the street, it might pass as a robbery that escalated into murder. But this way . . . This was an *assassination.*"

"You don't imagine it's the work of the IRA?" said Morris.

"I don't imagine anything. But what was Vinson doing on the cathedral grounds—we must assume—in the night? He completed his round of golf in late afternoon. That's all I know of his movements at the moment. But from my own experience with bodies, I shouldn't think he had been dead more than three or four hours when he was found at 4 A.M. Dr. Stewart will know more about that shortly. He must have been killed before the two kids who found him came onto the cathedral grounds, after one A.M."

"And it doesn't get truly dark until after 10 P.M.," Morris said. "Do you think it could have been a drug deal? I can't offer a kind word about Barry Vinson. But I never heard he was into drugs. Golf is a devilish game to play sober. No one can play it at the highest level even mildly drugged out. Or could it be an old debt was settled?" asked Morris, aware that he was rambling aloud.

"Maybe," the inspector said. "But it doesn't make a lot of sense. Vinson had been the Open champion of Britain and America. He was, in fact, a very rich young man, capable of paying off any imaginable debt."

"It could be a terrorist act," Morris said. "We just heard from Captain Tait . . . the technique used to kill him has been taught to armies and professional assassins for years. And if publicity is what the killer, or killers, are after, they will get it in every country in the world . . . before the sun sets.''

''But for what purpose?'' asked Emerson.

Morris could only shrug his large shoulders. Two phones in the room began to ring simultaneously. ''I better get out of your hair,'' Morris said. ''If I hear anything, or learn anything, I'll call you immediately.''

''Yes,'' said Inspector Emerson.

Morris stopped in the door. ''Do tell me, when you know, what the object is that was stuck in his throat.''

The inspector nodded and answered one of the phones while the other rang on.

Julia Sullivan had not stirred in the bed.

Morris touched her gently.

''I'm sorry, this bed is taken.'' She did not open her eyes.

''Oh, no. I have a room key right here in my hand.''

''That's different. Climb right in.''

Morris got under the covers, clothes and shoes and unopened umbrella.

''We don't have to be quite that formal,'' Sullivan said, hardly opening her eyes.

''Dead! Why didn't you tell me, John Morris?'' Sullivan sat up in the bed, which was a chaos of discarded clothes and a now-opened umbrella.

''I just told you.''

''You took your sweet time,'' Sullivan said, reaching for her own clothes.

''I did at that,'' said Morris, propped up on one large elbow.

''Tell me *everything.*''

Morris brought her up to the minute on all he had seen and learned. ''You remember Inspector Emerson?''

"Of course I do. The tallest, thinnest man in Great Britain. Not to be confused with some physiques I've seen." She pushed her elbow into Morris's considerable bulk.

"He's a good man, but you'd have to say he's a sack of bones," Morris said.

"In truth, who killed the boy, Morris?"

"It was no accident. Whoever did it, did it face-to-face; did it out of hatred."

"He was a strong young man. It would have taken some strength."

"Yes. Even in the dark, and unsuspecting . . . Vinson would be a formidable victim."

"Why would he have been on the cathedral grounds?" asked Sullivan. "He never struck me as the religious type."

"No. He had to be meeting someone. Question is, who?"

"Surely the boy wasn't buying dope. I've rarely seen him take even a drink. As I remember, he was some kind of health nut."

"You're right," Morris said. "I'd forgotten that. He even advertised a food supplement. Of course, he'd have put in a plug for Mr. Death if the fee had been right."

"Oh, it was right enough," Sullivan said. "He'll be pushing Mr. Death from now on." Her voice softened. "Maybe he would have grown up, Morris. Met the right girl and had a family."

"He'd already met most of the girls on seven continents. I don't think there was a 'right girl' for Mr. Vinson."

"Maybe it's a local custom," Sullivan said, "lovers meeting at night on the cathedral grounds. Maybe he was meeting a local girl. We know two lovers found the body."

"It's possible," Morris said. "But I'm sure he had a

suite—with champagne and soft lights—at the Old Course Hotel. Why meet in a cold, gloomy graveyard?''

''Why, indeed?''

''I'm hungry,'' Morris said.

''I'm starved,'' Sullivan said.

Murder seemed impossibly far away during breakfast in the sunny bay window of the dining room.

• CHAPTER FOUR •

Morris stuck his head into the press tent. Captain A.W.B. Tait stood at attention as questions ricocheted from every direction. Even the ever-correct BBC asked in understated tones: "It was not an accidental death? There is no doubt that Mr. Vinson was murdered?"

"No doubt whatsoever," said Captain Tait.

"How!" screamed an American broadcaster. "How was he killed? What could he be doing *legally* . . . at night . . . in a cathedral graveyard!"

"That information is not being released at the moment," Tait said.

The tent threatened to collapse under the frenetic shouting and pushing that jarred the poles that held it up.

Tait made it very clear: no, the tournament would not be canceled or delayed. Security had been intensified, on the course and off. New Scotland Yard was conducting the investigation into Barry Vinson's death.

Golfers were teeing off for the second round of the Open even as the turmoil mounted among the media.

"It sounds pretty crazy in there," said Sullivan, who had waited for Morris outside the tent.

"It's a feeding frenzy. You've seen it before."

"Tom Rowe wants to visit with you. He's waiting over by the R&A clubhouse."

Morris found him standing beside the great bay window to the Big Room of the clubhouse.

"Do you know Mark Bradley when you see him, old chap?" asked Rowe.

"Sure," Morris said. "He's a young guy. Medium height, dark hair, strongly built. Looks, dresses like a golfer. Never saw him in a necktie. He dropped out of law school at Berkeley. Represented that diver after the Olympic Games. Got him contracts like no diver had ever seen. Bradley talks big. But his clients sign big contracts."

"I'm supposed to meet him here," Rowe said. "I think it's his belief the *Times* would be more sympathetic to his reaction than our tougher-minded colleagues on the tabloids."

"I see he doesn't know you any better than you know him," Morris said. He pointed with his umbrella. "That's Bradley in the green sweater, coming from behind the temporary bleachers. Do you want me to hang around?"

"Please do," Rowe said. "You were much closer to his ex-client than I was."

"Sure. I almost had to whip his young ass. We had that together," said Morris, more than a little embarrassed to remember their last encounter.

Bradley had the chest of a body-builder under his light sweater. He'd cut himself shaving. And he had the confused look of a man who had lost a major meal ticket, but had, perhaps, inherited the whole enterprise.

Rowe introduced himself. Bradley remembered Morris, though he didn't offer to shake hands.

"Do you have a personal statement in reaction to Vinson's death?" Rowe asked, with a deliberate softball of an opening question.

Bradley didn't have to think a second. "Golf has lost

its greatest, most popular player, and I've lost a dear friend." He spewed out the words, by rote.

"Have you spoken with Inspector Emerson?" asked Rowe.

Bradley wasn't crazy about the second question. "Yes. He wouldn't tell me a goddamned thing. What kind of country is this?"

"A fairly safe one," Rowe said. "Murder is a rare thing in St. Andrews. When did you last speak to Mr. Vinson?"

"I told the inspector"—Bradley said *the inspector* with faint respect—"that I had a sandwich in Vinson's room . . . last night . . . at about ten P.M. We were both staying at the Old Course Hotel. We had contracts to talk over. Nothing out of the ordinary."

"Is it true he was leaving British Easywear?" asked Morris.

Bradley was even less crazy about that question. "It hadn't been decided," he said, too quickly, and not concealing his irritation.

Morris did not believe him for a minute.

"The two of you weren't meeting with Sir Arthur Maxwell?" asked Rowe.

"Not until tonight," admitted Bradley.

"What did you intend to tell him?" Rowe asked.

"We needed more money. We had a better offer on the table. Simple as that." Bradley's eyes had a way of drooping, as if he might fall asleep. It was a mannerism, no doubt born of his idea of a merciless negotiator.

"What were Vinson's plans for last night?" asked Morris.

"You two sound like *Scotland Yard,*" Bradley said, with all the contempt he could muster into the pronunciation.

Morris and Rowe waited for his answer.

"He planned to watch a little TV and turn in early. He

felt he could destroy holes seven through twelve and run away with the golf tournament. I think he was right.''

''What might have stirred his soul enough . . . to provoke him to leave his hotel suite *for a dark, chilly cathedral cemetery*?'' asked Rowe, with very little tender-loving-care in his very proper *Times'* pronunciation.

Bradley could only shake his head. He did not hazard an answer.

''A woman?'' asked Rowe.

''He never had a shortage of dames in his room . . . that I noticed,'' Bradley said, his droopy eyelids implying the opposite of sleepiness.

''Dope?'' Morris said.

Bradley swelled up angrily in his green sweater, Morris thought, like an overoptimistic bullfrog. ''Why the hell do you say that? Vinson was no dope-head. He didn't even smoke cigarettes. He was a health nut. He even converted me . . . said I would quit smoking or he would, by God, drop me.''

''Gambling debt?'' Rowe said.

''He bet fifty thousand pounds on himself to win the goddamned tournament,'' said Bradley, before he could stop himself, ''with a *licensed bookie.* It didn't put a hole in his walking-around money.''

Rowe made a note of this delicious tidbit.

''Then he went to pray,'' Morris said, with false reverence.

Bradley responded in all seriousness. ''I never saw him on a Sunday anywhere but the golf course, and usually high in the money.'' He said the last with a certain honest regret.

''Was he your foremost client?'' asked Rowe.

''He was *anybody's* foremost client,'' Bradley said, making no attempt to hide the speed of the money horse he had ridden.

"*Fortune* magazine reported that Vinson made fifteen million dollars last year," Morris said.

Bradley shrugged, as if it was a low-ball estimate.

"Where did he park his Jaguar?" Morris asked, the thought suddenly jumping into his mind; no doubt it had come to the inspector last night.

"I have no idea," Bradley said. "I don't know if they found it, or even if he drove it. He had copies of new contracts that aren't in his room . . . or so the *inspector* tells me. They must be somewhere . . . maybe in his rental car. Not that they mean a damn thing now." He did not hide the true disgust in his voice.

"Who was his next of kin?" asked Morris.

Bradley looked at him again, full of suspicion. "Only his old man, who he hated. His mother died when he was a kid. The old man married two or three more times . . . he's retired from the army . . . but none of the marriages worked out. That's how Barry learned to play golf . . . by himself, on military bases all over the damn world . . . like Moody and Trevino—and he was gonna be better than Trevino."

That had remained to be seen, thought Morris, but the bastard was plenty good. And better men than Barry Vinson had been buried in Scotland for a lot less than fifty thousand pounds, he thought.

"Then who inherits?" asked Tom Rowe, the ultimate question after any first-degree murder of any rich man in any country.

Bradley's lids slid over his eyes.

"Wouldn't *you*—as his agent—know who the beneficiary of his many contracts would be . . . if anything happened to him?" Rowe asked.

Bradley said, reluctantly, "Like I told the inspector, some of his contracts come to me . . . like some of my royalties would have gone to him. I don't know about his personal estate. You'd have to ask his lawyer in Orlando. Rice. Eddie Rice. Like I told the inspector."

Morris didn't believe for half a second that Bradley didn't know how Vinson left his money. "You wouldn't deny you stand to inherit a great deal, however he left his basic estate?"

Bradley admitted it was so with a nod of his head.

"I assume his life was insured?" Morris said.

Bradley nodded.

"And . . ." Rowe said.

"Some of it comes to me," admitted Bradley. "Look, I wasn't in the graveyard last night. I was in my hotel room, falling asleep, watching the boring BBC."

Neither Rowe nor Morris said a word.

"I can't prove it," Bradley said into the silence. "I mixed my own drinks from the bar in the room . . . with ice cubes no bigger than a pair of bloody dice. Look, America has lost its greatest young golfer. That's the story. Not how he left his goddamned money."

"But the second-day story, Mr. Bradley, will be *who killed him and why,*" Morris said. "And it will remain the story until whoever did is arrested and convicted."

Bradley had had enough of their "friendly" questions. He took a quick look at the reporters and broadcasters now spilling out of the press tent and turned into the crowd behind the 18th green, with just a lift of one hand to show that he was going.

Morris looked around, surprised to see a Scottish mist falling on himself and the second round of the British Open, which was starting not thirty yards in front of him, with Ben Crenshaw addressing his ball on the first tee with his driver.

Sullivan, who had been standing carefully to one side, monitoring their interview, shifted her umbrella to also cover Morris. He reconstructed their conversation with the reluctant Mr. Bradley, while Tom Rowe left to file a sidebar to the *Times,* leading with the titillating news that Barry Vinson had bet fifty thousand pounds on himself to win his second British Open. The bet, of course, was lost, along with his life, British bookies having no place in their dry hearts to weep for the deceased or their next of kin.

"So, what do you think, Morris?" asked Sullivan.

"No, what do *you* think?"

"Spoken like a true inspector," Sullivan said. "A *woman.* There is no other answer, Morris. He was eating a sandwich in his room . . . if we can believe Mark Bradley. He had his TV. He had his room bar. He had his telephone. And this isn't his first trip to Scotland. Somebody. Some *female* body, called him on the phone . . . or some *male* body called him about a *female* body. The one call our boy would answer . . . was the *mating call.*"

"I'm persuaded," Morris said. "But why in a graveyard? This is a lad who loves his comfort. And alphabetizes his women. And did the woman call of her own volition? Or did somebody call for her? Some pimp? Not that a woman couldn't surprise the man and strangle him . . . but it would take some doing, face-to-face. He was a strong kid."

Sullivan invented what she would say as she spoke. "Maybe he was going to pick her up . . . in his Jaguar . . . at the cathedral . . . and bring her to the hotel. And she persuaded him . . . into a little walk among the tombstones. You boys are very vulnerable."

"Tell me about it," Morris said. "But I've never gotten it done in a graveyard."

"Of course you haven't. I've never invited you," Sullivan said.

Morris reached over and closed the umbrella around them and kissed her on the lips.

"What . . . right in front of the Royal and Ancient?'' Sullivan said, and raised the umbrella again over their heads.

''They can take it,'' Morris said. ''There hasn't been an erection in that building since 1754.''

Sullivan almost lost her balance laughing, until the starter at the No. 1 tee stared her into silence.

''We best not forget the fifty thousand pounds Vinson bet on himself to win,'' Morris said. ''I don't care how little it meant to *him,* with his millions. He went off at odds of twelve to one . . . and immediately took a share of the lead. Vinson was no bohunk golfer. He'd won this baby before. Now some 'licensed bookie' was staring at a possible, even likely, payoff of *six hundred thousand pounds,* if my shaky mathematics can be relied on. Men have gone to the next world over a lot less.''

''True,'' Sullivan said. ''It's not an appropriate time to boast of it . . . but I laid our whack on another man.''

''Good word, *whack,* Sullivan. And a good decision. But which golfer?''

''Never you mind,'' she said, always one to keep her bet under her rain hat. ''If fifty thousand pounds 'didn't put a hole in his walking-around money,' then word might have gotten out that Mr. Vinson was a walking cash cow.''

''Ready to be milked,'' Morris said. ''The inspector should be able to tell us if any serious money was found on him.''

The rough touch on Morris's shoulder was from *A.P.* himself. ''What happened to the kid, Morris?'' Arnold Palmer asked, giving a strong hug to a willing Sullivan.

''He bought it in a graveyard. Convenient, huh?''

Palmer flinched. For so strong a competitor, he'd always had the heart of a pussycat when it came to another man's troubles.

''I think he would have preferred less convenience,''

admitted Morris. "But what the hell was he doing in the cathedral cemetery at night . . . and him leading the British Open?"

"I could guess," Palmer said in his famous croak of a voice.

"Couldn't we though?"

"Not the kind of guy you'd look up to have a drink with," Palmer said. "But he could play the game. He was young, Morris. Maybe he would have grown up."

"Maybe," Morris said, with little conviction.

Palmer left for the practice tee. Except for his score of 7 on No. 17, he would be leading the tournament at age forty-eight. He was still very much in it. He couldn't take two steps without signing an autograph, which he did with impossible patience.

"I'm not going to wash either shoulder," said Sullivan, lightly touching where she had been hugged.

"You are incorrigible," Morris said. "Listen, we might as well follow the tournament. Give the inspector time to solve the murder."

Sullivan nodded; she was game. "I wonder if Vinson took any calls in his room last night. Or if he had his phone shut off, like many of the guys do."

"Good questions," Morris said. "I'm sure Inspector Emerson is asking them. We'll catch him later in the day and see. I have an idea our boy Bradley didn't tell him about the fifty thousand pounds that Vinson had bet on himself. He only let it slip to us because he was angry at Rowe . . . for asking if Vinson was in the cemetery to pay off a gambling debt."

Morris, his cane in one hand and his sitting stick in the other, limping like a veteran of some foreign war, and Sullivan, sprightly as a young colt let out to pasture, hiked to the far reaches of the Old Course. They stopped at the brief little No. 7 hole, in the bend of the fishhook the course made before turning back against itself. They leaned on their sitting sticks and savored the light Scottish mist falling in silence. Only a few early, hardy souls kept watch with them over the No. 7 green, which sat, vulnerably, on a high plateau.

Through his binoculars Morris could follow the immense blind drive by Severiano Ballesteros. Its flight dared the line of savage gorse along the right side of the fairway and came to rest a bare forty yards from the green, which lay 372 yards from the tee. The young Spaniard, whose game vacillated between the brilliant and the erratic, was in full flight. He had just dropped an eighteen-foot putt for a birdie on the perilous No. 6, with the Loop, a vulnerable six holes, in his immediate path.

"Smashing," Sullivan said as Seve approached his ball.

"It was a drive of over 330 yards," Morris agreed.

"No. I mean the Spaniard," Sullivan said, lifting the binoculars to frame the young golfer who was as handsome as any movie actor in Europe.

Ballesteros, with the touch of a wizard, flicked his forty-yard pitch over the deadly Cockle Bunker, stiff to the pin on the enormous double-green for a birdie 3 . . . to a polite smattering of applause from the few huddled Scots, and a noisy cheer from Julia Sullivan, which actually turned his head in her direction.

Morris followed Sullivan following Ballesteros. His first putt on No. 8 died three dimples from the hole for an easy par 3. And after another uneventful par of 4, on the short 9th, Ballesteros removed his jacket—to Sullivan's vast satisfaction—to unleash his drive on the par-4 No. 10. He might have shot it out of an artillery piece. The length of the short hole named for Bobby Jones receded under the ball, until it came to rest *on the green itself,* 342 yards away. Ballesteros putted twice for a birdie 3 to go four under par for the day and seven under in the Open, taking the lead over the field. But it was early in the day in Scotland.

Morris and Sullivan drifted like the mist back toward the clubhouse, leaving Seve temporarily to his fate. They passed Palmer himself, raging through the front nine with four birdies to snatch the lead from Ballesteros. "But the days are long in Scotland," Morris reminded Sullivan again. They also drifted through the beginning of an immaculate round by Ben Crenshaw, so often wild off the tee but today driving it as straight as a Vicar on Easter Sunday, yielding not one stroke to par.

Sullivan put down her sitting stick opposite the tee on No. 17, as if come to watch a train wreck on the long-abandoned railroad track into St. Andrews.

Japan's Isao Aoki sent his drive over the trellis wall as if it were thin air and he could see the ball as it found the elusive 17th fairway. His long iron rolled to the edge of the green, and he two-putted for a rare par 4, then parred No. 18 for a round of 71—which gave him a two-day score of 139, which just might hold up for the halfway lead.

Several players with lesser scores massacred the 17th to Sullivan's satisfaction, and then came Ballesteros himself, with a two-stroke lead over the field. He backed away from his ball twice. Morris feared Sullivan, unable to take a breath, would faint from lack of oxygen. Finally, Ballesteros exploded into the ball and instantly split the air with a burst of Spanish that needed no translation. His ball flew crazily right of the stone wall, crashing against the shingled roof of the pub known as the Jigger Inn. Seve would have loved to stop for a shot of tequila. He teed up another ball and played the impossible hole in six painful strokes. Morris watched through his binoculars as Ballesteros finished No. 18 in par for a 70, tying Aoki for the Open lead.

A sortie of spring-fattened seagulls lumbered in the

damp air over the Old Course, hoping to land and waddle in the grass and heather and dry their wings in the occasional faint sunshine, but the unnatural throng of humans, standing and moving along the fairways, spooked them, and sent them screeing plaintively back toward the hostile sea.

Ben Crenshaw hardly paused over his tee shot on the 17th, before drawing it safely over the wall onto the fairway, then to the green, then into the hole in two putts for a priceless par of 4. He finished in 69 strokes, and not a bogey on his card, to tie Aoki and Ballesteros at 139.

Word swept through the gorse and the heather. Palmer, as in the days of his youth, had sustained his charge. Even with a bogey at the 14th, having driven into the Beardies, he was tied for the lead.

Sullivan might have been arrested for her smile when he touched her on the arm as he moved through the heavy crowd around the 17th tee.

Palmer had said to Tom Rowe before the day's round: "I'm putting better than I'm playing. And that hasn't happened to me in a long time." And today, he was putting *and* playing. The 17th hole had cost him the British Open in 1960, when he lost by one stroke to Kel Nagle. But Palmer was not a man to turn away from a challenge, or play the hole to a false par of five. He lined up his drive and tore through the ball with his familiar blocking action, to prevent a crash hook, but he played the shot too near the line of the old stone wall, and it never drew back in bounds. The oxygen seemed to go out of his lungs. Palmer again finished the Road Hole with a triple-bogey 7, and would never again lead the British Open championship, which he had won twice and restored to its international magnificence by coming from America to play for its then-modest first prize when he was the dominant golfer in the world.

Morris touched Sullivan, whose eyes had misted over,

and without a word they stood at the open door of time as it shut forever on the era of Arnold Palmer, champion.

They did not speak as they walked toward the 17th green. Behind them came the tousled hair of the champion of the New Age, Tom Watson, and his fierce drive into the 17th fairway. Watson arrived at the frightful 17th green in two shots and played a miracle putt "up hill and dale . . . along that dangerous route from the left bottom of the bank to four feet," to quote the ever-literate *Times* of the next morning. Watson made his second putt and finished the day with a strong 68, two shots off the lead.

Hiding among six players, four shots off the lead, was Jack Nicklaus, after a disappointing round of par 72. But every player in the tournament who hoped to win it would be pleased to finish one stroke ahead of Mr. Nicklaus.

Never had a draft lager tasted so good to Sullivan and/or Morris as they rested on their sitting sticks behind the 18th green, an historic spot reserved by their one authentic and one out-of-date Open press pass.

The hand on Morris's shoulder belonged to Warren Lightfoot, president of the United States Golf Association and one of the rare men tall enough to reach down and touch him, even when he was standing.

"Terrible business, Morris," Lightfoot said, and offered a polite handshake to Sullivan, who would have welcomed a hug from the tall, gray, aristocratic New Englander.

"Indeed," said Morris, who often found himself using words in the same manner as the person he was talking to, and Warren Lightfoot never used one word when none would suffice.

"Was the young man married?" he asked.

Morris thought Lightfoot just might be the only executive in golf who did not know Barry Vinson by reputation.

"No," Morris said. And could not resist adding: "I don't believe he had narrowed the field to any one *continent* of women."

Lightfoot's eyes widened at so unseemly a prospect. "Morris, I'm aware . . . you've . . . helped the police . . . in the past. May I ask your advice?"

"Don't confess. Get a lawyer," Morris said, immediately sorry for his flippancy when he saw Lightfoot's long face grow pale under his rain hat. "How can I help you?" he asked.

"I may have seen Mr. Vinson . . . last night," Lightfoot said.

Morris felt Sullivan touching his elbow. He rose to his feet, pushing himself up with his cane. "Where?"

"In front of the Old Course Hotel. I was getting out of my own automobile. I had first admired Mr. Vinson's green Jaguar . . . I believe it was Monday. He had parked it at the practice range. My wife does love that shade of green."

Morris waited without interrupting him.

"It was very near to one A.M. when I saw the Jaguar again," Lightfoot said. "In fact, it was within one or two minutes of one. I had eaten at the R&A . . . and there was a bit of a ceremony. . . ."

Morris knew the tall New Englander had been honored by the membership for his forty years of service to golf. He knew Warren Lightfoot to be a very proper man and a damn dependable one.

"Morris, I didn't actually see the young man. Or I don't remember seeing his face. I saw the Jaguar automobile. I *assumed* it was Mr. Vinson's. I didn't look at the license plate. I was interested in the deep shade of green and the rather clean lines of the automobile. I was thinking of surprising my wife with one just like it."

"You say you *don't think* you saw his face. What do you mean by that, exactly?" asked Morris.

"I . . . I'm not sure. My eye might have caught the driver . . . for an instant. But my mind was on the shade of green. I couldn't be sure I saw anyone. I only assumed it was Mr. Vinson's Jaguar in front of our hotel."

Morris ignored the mist, again falling on his rain jacket and in his thick black-and-gray hair, Sullivan having removed the umbrella so as not to inhibit their conversation. "Had you stepped out of your car when you first saw the Jaguar?" asked Morris.

Lightfoot thought. "No. I saw it as the valet opened my own door. I tipped the man, but did not take my eyes off the color of the Jaguar."

"Was it moving?" asked Morris.

Lightfoot thought. "Not at first."

"Were the doors closed?"

"Yes." He did not have to think.

"Were the lights on?"

"Yes."

"Did it begin to move toward you?"

"No," Lightfoot said, narrowing his eyes in concentration. "It moved away from me, but circled back, heading for St. Andrews."

"Was anyone sitting in the passenger seat?"

Lightfoot thought. "No. I'm sure there was not. . . . Now I remember I saw a *cigarette glowing* . . . over on the driver's side." He was excited to remember. "I certainly couldn't swear it was Mr. Vinson. But I never doubted it was he in the Jaguar. So long as the police understand that . . . I was sure it was him, but I didn't truly see him. I make a terrible witness, Morris. But I'm certain now I must speak to the police. I have no idea if they can make any sense of what I did and didn't see and what it might mean."

"You make an *excellent witness,*" said Morris, copying for him the name and phone number of Inspector James Emerson and the address of the police station, just a couple of blocks north and east from where they stood. "Warren, do go inside the R&A and call Inspector Emerson while this is fresh in your mind. Don't let whoever answers the phone hang up without connecting you to the inspector. You might recognize Emerson. A thin, rather tall man, not so tall as yourself. He's with New Scotland Yard and a fine golfer. He always takes a holiday at the British Open, and once came to our own Open, at Southern Hills. Tell him what you just told me. It's extremely important. Don't worry about what it means. Or *exactly* what you didn't see. Describe what you remember, *just as you described it to me.*"

Lightfoot was still nervous, but somewhat encouraged. "I think I did meet the inspector, Morris. You may even have introduced us in Tulsa. I remember he was dreadfully hot, if that was the inspector. I will call him now. Thank you, Morris." Lightfoot held on to the inspector's name and phone number as if it belonged to a future champion of the U.S. Open.

Sullivan, who had been sitting near enough to hear everything, said, "Morris, I'm impressed. You dragged out of him more than he ever remembered seeing."

"Good Lord, half the time with the old Associated Press, we had to drag it out of them on the telephone, when one or both of us were hung over. Sober, face-to-face, it's like stealing. We know this: Warren Lightfoot *saw the killer* at one o'clock, last night . . . driving Barry Vinson's green Jaguar."

Sullivan stood, not understanding his conclusion, as if it were too complex to figure out sitting down.

"Question is," said Morris, "who did our man see? And why would the killer take the terrible risk of driving his victim's distinctive automobile to his very hotel . . .

having just killed him? And with the body about to be discovered? Of course, he, or she, couldn't know that.''

Sullivan had the umbrella back over his head. She ignored the gentle mist falling against it while she whirred back through Morris's earlier conversation with Mark Bradley. ''I've got it,'' she said. ''Barry Vinson was a 'health nut,' according to his agent. *He didn't smoke.* Or tolerate anybody who did, including Mark Bradley himself.''

''Go to the head of the class,'' Morris said. ''You also were very much correct, Sullivan: There is not 'anything like a dame' to get to a sailor boy in the South Pacific, or a horny young golfer out on a chilly night in Scotland. Somebody rang our boy on the telephone and stirred his libido . . . or threatened it. And laid his natural ass on a gravestone.''

• CHAPTER FIVE •

"I don't know which feels best, Morris: the dry clothes or the dry martini." Sullivan lifted her glass toward the view of the North Sea out the window of the dining room of the St. Andrews Golf Hotel. "Here's to a people with a warm pub on every corner."

Morris touched her glass with his own. "And to a five-hundred-year-old golf course with a country wrapped around it."

She touched his glass again. "My God, why does anybody live anywhere but Scotland?"

They both drank to that.

Dinner was a brace of grouse and a running stream of interruptions. Writers, broadcasters, golfers (one-time champions and tour dropouts), golf executives, agents, merchandisers, punters, bookies, hangers-on of every persuasion, all stopped by their table, panting for information about the murder or offering "absolute inside knowledge of what really, by God, happened to him," including the "sure fact he'd had his throat cut by a jealous Scotsman."

After such a visitation by a traveling sporting goods salesman, Morris said, "They are singing your song, Sullivan, that our boy died making his last mating call. No cautious husband in Scotland is asking a roving wife if she spent last night in the cemetery."

Perhaps it was the pause in the noisy dining room, as

if every person at the same moment had stopped speaking, chewing, dashing silverware, to take a swallow of water, that caused Morris to look up and see Inspector James Emerson standing in the doorway. Morris signed their bill to their room and guided Sullivan toward the inspector, who was glad enough to agree to a round of brandies in what passed for a lobby but was truly a parlor, complete with a fire in the fireplace in July, and was curiously empty tonight except for themselves.

The inspector raised his glass to theirs.

"Your Mr. Lightfoot has been helpful," Emerson said. "As you know, it is possible he saw Vinson driving his Jaguar at one o'clock last night. But there's a problem: old Dr. Stewart believes the man was dead by one. Impossible, of course, to establish time of death more precisely than between 11:45 and one A.M., when the lovers entered the graveyard. So, he could have been alive at nearly one A.M. and driving his Jaguar away from the Old Course Hotel."

"Vinson was *not* driving the Jaguar," Morris said.

The inspector looked up from his glass at so absolute an opinion.

Morris said, "His agent, Mark Bradley, described him to us as a 'health nut.' Vinson *didn't smoke* and didn't allow Bradley to smoke in his presence."

"Dr. Stewart agrees he was not a smoker," the inspector said, rather puzzled, "but what does that . . .?" He paused. "You mean Mr. Lightfoot saw the glow of a cigarette in the car . . . but he did not mention it to me."

"I'm sure he simply forgot," Morris said. "I was careful not to coach him on it, or give it any importance. I didn't want to *shape* his memory, just stimulate it."

Emerson said, "I'll ring him tonight. Morris, tell me exactly what he said to you."

Morris repeated, verbatim, Lightfoot's recollection of

last night, beginning with his particular interest in that shade of green Jaguar as a possible gift for his wife. Morris quoted his own questions and Lightfoot's answers, including his seeing the lighted cigarette on the *driver's side* of Vinson's car as it moved toward the heart of St. Andrews and the cathedral. A lifetime of interviews had given Morris near-total recall.

"I'm afraid you embarrass me with the quality of your questions . . . and your recollection," the inspector said.

Morris offered no false modesty.

"Please don't encourage him, Inspector," Sullivan said, "he's already too full of himself."

Morris could not contain his smile.

"You believe Lightfoot saw the *killer*?" Emerson said.

"Or his accomplice," said Morris.

"I talked to a parking valet at the Old Course Hotel," said the inspector; "he knew Vinson—as a miserly tipper—and he knew his green Jaguar. He got the Jaguar out of the parking lot for Vinson last night . . . but *much earlier* than one o'clock. In fact, he's certain it was nearer 11:45 P.M. The doorman at the hotel agrees it was 11:45 P.M. He remembers that Vinson didn't tip him at all. He tipped the kid getting the car fifty pence. A real big spender, on his fifteen million dollars a year, your boy Vinson."

"Not *my boy,* Inspector," said Morris.

Emerson said, "The head clerk, working the front desk, insists that *no one* was given a key to Vinson's suite but Vinson himself. But somebody left a key in his room last night. And the room had been amateurishly tossed and rather clumsily rearranged. Somebody was looking for something and maybe found something."

"Was it a second key left in the room? Or was it Vinson's own key?" asked Morris.

"Vinson's. If we can believe the hotel staff," the inspector said. "They can account for the other four keys to room 605. No one was seen entering, or leaving, Vinson's room . . . after nine P.M., when sandwiches were delivered to him. The bellman saw Vinson and his agent, Bradley . . . who admits, as you know, he was there."

"Do you trust Bradley's account of last night?" asked Morris.

"No," Emerson said firmly.

"I would guess they were discussing British Easywear, the termination of the contract," said Morris. "And I'm sure Vinson was gloating over his round of golf. The bastard had a real chance to win on this course. But if he was meeting a young woman, I wonder if Vinson didn't let it slip. He didn't strike me as the strong, silent type. Did Bradley tell you that Vinson had bet fifty thousand pounds on himself to win the tournament?"

Inspector Emerson set down his empty brandy glass. "No."

"He let it slip," Morris said, "when Tom Rowe and I wanted to know if Vinson might have been in the cemetery to pay off a gambling debt. Before he could stop himself, Bradley said Vinson had bet fifty thousand pounds on himself to win the tournament and that it didn't 'put a hole in his walking-around money.' "

"Good Lord," said the inspector, making a note to call Bradley that night.

Morris added, "Vinson teed off at twelve to one, second only to Nicklaus and Watson among the favorites in the Open. When he shared the first-day lead, some 'licensed bookie,' as Bradley described him, was looking at possibly paying off *six hundred thousand pounds* to young Mr. Vinson."

Emerson let out a low whistle.

Sullivan broke her own rare silence. "Word must surely have spread over St. Andrews that Vinson was not short of 'walking-around money.' If his bookie didn't off him, maybe some plain thief did."

"No," Emerson said. "He was carrying five thousand pounds, untouched, in his billfold."

"Could he have been killed somewhere else and carried to the cemetery?" asked Morris.

"No," the inspector said. "The postmortem lividity is consistent with his having never been moved from where he died. You saw the torn turf at the foot of the gravestone. That same grass was found in his shoes. Whoever killed the young man, the question remains: *What was he doing in the cathedral cemetery between 11:45 and one A.M.*?"

"I agree with Sullivan," Morris said. "He could only have been answering the mating call. Or *answering for* his perverted mating call to some angry husband or father. Another round or two with Mark Bradley on the subject might be useful. Bradley said he'd never noticed 'a shortage of dames in his room.' Don't suppose Bradley could be arrested for his politically incorrect vocabulary . . . but what does he truly know about Barry Vinson's love life in St. Andrews?"

Emerson, his eyes reflecting his anger, said he would speak immediately with Mr. Bradley.

"Did anyone ring Vinson's room before he was killed?" asked Morris.

"The one switchboard operator can't possibly remember. She took hundreds of calls that night," said the inspector. "We do know Vinson did not make a call *from* his room. He would have been billed automatically."

"Did Dr. Stewart find anything stuck in the victim's throat?" Morris asked, suddenly remembering the possibility.

"Keep this among us," Emerson said, looking from Morris to Sullivan. "A *golf ball* had been forced into the back of his throat . . . while he was strangling but was still alive. It shut off his air supply and apparently killed him."

"Good Lord," Morris said.

"Yes. And no ordinary golf ball," the inspector said. "It was a *feathery,* and as you know, a very valuable antique."

"Who on earth would have a feathery?" asked Morris. Unspoken was the crueler question: Who would waste it on the already dying Barry Vinson?

"It's a grotesque fact that complicates everything," admitted the inspector.

Morris and Sullivan knew the feathery to have been the golf ball made famous by the Scots in the seventeenth or early eighteenth century, to replace the wooden balls that had been imported from the Dutch and in use up until that time.

A feathery was made of a bull's hide, soaked in alum and stuffed with goose feathers, that had been softened by boiling. The feathery would travel up to twice as far as the old wooden balls, which would rarely cover more than one hundred yards when struck. A feathery, even when invented, cost over twelve times more than one of the old wooden balls, as even an expert could not hope to make more than four featherys in a working day. Any surviving feathery ball was a collector's item, worth a great deal depending on its condition. The feathery itself had been gradually replaced by the gutta-percha ball, beginning in 1848.

"Did someone intend to stick the honorable game of golf down the throat of the dying Mr. Vinson?" asked Morris. "It seems excessive punishment, even for an American who would call the Old Course 'third-rate,' and refer to the tournament as a 'royal pain in the ass' and the club members as 'the ancients . . . running it.' "

"If the killer was intent on making a statement," the

inspector said, "then he succeeded. We won't release the details of the murder. Not yet. And maybe not until we've caught the killer."

Morris nodded his understanding. "Could we stick our noses in Vinson's room?" he asked.

"Certainly. We've finished with it. I'll leave word to let you look around. You might understand something we overlooked."

"Have you located Vinson's ex-caddy, Paul Mason?" asked Morris.

"He contacted us," the inspector said. "He was quite distraught. Several caddies in the old Fleming Hotel on Nelson Street swear they were drinking with him until after midnight."

Morris didn't ask about the young girl Mason met in the Bull and Bear pub . . . the girl Barry Vinson fired him over.

As if reading his thoughts, Inspector Emerson said, "The other caddies admitted there was a row in the Bull and Bear pub . . . between Vinson and young Mason . . . *over a girl* . . . and Vinson fired him on the spot as his caddy. The girl, apparently, disappeared. None of the caddies drinking with Mason are from here, and none of them knew the girl. Neither of the bartenders admits to being aware of the dustup, much less the identity of the girl. I understand the pub was full and loud and happy. But we are speaking with all the regulars we can find who drink there. Mason knows only that the girl was maybe eighteen and had red hair."

"That narrows it down to the female teenage population of Scotland," Morris said.

"We are checking all over St. Andrews and in neighboring villages. We should find her soon."

"Did you happen to ask Mason if he told the R&A about the illegal grooves in Barry Vinson's irons?"

"No," the inspector said, making a note of it. "I absolutely forgot the incident before the tournament began." He seemed disgusted with himself.

"I asked Mason about it, after he'd been fired," Morris said. "He denied telling the R&A anything . . . denied it rather hotly. And convincingly. Mason did say he told 'the lads' in the Bull and Bear about the grooves having been filed deeper . . . and said that he had intended to confront Vinson about it. But then he was fired. Anyone in the pub might have heard Mason and notified the R&A."

Morris added, "I spoke with Vinson before the tournament began. He laughed about the entire incident. Said he had been using other irons 'for two months.' That he just wanted to 'throw a little life into this goddamned past-tense country.' A sweet guy, Vinson . . . the kind of guy people sometimes murder."

Inspector Emerson nodded his understanding. "I'll speak to Mason tomorrow . . . and to the other regulars who were drinking in the pub. You two have been an enormous help."

"We will call you if we hear anything."

They followed the inspector out of the hotel and stood on the high steps, looking over the cold sea as he found his way to his car and driver, waiting at the curb.

"I bet you a quid . . ." Sullivan said.

Morris reached in his pocket and handed her a pound note. "When did anybody ever win a bet from you, Julia Sullivan?"

". . . That we can find the red-haired girl before the inspector does," she said, pocketing the one-pound note as her just payment.

Daylight was just now fading over the wide beach far below, and the sea darkened into a starless night.

Sullivan shamelessly left the breakfast table, having not touched the haggis (being a demonic concoction of sheep's entrails and oats, eaten only by practicing Scotsmen), but carrying a still-warm scone in her bare hand.

Morris could only shake his head. "I can't believe it. You've already eaten five."

"Counting, are you? Let's see, how many whiskys . . . ?"

"Never mind," Morris said. "Let's hike over to the Old Course Hotel. Work off our breakfast. We can ease over to the golf course later. The leaders won't be teeing off until the afternoon."

As they passed the 18th green of the Old Course, Sullivan said, "Do you think the killer is a member of the Royal and Ancient Golf Club? Who else would have a feathery?"

"It's more than possible. It would be interesting to see if a feathery is missing from the R&A's great museum collection. We'll have to ask our Mr. Tait."

The inspector had not forgotten to leave his permission for them to enter Barry Vinson's room, but it took a bit of convincing, all the way up to the manager, for Morris to get a key to room 605. Vinson had been given a prime corner suite, overlooking the dreaded 17th hole and the Royal and Ancient clubhouse in the far distance.

Looking down on the open-trellis fence, old stone wall, and the Jigger Inn beyond it, Morris said, "If we could move the wall and the out-of-bounds, I bet we could sell the real estate to Palmer for the price of Latrobe, Pennsylvania."

"Oh, yes," Sullivan said. "But if you took away his courage to risk the tee shot, he might never have been in contention for the British Open or any other championship. And he would be some other lesser person and golf would still be just a rich man's fancy."

Barry Vinson proved to be a neatnik. His clothes hung in the huge walk-in closet as if on parade; his shoes were lined up as if for inspection. Two huge, expensive suitcases were closed and tucked precisely away in the closet. They checked them immediately. Both were empty, except for his first-class plane ticket back to America.

Morris opened each dresser drawer with Sullivan watching beside him, a keen voyeur of the hidden life of the late Mr. Vinson. Most of his casual clothes came from British Easywear. All of them seemed to be too new to have been cleaned even once. Oddly, the stacks of shirts had been tossed as if from a distance into a drawer and his socks looked as if a cherry bomb had gone off among them.

"Something's wrong all right. This boy was seriously anal retentive," Sullivan said.

Morris couldn't help smiling.

"What are you smiling at?"

Morris did not say that such a description would never fit Julia Sullivan. Nor did he say that, on the other hand, he did admit that none of her own clothes had ever been found on the ceiling of any room. She punched him for what he was thinking.

They went through every drawer meticulously, aware the police had been there before them.

Sullivan reached into a stack of pajamas and lifted out an old stuffed animal, so worn that the stripes identifying it as a tiger had almost vanished, as if it were an endangered species. She held it on her two open palms, forever abandoned. A great tear slid of its own volition out of her eye and down her cheek. "He was plenty nasty. But he was just a boy, Morris." She suddenly wondered when his mother had died. "Nobody had the right to kill him."

"No," Morris said. He touched the sad tiger, as if he expected it to gnaw on his large finger like a kitten.

Vinson's expensive accessories were carefully placed,

including a variety of thin, gold watches in a large jewelry box.

"He must have had a separate watch for every day of a tournament, including practice rounds," Morris said.

Nowhere in the room did they find an address book, or a day planner, or a working calendar of any kind. Unless the police had found it first. And perhaps the killer had been looking for exactly that.

There were no letters in the room either, or postcards, or photographs, or books, or even magazines. Barry Vinson might have been an orphan boy who could not read or write, had no friends or relatives, and was lost in the world of golf, like the three balls untypically loose on his sitting room floor.

They went back to the large closet and Sullivan began running her slim hand into each trouser pocket, and then into each coat pocket, turning them all carefully inside out. Her fingers touched no solid thing, not even loose change. She emptied the right pocket from a blue blazer. Nothing, so far as Morris could tell. But Sullivan followed a patch of whitish fluff drifting aimlessly to the floor. Morris would never have seen it. She lifted it from the closet carpet as if it were a rare specimen of collectible lint.

"Look," she said, tugging at the ends of the fluffy material, which was made up of tiny white threads.

"What?" said Morris.

"See them spring back. They are elastic."

"So?"

Sullivan took his large hand and guided it down inside her dark trousers.

"Listen. We better not. This room . . ."

"Hush," Sullivan said. "Feel that elastic."

"To hell with the room," Morris said, reaching with his large fingers.

She lifted his eager hand away. And then unzipped her

trousers and plucked at the inside of the elastic band on her white panties until her fingers came away with a long strand of fluff, exactly like the patch Morris was still holding in the palm of his hand.

"You think . . ."

"I think our boy burst some girl's undies and, maybe, put them in his pocket as a trophy," Sullivan said, now ashamed of the tear she had spilled over the worn tiger.

"And somebody garroted the bastard and came looking for them?" Morris said skeptically. "Why take such a terrible chance coming here?"

"Maybe the girl meant the whole world to somebody. Maybe the idea of her honor in Vinson's coat pocket was more than he could stand," Sullivan said. "I don't think a killer who would stuff a two-hundred-year-old golf ball down a victim's throat is behaving like your average Jaycee."

"But today? In 1978? In a free-love society?" Morris said.

"And what if we are speaking of rape, Morris? I think Scotland frowns on it."

He thought about it. "I see what you mean. A husband, a father, a lover. Might turn murderous . . . to teach an infidel respect . . . for a beloved young woman . . . and even for the ancient game of golf."

"I believe you have it," Sullivan said, taking the springy fluff back and placing it in a stamped envelope she carried in her purse.

"Of course, that could have been in his pocket for days or weeks or months," Morris said.

"True. But our boy was only killed once . . . two days ago."

"You've got a point there. I think, Sullivan, now is the time to earn that quid I paid you last night."

"And find the red-haired girl from the Bull and Bear," Sullivan said.

* * *

It was a bit early in the day for a full pint of lager. "We'll just have to choke it down," Sullivan said, wiping the mustache off her lips with pleasure.

The Bull and Bear had never required the fake charm of an imitation eighteenth-century public house, with newly distressed brass lamps and falsely scarred tables . . . or even a reclaimed two-hundred-year-old bar from some ex-tavern . . . for the Bull and Bear was heavy with age and old, ruined wood and true brass lamps that had been converted from gas; fourteen generations of Scotsmen had drunk to good and terrible times in this old room, thick today with smoke and talk of golf and murder.

Morris recognized a long table of weathered faces as belonging to licensed St. Andrews caddies, no longer used by the professional golfers who flew their own full-time bag-carriers from as far away as Australia. It seemed to Morris that the table of caddies was avoiding his eyes, and he'd lifted a beer with many of them over the years. Old Alec MacLaine was not among them. The young American, Lowrey, whose bag Old Alec had caught, was well up in the field at level par, with a real chance to win the tournament. Lowrey would not be teeing off for another four hours.

Neither of the two bartenders would ever see this side of seventy again. Both of them knew Morris's face but were not sure of his name, as there were five to seven years between British Opens at St. Andrews. The woman owner, Issette, always recognized Sullivan and wouldn't let her pay for a beer. Golf addicts of every persuasion filled the pub, some of them lifting their first glass in the town of St. Andrews. Morris was sure most of the locals had taken to more distant pubs to escape the outsiders, who were thick on the ground this week.

"Do you mean to tell me," said Sullivan, "that those

two lecherous old bartenders, and that table of sun-ruined caddies, wouldn't know a beautiful, red-haired dolly bird the moment she took her first step into this old, smoke-drenched public house, and know her father and her grandfather and her great-grandfather before her?"

"I would not tell you that," Morris said.

"Surely the inspector didn't believe them."

"Surely not."

Morris had a go at the older of the two bartenders, who he knew had been drawing beer in this pub at least since 1960, the year Palmer lost to Kel Nagle by a bare stroke. Morris and Palmer had shared a draft drawn by the very man himself. Morris waited until the delicate task of measuring the head in his mug was done, then recalled that time and moment with Palmer to the old man, who admitted to the name of Laidlay, and who grunted his memory of those two beers.

"Gowf is a way o' killin' a man . . . an' nae mair 'ope for Mr. Palmer. 'E's left 'is 'eart on the Road 'ole these eightin years," said the old man.

"True," Morris said. He let his beer rest on the bar without tasting it. "Mr. Laidlay, a young red-haired woman came into the Bull and Bear two nights ago. There was a bit of a flare-up at her table. I believe you have been asked about her. It's terribly important that we find her. I do not believe her to be guilty of anything. But I know New Scotland Yard will not rest until she's found. It will go better for her and her people if we find her first."

Laidlay's face might have turned to stone. Even his eyes were lifeless. He did not speak. And Morris knew that he—nor any man in the room—would never speak to him of the phantom girl.

* * *

Sullivan waited until the woman she had known only as Issette for twenty years, tall and still athletic but now entirely gray, moved toward the women's loo. Sullivan knew her to be owner, bookkeeper, and sometimes temporary scullery maid, when the pub's help failed.

"Issette," Sullivan said, almost in a whisper.

Tears were already threatening in Issette's eyes.

Morris returned with his beer to their table. Sullivan was nowhere to be seen. Well, she was never one to pass up a lady's room, even one as grim as the Bull and Bear's. Ah, yes, here she came. But the look on her face frightened him. He had first seen it years ago, when he woke up in the hospital after the terrible automobile crash; even before she'd spoken he'd known that Monty Sullivan was dead.

"Let's get out of here, Morris," she said.

He followed her outdoors, which was unnaturally sunny.

"What?" he asked.

She told him. Issette, an old friend, who had owned and worked in the pub for a generation, had been weeping for two days. She had been unable to come to work yesterday in her grief . . . and had not spoken to the police. Not yet. Sullivan had hugged her and comforted her and learned what she knew in a matter of minutes . . . with a promise only to visit the girl before recommending to the family what it should do . . . or going to the police.

"Neither Issette nor the girl fears us," Sullivan said. "They are terrified of Scotland Yard."

The two of them hardly spoke walking back to the hotel. Morris cranked the small Ford and weaved through spit-and-snarl traffic out Pilmour Links Road. Golf along the Old Course might have been playing in another century. Morris parked outside the old stone house. Sullivan touched his hand and left him alone in the bright sun coming through the windscreen.

Anne Kirkcaldy looked astonishingly like her daughter, Sharon, who might have been taken for her younger sister. Her eyes were afraid, but entirely dry. She had no more tears to weep. She hugged Sullivan like the mother she could hardly remember, then took her inside and left her at the door to her daughter's room.

Sharon's face was turned to the wall. Her bright red hair spilled on the pillow, as if denying the sorrow in the room. Sullivan sat on the edge of the bed and gently turned her fragile shoulders toward her. Sullivan did not flinch from the blue and yellow bruises under her eyes or her still-swollen lips.

Sullivan held her for a long time while she wept new tears. She was light and trembled like a frightened bird in Sullivan's arms. Sullivan dried her tears, which spilled among her freckles; she might have been a small child who had taken a bad fall in the schoolyard, rather than an eighteen-year-old who had passed her O-levels and was ready to be off for university and had been beaten and brutally raped three days ago by the late Barry Vinson.

After a long silence Sharon, in a soft Scottish voice, began telling Sullivan what had happened to her, a ghastly story she would never be able to tell her own mother. Sullivan sat with her, patting her, soothing her, like the child she'd never had.

Despite his anxiety, Morris, after an hour of sitting in the sun-warmed Ford, fell asleep. Sullivan opened the car door and ran her hand through his thick hair. "Wake up, old man. It's time to go."

Sullivan described to him the fragile Sharon lying in her arms, until tears came to Morris's eyes . . . to be replaced by anger so murderous he hesitated to start the car.

Sullivan re-created what had happened: After the dustup in the Bull and Bear—where Sharon was permitted to go, even at the tender age of eighteen, because of the protective presence of her "Auntie" Issette—Sharon had left the pub. It was several miles home, but a walk she'd made many times. She didn't want to bother her mother, who got up early for her job in Burns's Sweet Shop.

Barry Vinson had pulled alongside her in his green Jaguar, with a friendly smile and an apology for what had happened. He was a famous American golfer. An Open champion. She had known nothing but pleasure from golf, oftentimes following her grandfather around the links when he caddied for Captain Tait, or some other member of the R&A, who knew her to be a lass as quiet as the heather and who never had to be reminded where not to stand or jostled to keep up. And she played a smart game herself, despite her fragile size.

Vinson had turned up the rock music on the radio and whipped the Jaguar through the dark countryside, seeming to enjoy Sharon's delight in the splendid automobile. Even when he pulled into a lonesome lay-by and stopped, the headlights were still on, the music playing, and he was smiling, friendly as any American. When he kissed her once, it was done lightly and in good fun, and she would have a moment to tell her mates about. Then the headlights went dark, by themselves, as if the automobile were threatening her. He pulled her against him, his arms too powerful to resist, and kissed her roughly. She cried out, and he slapped her so hard that tears came to her eyes. His arms and strong hands . . . she fought but couldn't stop him. When she screamed, he hit her with his fist, and she thought her face was broken. And then he hurt her for a long time until she couldn't cry anymore.

Home was the only word she could say. And barely point the way, hurting, her clothes ruined. He opened the door and pushed her out. It was not late. Her mother was not even worried until she saw her in the door, weeping, bleeding, unable to stand alone. Old Alec had sent for the family doctor, who took the girl to Gipson Hospital in her grandfather's arms.

Morris said, "I'm betting Old Alec *called Barry Vinson on the telephone from the hospital.* It's only a couple of blocks from the cathedral. Maybe he threatened him with the police. Rape is not a two-stroke penalty and a free drop in Scotland. Vinson could have served twenty-five years in prison. Maybe Old Alec pretended to blackmail him. Maybe that's why Vinson had so much cash in his pockets, which went untouched by his killer. None of the family heard what Old Alec said. He kept them out of the room. For whatever reason, Vinson agreed to meet Old Alec in the graveyard. No doubt he killed the son of a bitch, then drove Vinson's own Jaguar to search his hotel room."

Morris thought, Old Alec could kill him, too. A half-century of shouldering two seventy-pound bags of clubs for four miles, his arms like steel bands.

"And the feathery ball," Sullivan said, closing her eyes at the thought of its being crammed down the throat of the Ugly American.

"All these years looking for lost balls in the heather and gorse," said Morris, "I'm sure Old Alec found featheries, lost for more than a century, and so must his father and grandfather before him, both of them caddies here all of their lives. What the hell should we do, Sullivan?" Morris slapped his open palm on the steering wheel of the motionless Ford.

Sullivan said, "Who is the man I sleep with who's

always saying, 'Never come to a conclusion before you know the essential facts'? We don't *know* that Old Alec MacLaine killed anybody. We know how much he loved his granddaughter. We know what Barry Vinson did to her. We believe Old Alec called him on the phone. We know how powerful Old Alec is, despite his age. We know finding golf balls are his business. But we don't *know* that he owned a two hundred-year-old ball. We don't *know* where he was two nights ago. We don't *know* that he killed anybody."

"This man you sleep with doesn't always do as he says," admitted Morris. "But it doesn't look good for Old Alec MacLaine. You have to admit that."

She sighed. "You know what I need. I need some golf."

"Yes. We can't even talk to Old Alec until his afternoon round is finished . . . and do we truly want to talk to him at all? The police, you can be sure, in the history of the organization, have never asked the moral question: *'Did the man need killing?'* Maybe we let them sort it out for themselves," Morris said. "The old men in the Bull and Bear have made up their minds to never speak of the crime or the punishment. And, by God, it's their country, not ours, however much we may love it."

"Take me to some golf, Morris. I've had enough of the world for one day," Sullivan said.

The silence of the play, even the absence of wind, seemed surrealistic after the violence of the week. Though the course appeared vulnerable without its protective winds, the Pin Placement Committee had secreted the cups in every deadly swale of the greens, so that the golfers were making their first putts from painful distances.

Sullivan and Morris, with their spirits drooping, watched Crenshaw, with every daring, thread irons to within four feet of the pin on the 3rd and 4th holes, but the small man with the great touch drew his putter back as slowly as regret and brought it smoothly forward . . . only to miss both putts. His confidence suffered, and only his nerves got him around the course, one over par and a shot out of the lead he had held after the second round.

There was an unfortunate landing and taking off of helicopters, depositing and removing self-appointed VIPs from the Old Course. Nicklaus backed away from a thirteen-foot putt on No. 1, and backed away again. If looks could have brought down a helicopter, one would be swimming in St. Andrews Bay. Jack missed the putt. But on the fourth hole, in a rare absence of helicopters, he drained an eighteen-foot putt for a birdie.

Morris and Sullivan followed his high, high immaculate drives, which resulted in pars until he reached the short, par-3 No. 8. Jack bent over a birdie putt and backed away three times because of a hovering helicopter. Finally, he three-putted for a bogey 4. After the round, Nicklaus said, "I counted eleven separate helicopters. They drove me crazy."

But even an insane Nicklaus is a force to be reckoned with. Birdies escaped him through the easy holes of the Loop—which brought him, downcast, to the fearsome, par-5 14th, with out-of-bounds squeezing in from the right, the Beardies bunkers to the left, and Hell Bunker up ahead. Nicklaus would have no part of any of them, driving into Elysian Fields, laying up intelligently with his second shot, and spinning a wedge six feet from the hole. Jack stared the putt into submission and willed it into the hole and recovered his momentum.

His drive on No. 15 scraped the sun and left him a short iron to the green, and with his instinct for the jugular throbbing in his hands, he drowned a twelve-foot putt for birdie.

Sullivan beat Jack to the 17th tee, with Morris poling his bad leg through the innocent masses to keep up. Nicklaus took no time in dispatching a huge drive over the trellis wall and following it with a two-iron from the light rough, which nearly reached the upper surface of the green. A bogey on the Road Hole left him four under par for the day. Nicklaus had passed fourteen players and eleven helicopters and found himself only two strokes off the lead going into the final day.

Sullivan was thankful they had gotten to the 17th tee too late to see Palmer, again, drive his ball off the Jigger Inn and take another 7 and destroy another good round and any lingering championship hopes. The finishing holes also damaged the round for Tom Weiskopf, but he, like Nicklaus, lay only two strokes back at 213, with Tom Kite, Nick Faldo, and John Schroeder.

No player, in all of the great history of the Old Course, ever suffered so grievously on the fearful 17th, the Road Hole, as did Japan's Tusneyuki Nakajima. He arrived on the 17th tee one under par, and very much in the chase for the Open title. Nakajima's drive blew down the fairway, and his two-iron miraculously found the green, but came to rest above the hole. His first putt skirted the cup and, sadly, ruinously, continued down and off the green into the Road Bunker.

Through his binoculars, Morris saw sand erupt in the bunker: once, twice, an astonishing *four* times, until Nakajima staggered off the 17th green with a *nine* and a 76 on the day. To this hour, the sand in the Road Hole Bunker is known over all of Scotland as *the sands of Nakajima.*

Tusneyuki's countryman, Isao Aoki, survived the day with a 73 (212), one stroke off the lead, and tied with Simon Owen of New Zealand, who shot the day's best score of 67.

And the leaders? Tom Watson and Britain's Peter Oosterhuis at 211.

"We might have missed seeing the champion, Sullivan," Morris said. They did not see Watson make even one of his 70 shots, or Oosterhuis one of his 69.

"Not to worry," Sullivan said. "I didn't place our whack on either man." But the fun had gone, even out of their bet—though the golf helped, if golf could be said to help a sinking man's spirit.

At the 18th tee Morris and Sullivan caught up with the young American, Lowrey, being handed his driver by Old Alec himself. Thoughts of murder, which had dissipated somewhat with the silence and the old, grand rituals of golf, flooded back through them both.

Lowrey struck a monstrous drive within ten yards of the home green.

Sullivan and Morris could only watch the unchanging concentration of Old Alec, who already had his gnarled hand on the eight-iron he intended Lowrey to use in running his ball up the Valley of Sin, for a putt at a three and a tie for the British Open lead after three rounds. Lowrey waved off the eight and took a sand wedge and dumped it into the Valley of Sin, and was short on his first putt, and bogeyed the simple hole to his own disgust.

Old Alec MacLaine never changed expressions, his face battered by time and wind but tolerant of youth and human frailty. He patted Lowrey on the shoulder, a young man with the world of golf to learn, but still only two shots off the Open lead.

At that instant, Morris did not have to look at Sullivan to know that New Scotland Yard was on its own in its investigation into the death of the American golfer Barry Vinson.

• CHAPTER SIX •

"Here's to Ma Bell's Tavern," said Sullivan, who sat at the bar like a local.

"Here's to our hotel, which is wise enough to have its own tavern," said Morris, standing behind her, eating pretzels off her plate.

"Isn't it wonderful when the earth turns on its axis and that terrible decision *you no longer have to make* is on the dark side from the sun?"

"I'll drink to that and to all Scotland," Morris said. "It'll be something to drink to when we're old and can't remember who won the 1978 British Open."

"Here's to the leaders: Watson and Oosterhuis."

"It's fun to say *Oosterhuis,*" Sullivan said. "*Oosterhuis, Oosterhuis.* It sounds like a German automobile."

"Did you put our whack on Oosterhuis?"

Sullivan turned on the stool and looked up at him; if she had been wearing glasses, she would have been looking disapprovingly over them, like his sixth-grade teacher when he'd neglected his lessons.

"You're sure you got down with this bet," Morris said. "Or was it lost in the 'sands of Nakajima'?"

Sullivan did not waste a contemptuous look on such a possibility.

"Do you think we will ever wake up in the night with a terrible regret?" asked Morris quietly.

Sullivan thought about it. "What the hell? Everybody should have one regret. Or maybe we already do. How do you know when you have one, Morris?"

"I think they come on you like a car wreck," he said.

"Oh. Nobody can unwreck cars." She turned around and pulled his head low and kissed him.

"Och," the bartender said. "The lass deseruv's a whisky."

"And you as well . . . on me," Morris said, lifting his own glass to the young bartender, who poured one for himself.

The tall, thin man in the mirror standing behind Morris was Inspector James Emerson.

"And a glass for Mr. Emerson," Morris said.

The inspector, who looked as if he'd grown even thinner with lack of sleep, raised his whisky to their own.

Morris and Sullivan had not collaborated on how they would answer any questions about the late Barry Vinson. Morris was determined not to ask any questions of his own or offer any fraudulent answers.

It was left to the inspector to say, "There are 30,000 people here for the Open . . . and 156 players. Is there one person among them all who is not a suspect in this case?"

"What have you learned?" asked Sullivan, without an ounce of conscience.

"Half the members of the Royal and Ancient Golf Club fought in the Big War, and the other half have fought in the lesser wars since. Not a crowd you'd want to slap in the face with an insult. Even Captain Tait—every inch the gentleman—parachuted into Normandy the night before the invasion. The medals he won would sink an Olympic swimmer. But then, when you take a critical bridge by *garroting* four German soldiers in the dark, Field Marshal Montgomery himself might pin a medal on you. Which, in fact, he did."

The inspector held up his glass for a refill. He looked at the two of them, as if weighing the odd silence between them.

"We did locate the 'licensed bookie' who took Vinson's fifty thousand pound bet . . . a George McCormack," Emerson said. "It's quite true: Vinson took himself to win, at twelve to one odds. Fancy that much confidence."

Sullivan's mouth flew open, but she didn't speak.

"I expect you met a happy man in McCormack," Morris said.

"He did not conceal his relief that he wouldn't be facing a six hundred thousand pound payout, though he'd laid off a great deal of the bet on Edinburgh bookies." The inspector described McCormack: "Huge man with a great round stomach, arms like cables, quick with a drink for the house, a cigar, and a lively story, but a merciless man to owe money to. There's a saying in St. Andrews: *Aye, owe the divil, chust pay McCormack.*" The inspector said the bookie had spent five years in the Queen's prison for manslaughter. "He doesn't deny it was done with his bare hands. A workingman 'forgot' his wager with the cheerful Mr. McCormack." Emerson added, "McCormack has no alibi, except he was sleeping the sleep of the innocent, he says, in his own flat. He says he does not collect golf memorabilia, though he once accepted a feathery ball as payment on a significant bet. Doesn't remember who he sold the feathery to, or even what year it happened."

Sullivan kept a careful face, saying nothing.

"Sounds like a genuine suspect," Morris said, despite his resolve not to comment. "But why kill Vinson after the *first* round? He might have shot himself out of the tournament in the second or third rounds."

"McCormack raised the same question," the inspector said. "Then again, if Vinson continued to lead the tournament, things would be even hotter for his bookie than they presently are . . . if Vinson turned up dead on the cathedral grounds."

"Is there a feathery missing from the R&A collection?" asked Sullivan, her smile offering nothing.

"No. Absolutely not," Inspector Emerson said. "Captain Tait and two other officers of the club walked me through their entire collection of golf artifacts. No feathery ball is missing from their museum collection in the South Room."

Morris knew the Royal and Ancient collection was carefully watched over and would one day make up the core of the British Golf Museum, to be built directly behind the R&A clubhouse.

"Have you spoken with Sir Arthur Maxwell?" asked Morris, before he could stop himself.

"Yes," the inspector said. "He's very much distressed. Barry Vinson's line of clothes was, indeed, his most profitable. He'd planned to offer him more money . . . against the American offer."

"Not a likely suspect," said Morris, unable to bite his own tongue.

"No," Emerson said. "And yet, Sir Arthur was heavyweight boxing champion of Cambridge and won serious medals for valor in Vietnam."

"Are there no cowards in Great Britain?" asked Sullivan. She answered her own question: "We must remember these small islands dominated the world for two hundred years. There's a statue at every intersection in London to some hero who led ten thousand to their willing deaths."

"Desperation is different from cowardice," said Morris, mentally telling himself to hush.

"Yes, indeed," the inspector said. "If the clothing line was lost . . . if his company was lost . . . could Sir Arthur have taken out his humiliation on Mr. Vinson?" The inspector thought about it. "Doesn't seem likely. But then again, Maxwell claims to have been working on the company books in his room at the Old Course Hotel late into the night. No witnesses, of course. Captain Tait retired early. He's a widower and sleeps alone. Your USGA president, Warren Lightfoot, having seen the green Jaguar leaving the hotel, ate a late sandwich in his room and fell asleep watching television."

"So much for a rowdy night in old St. Andrews," Sullivan could not resist saying.

Inspector Emerson put his glass firmly on the bar. "And what were you two about all day long?" he asked, as if suddenly realizing the night's conversation had been very much one-sided.

Morris had the uneasy feeling that Emerson suspected more than his eyes betrayed. With Sullivan pitching in when he faltered, Morris described the golf they had seen and absorbed during the third round of the Open. If the inspector realized that each of the golfers they had followed had teed off *in the afternoon,* he did not give it away, nor ask them what they had done with their morning. Morris had the feeling the question was in the air . . . only that it was unspoken.

The inspector did ask, "What are the golfers saying?"

Morris told him what they had heard. Including that Barry Vinson was nobody's best buddy. Golfers wouldn't look him up for a drink. But the kid could play. And maybe he would have grown up. "*Maybe,*" Morris quoted himself, doubtfully.

"What's the mood at New Scotland Yard?" asked Sullivan. Morris kicked her shoe under the bar. Sullivan kicked back, much harder, stinging his ankle.

"Nothing beyond absolute hysteria," Inspector Emerson said. "There's even been a call from the Royal family. Caused a bit of a stir. Enough to dispatch five more inspectors to St. Andrews. God knows what I will do with them. We are drowning in inspectors. We need one sure lead.'' He looked up, as if aware of being betrayed here in Ma Bell's Tavern.

And so he is, thought Morris, but he was in no way tempted to reveal Old Alec MacLaine as the prime suspect in a killing all Scotland would applaud.

''Inspector, have you identified the red-haired girl?''

Morris could have poured his lager in Sullivan's lap. Of course, it was the question that had to be asked.

''No,'' said Emerson, looking down at his empty glass and looking up again at them both. ''I have no doubt she is known by every old bastard who was drinking in the Bull and Bear. We are calling them in, one by one.'' He looked at his watch. ''Even as we speak. Someone will talk, finally. Someone always does.''

Morris did not know if the inspector's eyes were accusing them, or if his own heavy conscience gave him that impression.

''Did any of the players see Vinson leave the hotel?'' asked Morris. *What the hell,* he thought, *we're subverting his investigation, we might as well sound convincing.*

''Yes,'' Inspector Emerson said. ''A young British amateur saw him walk through the lobby and out the front door. About 11:40 P.M.,'' he added, without being asked.

''More than an hour before Warren Lightfoot saw his Jaguar pull away from the hotel,'' said Morris.

''Plenty of time for someone to kill him and drive his Jaguar back to search his suite,'' the inspector said. ''Did you two notice anything in his room that we might have overlooked?''

Morris was relieved that Emerson looked directly at Sullivan, who never blinked.

''Yes,'' Sullivan said.

Morris nearly choked on his beer.

"Where was his putter?" she asked. "Vinson was one of those players, like Trevino, who always carried his putter to his room . . . to practice on the carpet. We saw several balls on the floor and an upturned drinking glass Vinson was putting into. But no putter!"

Morris could have kissed her on the spot. He'd seen the balls and the drinking glass and immediately had known why they were there, but hadn't thought about the missing putter.

Neither had the inspector. "But why take the man's putter?" Emerson asked, as if to himself. "Vinson was garroted, not bludgeoned. The putter couldn't possibly be evidence."

"We're assuming the putter is not safely in his bag in the clubhouse," Morris said. "But then . . . if he had been putting the night *before* he was killed, surely the maids would have picked up the glass, if not the balls. Your question is a good one: Why would the killer risk carrying the putter out of the suite?" It was a question Morris couldn't begin to answer for himself.

"We'll check his golf bag and talk with the maids," said the inspector.

Morris said, "Well, a hundred years from now, the murder will be a forgotten footnote in the history of the 1978 British Open championship."

"Oh, no," said Emerson, lifting his hand in a parting salute. "We are a people who love a murder more than a champion. But especially an unsolved murder . . . which this one, I swear in the Queen's name, *will not be.*"

Morris lifted his glass, as if to the challenge, as the inspector left Ma Bell's Tavern and the hotel.

Sullivan waited until the inspector was out of sight. "Morris, we may have to collect from 'the divil'—this McCormack. That's the licensed bookie I placed our bet with."

"Terrific, Sullivan. If we win, maybe we can arrange to be strangled together. Where did you run into him?"

"I didn't. I looked him up. He has a betting shop just off the 18th fairway of the Old Course. Not a cheerful man, this McCormack. He took my cash and gave me this marker." She held it up for Morris to see, but not near enough for him to see just how large their bet was. From much experience, he knew it wasn't any larger than the gross national product of Scotland.

"So if we win, you'll send me to collect from this convicted killer?" Morris said.

"You're quick," Sullivan said. "Do you think the inspector suspects us of holding out on him?"

"He doesn't suspect. He *knows,*" Morris said. "He just doesn't know *what* we're concealing. Or maybe he thinks we are just bored with it. He's known us a long time, but he doesn't know us very well, Sullivan."

"I'm not so sure."

"Listen, you never mentioned the missing putter," Morris said. "And I never thought of it."

"Neither did I, until just this minute," Sullivan said. "I was turning over in my mind how to answer his question . . . *did we see anything the police had missed* . . . and it just came to me . . . Morris, do you think Old Alec took the putter?"

"He must've. The maids would have picked up the glass, and probably the balls . . . if Vinson hadn't left them there the night he was killed. Why the hell would Old Alec take such a risk to steal a mallet-head putter?"

Sullivan thought. She shook her head. "We know what Old Alec came for . . . and took from Vinson's jacket. I'm sure of it."

"Then he took the putter as some kind of steel-shafted trophy? Stuffed it under that evil old sweater of his? For God's sake, *why*? It meant nothing. Now it's evidence that could send him to jail for life."

"There's only one way we'll ever know," Sullivan said; "if they catch him."

"Oh, they'll catch him. The inspector will light a fire in somebody's whiskers, which will show the way to Sharon Kirkcaldy and the old man's motive for murder. Question is, can they convict him? Expect anything, Sullivan. But don't expect a confession. That old Scot doesn't even speak if you decline to chip with the eight-iron he hands you on the 18th hole. Ask young Lowrey."

Morris brooded for a minute. "If I don't think about Vinson's body lying faceup in the graveyard, Old Alec's killing him doesn't bother me so much. Though I don't ever want to shake the old man's hand again."

"I know how you feel. Alive, Vinson was such a son of a bitch. And what he did to that girl . . . I might have killed him myself." Sullivan sat in silence. "To be honest, I don't like to remember the old, ruined, stuffed tiger among Vinson's things, or think of him as a boy, alone, playing golf on some military base in some country to which he would never belong."

"No," Morris said. "But it's up to a man, finally, if he chooses to belong somewhere."

Sullivan finished her drink and stood up. "I belong in bed. Do you know of one in Scotland where I am welcome?"

"Oh, yes, it's a tolerant country."

The morning sunlight burned itself into sound, tearing into the room. Morris picked up the phone before he was awake.

Captain A.W.B. Tait of the Royal and Ancient Golf Club identified himself, as much with his Scottish tongue as with his proper name. "Ol' Alec . . . he's deid, Morris. An na' innis sleep. A guid man killed innis own 'ome . . . by the same 'and as done Vinson." Tait gave him a straightforward account of what he had seen, then said, "Ah, 'orrible work of the divil 'isself. What d'ye make of it, Morris?"

Morris finally realized that the captain could not see him shaking his own head. "I'm . . . amazed," Morris said. *Amazed* was a word Tait could not be expected to understand, not knowing who had killed Barry Vinson. ". . . And sick," Morris quickly added. In truth, he was too amazed at the moment to be anything else.

Tait said that he would be releasing information—but no details of the murder—much later in the day. The inspector wanted to work undisturbed for as long as possible. Old Alec would not be missed until the young American, Lowrey, would need his clubs to prepare for the afternoon's final round of the Open. The R&A would see that Lowrey was furnished a proper caddy. Of course, there was "niver but one Old Alec MacLaine."

Morris agreed, still too amazed to trust his own thoughts.

Tait said, "Dinna tell the inspector tha' I called. 'E doesna' want the press thair."

Morris was now awake as if he'd never slept in his life. He sat up so abruptly as to wake the unwakeable Sullivan. He spun out the story to her as if it were a recording. Captain Tait had been called by Inspector Emerson. He had gone to Old Alec's ancient croft house on Pilmour Links Road, where the body had been found by his daughter, Anne Kirkcaldy, who'd come from next door to cook his breakfast, as she often did. Old Alec had been murdered, *garroted,* in the same manner as Barry Vinson, only the implement of his death was still around his neck.

Sullivan pried every word out of him, as if she were a sitting grand jury. "How could we have been so wrong?" she asked.

Morris could only shake his head. Even after a cold

shower, he couldn't imagine what had happened . . . who had killed them both . . . and why?

"I don't need any breakfast," Morris said. "I'll be eating crow for the inspector. I shouldn't be surprised if he throws us out in the street . . . if he doesn't arrest us for obstructing an investigation."

Sullivan felt the same remorse, but not so strongly that she didn't snatch up a handful of warm scones and a cup of hot tea on the way out of the hotel.

It was too early even for the first golfers to be teeing off on the Old Course. Only the ground crews were out, mowing the greens and fairways; and the Pin Placement Committee, with Gerald Balfour-Melville Dougall presiding from a golf cart, was kneeling, setting the cups in all the awkward places, as the oldest Open went about identifying with the cruelest possible challenge the greatest champion in the game of golf. All of the committee looked to their separate tasks, unaware of the death of the old man who had caddied these seaside links for forty-nine of his seventy-two years.

Morris parked the small Ford outside the low, dark house, which might have been built of the same stones as the old bridge over Swilcan Burn. No bright tape had been put up to mark the crime scene. Anonymity was what the police hoped for at the moment. Morris walked straight up and knocked on the low front door as if to confess to the crime.

Inspector Emerson surprised him by not changing expressions, or even warning him what not to touch in the doorway. He nodded toward Sullivan, who stepped up beside Morris, as if an accomplice in the crime. "I'll be right out," said Emerson, no hint of anger in his voice. His eyes did not accuse them or ask how they came to be standing at the crime scene at the break of day.

The inspector closed the heavy door behind him. "I've met the *red-haired* granddaughter," he said, looking directly at Morris. "I haven't yet questioned her at any length. What can you tell me *that you wouldn't tell me last night*?" There was severity in his voice.

Morris told him everything they knew of the terrible rape of the fragile girl that night in Vinson's Jaguar. Sullivan even presented the wisp of white elastic from Vinson's coat pocket, which she had preserved in a stamped envelope in her purse.

"So, the two of you did not imagine that Great Britain might be able to sort out justice for itself?" Emerson said. There was as much sadness as anger in his voice.

Neither Morris nor Sullivan denied it. Or offered a false apology.

"And the victim an American," the inspector said, "if a particularly unsavory one." His tone now indicated there might be at least two other unsavory Americans presently in Scotland.

Morris only nodded.

"You also did not imagine that *you could be wrong,*" Emerson said, now truly accusatory, his thin hand trembling on the doorknob to the old house.

Morris and Sullivan nodded that it was regrettably so, like two children brought before disappointed parents.

"And maybe this man would be in jail," Emerson said, "but surely he would *still be alive.*" And now there was only regret in his voice.

Morris could not imagine the pain showing in his own face.

The inspector was silent for a long time. "If I had known what the two of you knew . . . I would have come to the same conclusion," he admitted. "I can only hope I would have seen clear to do my duty as a citizen." The inspector looked at first one and then the other. "Do not imagine you are the only two in St. Andrews who loved this old man, or *the fact of him,* speaking for those of us who didn't know him so well as you.

I've seen him on the Old Course, or in a pub, almost every time I've come to St. Andrews. And I read two of the pieces you wrote about him some years ago, Morris. . . ." Inspector Emerson had crossed some river of anger and distrust regarding the two of them; perhaps out of friendship, perhaps out of fearful necessity . . . a second man garroted, with the bloody world looking on, and he farther from a solution than the time of the first murder. "But how do we explain *this*?" Emerson pointed toward the closed door and the body of the old man, unseen, behind it.

"I'm amazed," Morris said, for the second time that morning.

"Yes," agreed Emerson.

"Old Alec . . . if he didn't kill Vinson . . . might have known who did," Sullivan said.

"Not likely he would have told in this life," Morris said.

"No. But he might have confronted the killer," Sullivan said.

Morris nodded. "Threatened him? With blackmail? The man who avenged the rape of the granddaughter he loved beyond anything?"

"Not likely. But the killer couldn't be sure of that," Emerson said, as if all their words were one puzzled monologue.

"Why," Morris asked. "Why kill Vinson, if not for what he did to the girl?"

"The man insulted golf, the Old Course, the Royal and Ancient Golf Club, and all Scotland," Sullivan said. "You said yourself, kings and queens have died for less."

"There's truth in that . . . even if I said it."

"But why kill Old Alec? For any sane reason?" said Sullivan.

"Not so likely, either, that we have a madman loose in

the population,'' the inspector said. ''What common insanity would kill a nasty young golfer from America and a well-loved old caddy from St. Andrews?''

Morris could offer no logical explanation.

''Come look at the murder scene,'' the inspector said, pushing open the heavy door, and pushing away any lingering resentment against the two of them for what they had not told him.

The photographers had snapped their last shots. Old Dr. Calvin Stewart, his words all grumbles, waited to get his hands on the corpse of the man he had known for half a century.

Under the one naked bulb, hanging from the low ceiling, Old Alec MacLaine lay on his face, his beard crushed into the stone floor, his left eye bulging open, as if staring over his shoulder in fury at his murderer. Two smooth round wooden handles crossed one another on the back of his old wool sweater, the single wire loop connecting them buried in a bloody circle around his thick neck. Just the one straight-backed chair had been toppled over in the struggle, which could not have been long, or sprawling, with the other heavy furniture still obviously in place in the stone room.

''Is there a feathery . . .'' began Morris.

''Ball in his throat?'' Inspector Emerson finished. ''There seems to be. I could feel something, maybe a ball, with my finger. But I was very careful not to disturb him until he could be photographed and the doctor could examine him.''

''Then it would have to be the same killer,'' Morris said. ''You never released the details of Vinson's death.''

''No. But a number of people . . . with the ambulance crew . . . in the morgue . . . with the police—and I'm sorry to say, with New Scotland Yard—know the details. And the aspects of Vinson's murder and this one are so . . . dramatic. They are bound to be repeated,'' the inspector said. ''And probably already have been.''

Morris propped himself up with his cane. ''No small job, killing Old Alec with your two hands and a garrote.''

''He was careful to take him from behind,'' said Emerson. ''And this time, the wire cut deeply enough into his neck to strangle him. The ball, if it's truly in his throat, wasn't needed. Still, it took nerve enough. Old Alec was a powerful man, even drunk, and might have turned to face his killer at the critical moment.''

The smell of whisky still mingled with the smell of death.

''He was drinking,'' the inspector said. ''No doubt. The bottle on the table is nearly spent, and a twenty-year-old whisky at that.''

''I've drunk with Old Alec,'' Morris said. ''Never saw him lift a glass of twenty-year-old whisky . . . in fact any whisky *that he paid for.* He was a close man with his advice to a golfer, and with his spending money.''

''He was drinking another man's whisky last night, you can be sure,'' the inspector said. ''The same man who looped the wire around his neck, I would imagine.''

''Had to be someone he knew well,'' Morris said, ''for the man to be here . . . even pouring his own fine whisky. But for what purpose? What could have been said here, or done here, that led to the murder . . . or did the killer *bring his intent with him*?''

The inspector nodded his own puzzlement.

''Is this the same . . .'' began Sullivan, pointing to the corpse.

''Garrote? That killed Barry Vinson? It's very possible,'' Inspector Emerson said. ''We'll know soon enough . . . unless it was scalded clean after Vinson's death. And it doesn't appear to have been cleaned at all.''

Morris knelt to look closely at the two smooth handles and the wire, all of them dark with age. ''I swear this is a military weapon,'' Morris said. ''It doesn't have a home-made look about it.''

''No,'' Emerson said. ''I'm thinking it dates to World War Two. I've seen them in the military museums.''

''Old Alec himself was a commando,'' Morris reminded him.

Emerson nodded. ''One strong reason you were so sure he killed Barry Vinson.'' It was a statement, not an accusation.

Morris nodded yes. ''But half the membership of the Royal and Ancient Golf Club distinguished itself in that war. And God knows how many other men here in St. Andrews did the same. Though anybody who fought in World War Two would likely be sixty years old or more.''

''Of course, Old Alec was seventy-two and strong as the whisky he was drinking,'' Sullivan said. ''Inspector, you said his daughter found him?''

''Yes, this morning. Before daybreak. Anne came over to fry up his breakfast. Found him just like this. Put her in a terrible state. It took her own daughter, Sharon, nearly half an hour to calm her down enough to tell her what happened so that she could call the police. The mother is still too hysterical to be interviewed.''

''Had you suspected Old Alec . . . in Vinson's death?'' asked Morris.

Emerson shook his thin head. ''We hadn't gotten that far. But I had an appointment today with the owner of the Bull and Bear . . . Issette Locke. I meant to find out the identity of the red-haired girl . . . or hold her as a material witness.''

"But you would have been a long way from a confession," Morris said.

"Indeed," said Emerson. "We would have needed this weapon to prove anything." He indicated the wooden handles and the deadly wire, which Dr. Stewart at that instant was unwinding from the circular gash around Old Alec's neck.

"So now . . . you question the Old Guard in the R&A, and all the local and international world of golf—which is just about every person in St. Andrews," said Morris.

"And the bloody tournament ends *today,*" the inspector said, bending his thin head downward, as if in obeisance to the darker fates. There was a knock on the heavy wooden door, and five young officers, with that many assistants, were waiting to take the room and the entire house apart.

"Morris," Emerson said, pulling him aside. "I intend to call on you two—and your knowledge of the golf world—if the evidence leads to the Queen Mother. May I count on your candor?"

"Yes," Morris said, and meant it.

"Inspector, could I look in on Sharon and her mother?" asked Sullivan.

He nodded, warning her the mother might still be hysterical.

Sullivan stepped inside next door, only long enough to hug both mother and daughter, who were huddled together on the same bed in their shared misery. It did encourage Sullivan to see the recently traumatized Sharon Kirkcaldy soothing her weeping mother.

Morris waited outside the old wooden door.

"The man who did this . . . must pay for it," Sullivan said. She was too outraged to ride as a passenger and drove the small Ford back to their hotel, lucky to find their parking place still empty in front of the hotel. The short drive had calmed her anger. "Morris, I don't think I could have forgiven the two of us as readily as the inspector did."

"No," Morris said, hoping to break the gloom in the car by needling her a bit. "You still remember my crush on the young woman journalist from Australia at the 1969 British Open. And I only changed a ten-pound note for her so she could buy stamps."

"Yes, and don't ever let me see you again throwing big money at some Australian journalist, batting her false eyelashes."

"Her eyelashes weren't false."

"How do you know?"

"She closed her eyes when she kissed me good-bye."

"John Morris! There have already been two murders in St. Andrews. You wouldn't want to go for a third?"

"No." Morris laughed. "I don't think you would have been as generous with the two us. All we imagined we were doing was helping an anonymous old man get away with killing a famous young man."

"A famous *rapist,*" Sullivan said.

"If we were wrong about Old Alec . . . could we have been wrong about his granddaughter?" asked Morris.

"No. Sharon Kirkcaldy was too near a complete breakdown to even imagine telling me a lie," Sullivan said. "Remember, Morris, we never spoke to Old Alec about Vinson's death. And we never would've. We can only imagine how he would have reacted."

"I still don't understand anything," Morris said. "We can hope forensics will tell us something."

Captain Tait was waiting for them in the dining room of the St. Andrews Golf Hotel, his face strained with the knowledge of a second murder.

"D'ye keen Ol' Alec and 'im deid?" asked Tait.

"Makes no sense to us," Morris said, "or to Inspector Emerson, either." Morris then explained why he and Sullivan had suspected Old Alec of killing Barry Vinson. Tait had known young Sharon Kirkcaldy since she was a barefoot child, and tears of outrage sprang to his eyes. He swore on his honor as a Scotsman never to mention the incident. "Pity we canna' blow the aiyer back in the bastard Vinson an kill 'im o'er," he said.

Sullivan could not suppress the thought that the captain might be confessing to having put him down the first time.

Tait hesitated to speak further, and then leaned nearer to Morris. "I was oot, Morris. La' nite, lookin' for ma guid cronies at the Bull an' Bear, a motley lot. An' I met wi' a widow. Too much aloone, d'ye ken?"

Widower that he was, thought Morris. Plenty of old cronies at the Royal and Ancient Golf Club, but maybe none of them comely and needing companionship. *God bless you,* Morris almost said.

Tait said he had spoken with Old Alec after the third round. He said, "The toornament an' 'is American lad, Lowrey, wa' oon 'is mind. *'E cuid run awa' frae the field, tha' one,* 'e said."

Morris listened closely to understand what else Captain Tait and Old Alec had discussed. Old Alec had believed that the winds would shift around from the westward, opposite of how they had blown for the three opening rounds. Players who did not know the wind from Guardbridge would suffer mightily. Captain Tait, despite all that had happened, confessed he was pleased to step outside this morning and see that Old Alec had been correct; the winds had shifted from the westward, proving all the meteorologists mutton-headed, and putting a welcome uncertainty into the minds of the golfers. The Old Course was fighting back, as it had for five hundred years.

Morris hated to shift the captain's mind from "gowf" to murder. "Had Old Alec been drinking last night? I mean, seriously?"

"Oo, yes." The captain had never seen him so pissed.

"Who had he been drinking with?" asked Morris.

Tait hesitated again, then blew out his breath and admitted that Old Alec had forgotten his wool cap at a long table of locals, including the punter, George McCormack, who was buying the drinks as often as not. Tait did not remember exactly when Old Alec had left the bar. He didn't think it was later than nine P.M. But he was only guessing. He just looked up and Old Alec, who had drunk more than his share, was gone. He didn't remember what happened to the cap.

"Who else was at the table?" asked Morris.

Tait remembered, with distaste, the young caddy Peter Caldwell, who had recently been suspended from the Old Course for a month . . . suspected of nudging a ball in "the ruif" in a lively four-ball match between R&A members for a rather large bet. It seems young Caldwell had himself bet ten pounds on the side. "The members wa' ootraged," said Tait.

Morris did not know the young man. Old Alec would certainly have known him. And if the lad cheated on the golf course, Old Alec would have hated him.

Tait said, with no insinuation, that Sir Arthur Maxwell was sitting at the far end of the table, but added he did not have a chance to speak with him "bafoor 'e was goone."

"Any other member of the R&A in the Bull and Bear?"

Tait insisted it was crowded with smoke and conversation and great quantities of laughter. Then he remembered that Gerald Dougall was sitting across the room when he first entered.

"With whom?" asked Morris.

Tait admitted, reluctantly, that Dougall was with a young woman, but he did not know her.

Morris was aware that Dougall was a married man and one of the richest men in Scotland . . . and a most unpleasant one. He remembered how Dougall had enjoyed too much his power over Barry Vinson and the illegal grooves in his irons.

"Did you leave alone?" Morris asked Captain Tait without an apology.

Tait looked him straight in the eye. "Nae." Tait said he'd left with the widow from London, who stopped by her flat to get some things and came to his room later and spent the night there.

"How much later, would you say?" Morris did not have to add; the inspector will be asking you the same question.

"Aroond eleven P.M.," the captain said with much dignity. He added, "In the wee hours o' my drinkin' yeers, I might've caught the scoundrel oo' killed Old Alec."

And maybe Old Alec was already lying dead when the widow got there, thought Morris.

Captain Tait could see it in his face. "I niver killed 'im, Morris. I luffed 'im."

Morris believed the captain. But men had killed the things they loved, long before Oscar Wilde wrote "The Ballad of Reading Gaol," the poem of the same expression.

Morris was never a man to forget old friends and old debts. Tom Rowe of the *Times* was lurking near the first tee of the Old Course, though only the lads far back in the field, hoping to make a paycheck, were teeing off this early on the final day.

"John Morris, I can see there's news in your face

. . . and it's not friendly news,'' said Rowe, ever the gentleman in his coat and tie.

Morris nodded. Sullivan touched Rowe's arm. The three of them shared the anonymity of standing among old R&A members, caddies, players, Open officials, reporters, and photographers coming and going in front of the great bay window in the R&A clubhouse—the first tee a bare few yards in front of them, as golf played on, uncaring, if even a Third World War had broken out.

''The news is wretched,'' Morris said. ''Someone killed Old Alec the caddy. Last night. In his own house. With their own hands. Almost certainly using the same garrote that strangled Barry Vinson.''

''My God,'' Rowe said.

''And the divil,'' Morris said; ''the two of them still locked in combat after all these years. That last, about the wire, is very much off the record. As you know, Inspector Emerson has never released how Vinson was killed.''

''Did the same man kill them both?'' Rowe asked.

''It would seem so,'' Morris said. ''The handles and the wire on the garrote appear to be World War Two vintage. But that is also classified information.'' Rowe nodded his agreement. ''Forensics will know, perhaps, if it is the same weapon that killed Vinson.''

Morris, accepting another nod of agreed silence, told Rowe why he and Sullivan had suspected Old Alec of killing Vinson. Rowe's eyes reflected the same pain that had distorted their own judgment. Rowe had often written of Old Alec and had once even photographed him with his granddaughter in his lap.

''So the two of you would have kept your silence?'' Rowe asked, looking also at Sullivan.

''Believe it,'' Morris said. Even now, he kept another silence . . . of Captain Tait's narrative of what he'd seen last night at the Bull and Bear, including his encounter with a very drunk Old Alec.

"I'm glad I never knew what the two of you suspected of Old Alec," said Rowe. "It would have been hell to make the decision about what to print. No man in golf despised Barry Vinson more than myself I'm embarrassed to say."

"It was as clear as ice in a glass—what not to say—*until you closed your eyes and thought about it,*" Sullivan said.

"Captain Tait won't release Old Alec's death to you fellows until he has to," said Morris. "That won't be until after lunch, when the American player, Lowrey, will be looking for his caddy. So you've got a running start, old man. But not to release anything until after the press conference."

"Indeed," said Rowe, who would alert his editors that he had a major, major front-page story coming up for the first edition . . . so they should save a vast hole for it; the good, gray *Times* might even go all the way and run a thumbnail photograph of Old Alec.

"Morris, who the blazes is killing our people?" asked Rowe. "Vinson was a bastard, at best, if a talented one. But Old Alec was a national treasure, as were his father and grandfather before him. Vinson and Old Alec don't belong together on the same obit page."

"*Who is killing our people?*" repeated Morris. "That is a terrible question, which I have heard put to music before at the U.S. Open. And just last night, Sullivan and I were very smug—and apparently, very wrong—in our assumptions. I don't know, Tom. You are absolutely right: the two deaths make less sense together than they do separately."

Rowe left for the press tent, still shaking his head, his cowlick waving in the breeze.

* * *

The sun had broken through the cloud cover, but the multitude of Scots were still decked out in caps and long-sleeved sweaters, fearing the westward wind would blow ever cooler as Sunday wore on. It was entirely too early for a draft beer. So Morris bought only one, until Sullivan lifted it out of his large hand, sending him back for a second. Another hand reached out of the crowd to tug on Morris's sleeve. It was the young ex-caddy from Georgia Tech, Paul Mason. His appealing grin was in place, while his mop of dark hair blew in the gathering wind.

"Mr. Morris?" the boy said.

"Morris will do."

"Could you help me?"

"Your money didn't get here from home?" Morris said.

"Oh, no. I got it, thanks. I . . . I think I know who the young girl was in the Bull and Bear," Mason said. "But I don't know how to get in touch with her."

Morris winced, not sure how to answer him. The kid had no idea what had happened to Sharon Kirkcaldy . . . or that her grandfather had been murdered.

Sullivan saved Morris from his indecision. "Who do you think she is?"

"Her name is Sharon. Sharon Kirkcaldy, I believe. One of the local caddies I've spoken with knew her name. He didn't know, or wouldn't tell me, where she lives. She doesn't seem to have a telephone. Her grandfather is the famous caddy here, called—"

"Old Alec," Sullivan said. "Yes, Paul. I know his granddaughter. She's eighteen. And she has beautiful red hair."

Morris could see that Sullivan's romantic heart was in full bloom. But what could she tell him? Sullivan never missed a beat. "There's been a death in her family, Paul. She will be in deep mourning. But I'll see her today.

And I'll tell her that a very appealing young man from Georgia Tech would like to see her again."

Paul Mason blushed in spite of himself.

"When are you going back home?" asked Sullivan.

"My ticket was for tomorrow. . . ." He hesitated. "But I had to change it. Inspector Emerson asked me to stay here until he's further along in his investigation into who killed Barry. You know I despised Vinson. But I can't imagine my killing him or anybody else. And Barry would have been tough to kill," Mason said, as if considering the idea as a practical matter for the first time. "All you had to do was see him hit a high one-iron to know just how strong he was."

How did Mason know he wasn't killed by gunshot? wondered Morris. And maybe he didn't know. "Are you staying at the same hotel?" Morris asked innocently.

"Yes."

"Were you guys hanging out again at the Bull and Bear last night?"

"The guys were. But I left early. Took a long walk. But I got lost. How the devil do you get lost in a city as small as St. Andrews? I wound up on the outskirts, on something called Pilmour Links Road. Must've walked up it a half mile. I didn't get to my room until after midnight."

"I know that road," Morris said. "By the way, Inspector Emerson wants you to call him. He's talking again with everybody who knew Barry Vinson." The inspector hadn't spoken to Morris about Mason, but he was sure to be interested in when and why the boy was "lost" on Pilmour Links Road . . . and what he might have seen while Old Alec was being murdered.

Morris asked him, "Did you see much traffic on Pilmour Links Road last night?"

Mason looked at him strangely. Then he made a physical effort to remember. "No. It was past ten. Just the occasional car."

"Any particular makes or models strike your fancy?" Morris thought a Georgia Tech engineer ought to be interested in what machines the locals and the visitors were driving.

"I did see a Citroën, the French luxury car. Pretty unusual, even for Scotland. I'd love to get inside one. It sinks lower as you gather speed. Pretty interesting concept." He thought a minute longer. "Plenty of heavy metal in town for the tournament. Most of it English. I saw at least one Bentley. Must've weighed four thousand pounds. A couple of Jags. I wasn't hitchhiking or anything. Oh. A motorcycle blew by me, headed into town. I swear it was doing a hundred miles an hour. I swear it. About ten P.M. In the dark, it seemed like it was going two hundred. It was on me and gone before I could blink."

"A man or a woman riding?" asked Morris.

"All I saw was a blur of light and noise in the dark."

Morris waited to see if he would call up any other memory of the night's traffic. But Mason could only shake his head, remembering the furious motorcycle.

"Paul, do call Inspector Emerson immediately. Tell him that I told you he wanted to speak with you. Tell him exactly what you just told me. And anything else you remember. Trust me," Morris said.

"Sure," said Mason. "I'll call him." He was puzzled, and more than a little worried. "I'm not in any kind of trouble, am I?"

"Not that I'm aware of," said Morris. "Not if you are absolutely candid with the inspector."

Mason nodded his promise and moved toward a bank of pay phones at the intersection behind the 18th green.

"Who do we know, Morris, who rides a motorcycle?" asked Sullivan.

Morris couldn't think of anyone in Scotland. Plenty of British Open officials and players were driving courtesy Jaguars. Bentleys and Rolls-Royces were much in evidence for the tournament. But Morris had not seen—or remembered seeing—a Citroën.

Morris and Sullivan moved through the press tent, Sullivan's out-of-date press pass working as it had for years. The ink-stained wretches were at their typewriters and word processors, those not still nursing hangovers in their rooms. Morris was stopped by old friend, Furman Bisher of the *Atlanta Journal-Constitution,* never a man to ignore his assignment, even six thousand miles from home.

"Anything new on Barry Vinson's murder?" asked Bisher, still one of the most stylish writers among sports columnists in the American colonies.

Morris looked at his watch. The kid, Lowrey, would be at the practice range in half an hour. Captain Tait couldn't wait longer than that to make the announcement of Old Alec's murder. After a promise of confidentiality, Morris told Bisher that Old Alec MacLaine had been killed in his home last night. He did not offer any details of his murder. Bisher, ever the professional man, was able to reach into his briefcase and pull out a column he had written about Old Alec in 1970, the year Nicklaus defeated Georgia boy Doug Sanders for the British Open title, here in St. Andrews.

"A grand old man, Old Alec," said Bisher, who loved the keepers of the tradition of golf—and woe be to anyone who trampled on it, in high or low places. "Do the police consider it to be a double murder?"

"I don't know," Morris said honestly.

Bisher got on the horn to Atlanta to alert the Sunday night sports staff that he would have a zinger of a story for Monday morning, in addition to who won the golf tournament. He was careful not to break his word to

Morris and speak of a murder before Captain Tait made his announcement.

"Here comes the captain now," Morris said. He and Sullivan found empty seats in the row behind Bisher.

Tait, coached carefully by Inspector Emerson, said that Old Alec had been murdered in the night in his home. Tait fought off a blizzard of questions as to the details of the murder, saying only that New Scotland Yard admitted there were *aspects* of the murder of Old Alec that *resembled* the murder of Barry Vinson. Tait declined to answer any questions as to those specific aspects, prompting a firestorm of resentment, especially from the British tabloid press, whose reporters were jumping out of their skins to blast the story over merry England with every imaginable invention . . . but nothing, Morris was to note, as macabre as the true details of the two murders.

Captain Tait finally looked at his watch and declared the press conference at an end. The British Open, of course, would continue.

Morris waited for Tait at the entrance to the Royal and Ancient clubhouse, being sure he would seek it out as a refuge from tabloid mania. Sullivan agreed to meet him later, the inner sanctum of the Royal and Ancient clubhouse not open to *violation* by the opposite sex except on specific occasions. "No doubt the reason the hapless men lost the Empire," said Morris.

Captain Tait did, indeed, invite him in for a desperately needed drink. Morris loved the Royal and Ancient clubhouse, which had opened on Whit Sunday, 1854. He could imagine the rounds of whiskies and Scottish toasts lifted in mid-century. It would have been as much fun as dining on haddock and mutton chops at Glass's in St. Andrews, in 1773, with the redoubtable Dr. Samuel Johnson and his biographer, James Boswell. Morris only wished that Dr. Johnson had taken the occasion to make some recorded statement on the humbling game of "gowf."

The Big Room of the clubhouse was paneled in wood, but only to a height of six feet. And the floor-to-ceiling bay window on the west wall looked out over the 1st tee and 18th green of the Old Course, the tournament playing on silently in the distance.

Grand old portraits hung in the clubhouse: John Whyte-Melville in the nineteenth century, in his mustache and side whiskers and red member's coat of the era, with black tie and black hat, standing near the Old Stone Bridge over Swilcan Burn, while his caddy kneeled to tee up his ball on a small mound of sand on the No. 2 hole. Samuel Messieux, looking very grand in his red coat and black bowler and starched collar and tie, addressing the ball as though it would be impolite to strike it. Old Tom Morris, the original R&A club professional and four-time British Open champion, painted by Sir George Reid with his vast white whiskers, his cap, coat and tie, and with an iron club in his huge right hand and his left hand thrust into his trouser pocket, with his gold watch fob swinging below his vest, which buttoned over his substantial stomach. And the century-old painting of Allan Robertson, the club's talented maker of feathery balls, sitting like a banker in his coat and tie and Captain Ahab whiskers, balancing three clubs and a feathery in his strong right hand.

In the South Room of the clubhouse was the museum, conceived in 1864 by Admiral Bethune, and subscribed to by the committee as a record of the game of golf as we know it, which, of course, owes its origins to Scotland. The clubs and balls and artifacts in the room were only *priceless,* including the oldest club known to be in existence, a play-club made by Samuel Cosser in 1760.

Morris longed to lift it up, illicitly, in his own big hands and *feel* the origin of the game in his fingers.

Wooden clubs preceded iron clubs in the history of golf. And James McEwan and family began carving wooden clubs in the eighteenth century. The McEwans were paid two guineas a year to attend spring and autumn meetings in St. Andrews. Their clubs rested about the museum as beautifully and as timelessly as thin sculptures. Before the rules of the game inhibited imagination, clubs of an astonishing variety were invented, including niblicks with a hole in the face so that water from Swilcan Burn could pass through the club while the feathery ball was struck safely onto dry land.

All around the South Room museum were favorite clubs by great and historic golfers: an entire hickory-shafted set swung by the immortal Bobby Jones in his winning of Open championships; and the five-iron used by Gene Sarazen for an ace at the 8th hole at Troon, in the first round of the 1973 Open, after Sarazen was in his *eighth decade* of his life.

The collection was historic and wonderfully eccentric, from a Persian carpet from the Agbadan Golf Club to a ball, offered by one K. L. Keyser in 1892, that had been "chewed, swallowed, and evacuated by a cow." Morris loved it all too much to make a sound. He knew that Sullivan would love the sight of him loving the museum.

Captain Tait said that Old Alec MacLaine and his father and grandfather before him were known to have saved many an artifact from the old days at St. Andrews, but that Old Alec would never entertain an offer for them or even allow them to be seen, except by a few old caddy friends who wouldn't discuss them. Tait was sure Old Alec had owned a fine collection of antique golf balls. There was no hint of accusation as to what might have been done with two of the featheries.

Captain Tait showed Morris through the offices of the

official staff of the R&A, from which were administered the modern rules and the very code of the game of golf in the world, in concert with the United States Golf Association.

Tait led them to a table and two good Scotch whiskies, taken neat in the glass. The burn of the whisky made possible the turn of thought at the table from golf to murder.

''Morris, I firgot a' face . . . a' the Bull an' Bear. Yer oon Warren Lightfoot, a' gintleman o' the gemme,'' said Tait. He signaled for two more whiskies, which were delivered in their glasses as precisely as if measured out by a dedicated chemist.

Tait said that Lightfoot, president of the USGA, had been deep in conversation with a young man he himself had seen in St. Andrews but did not know. He described the young man as short and thick and red-haired and very much a Scotsman.

Morris was sure Inspector Emerson would be keen to know the name of the young man and why he was talking with Lightfoot. Morris could not imagine the tall New Englander as a double killer . . . but he had been fooled before by a gentleman he'd known far better than Warren Lightfoot. Could it be that Lightfoot himself drove Barry Vinson's green Jaguar away from the Old Course Hotel the night he was killed? Morris found it difficult to swallow his whisky and impossible to swallow that notion of Lightfoot as a strangler . . . without a great deal more evidence.

''Captain,'' Morris asked, ''do any of your members ride motorcycles for pleasure?''

Tait was obviously taken by surprise at the question. He sat down his whisky and thought. ''Nae.'' He shook his head. He did say it was the habit of several club members to *bicycle* across the countryside, despite the fierce traffic and the narrow roads.

"Any local golfers of note, or caddies, come to mind who ride motorcycles?" asked Morris.

Tait rapped on the table. "I dinna mean tae forgit the yoong bastard Peter Caldwell. Aye, ye'll heer of 'im roarin' 'is motor up to the Old Course, somethin' awful."

Morris remembered that Caldwell, a caddy he'd never met, had been suspended from the Old Course for improving a member's lie in "the ruif," with a rather spirited bet riding on the match. And Tait himself had seen him drinking last night in the Bull and Bear. Caldwell was a young man for Inspector Emerson to find, if Morris and Sullivan didn't run across him first.

Tait, without so much as a blush, said again he'd spent last night in his flat with a widow he'd known for some time. He'd spoken with her, and she'd agreed to talk with Inspector Emerson, and after that with Morris also, if it would be helpful. Her name was Agatha Burns. Her grandmother had claimed to be a distant relative of the great eighteenth-century poet Robert Burns. Tait smiled, indicating he was prepared to believe it himself.

Morris sat down his glass and recited:

> Of a' the airts the wind can blaw,
>   I dearly like the west,
> For there the bonnie lassie lives,
>   The lassie I lo'e best:
> There wild woods grow, and rivers row,
>   And monie a hill between;
> But day and night my fancy's flight
>   Is ever wi' my Jean.

To Morris's astonishment, great tears streamed down the rugged face of Captain A.W.B. Tait, who made no effort to blot them or hide them.

"Oh, my," Morris said, handing him a fresh napkin, which he used without embarrassment.

"The la' too lines be carrved oon ma' Jean's gravestone," he said, touching Morris's hand to let him know they were long-loved lines, often wept over.

The two of them raised their glasses in a silent toast to the absent Jean. Murder never seemed so insignificant.

"Morris, I need a golf fix," said Sullivan, waiting outside the clubhouse, blinking at the sun, which had broken through the light cloud cover. "We came to Scotland to see a golf champion crowned, and by God, I mean to see one!"

She took Morris by the arm and led the way through the standing, milling thousands, toward Swilcan Burn and the first green of the Old Course. Morris repeated all he'd seen and heard in the R&A clubhouse.

"Then we will find this Peter Caldwell and put him and his motorcycle on the rack," said Sullivan. "But that's enough of murder, let's watch the golf."

They were too late to see Jack Nicklaus, in a colorful long-sleeved sweater, shake hands on the first tee for the first time in his life with his twenty-seven-year-old playing partner, Simon Owen, hardly known outside of his native New Zealand.

In the final round of the Open ten players had teed off within two strokes of the leaders, Tom Watson and Peter Oosterhuis, who made up the last twosome.

Morris lifted his cap to feel the freshening west wind in his hair, reversing, he knew, the play of the back nine holes from the first three rounds, bringing them all downwind. Morris remembered 1970, when Nicklaus won here on the final round, played under the exact same wind conditions. One big difference, thought Morris: the bigger American ball, never before allowed in the British Open. Most of the field were playing with it, and the following west wind would blow more formidably against the larger surface of the ball.

"Let's catch Nicklaus," Morris said. "Whoever finishes ahead of him will put both hands on the old Silver Claret Jug."

Sullivan, like a native salmon come home to spawn, swam them through the thirty thousand free-floating spectators. As they beat their way up the front nine among the streams of fans, they could follow the demise of the defending champion, Tom Watson, from the low moans behind them, as if an entire people were suffering the loss of a favorite son. The scoreboards, like stationary fate, confirmed the implausible: Watson suffered bogeys on holes 4, 5, 6 and 7, destroying his chances for a third Open title. His playing partner, Oosterhuis, clung to par and at least a share of the lead through the first nine holes.

Morris and Sullivan caught their breaths and Nicklaus on the 12th tee. Young Simon Owen had the honors, having birdied the 10th hole. Nicklaus held a one-stroke lead over Owen and was, at the moment, himself one shot behind the leader, Oosterhuis.

Nicklaus stood over his ball, his driver in his unusually small hands. Morris could not remember when Jack began to hover his clubs, never grounding them as he addressed the ball. Nicklaus turned his blond head until only his left eye fixed the ball on the tee with a cold stare. And now the club was swinging back in a great arc, his hands reaching over his head as though to rip power physically from the air—even his right elbow flying upward as in a daguerreotype from the nineteenth century—and now the club was flying down, too fiercely to be seen, and only the passing of it heard, tearing the air, the ball exploding skyward, a tiny, shining thing in the sunlight, until it exhausted itself toward the earth, striking, rolling, stopping, not twenty yards from the

12th green. Old Scots lifted their wool caps and others applauded carefully, in full knowledge of the greatness of the shot.

Owen played a powerful drive and a splendid wedge to within three feet of the pin and an unmissable birdie, to considerable applause.

Nicklaus, unmoved, bent and stared, never deviating from his deliberate obsession, then flicked his own wedge, and his ball spilled onto the green, stopping five feet from the cup. Nicklaus reached the green and turned his head to look blazingly down at the motionless ball, as if its very silence offended him. He bent to his work, easing his blade putter behind the ball, his head fixed far behind the blade, as if he would watch his own stroke from a near-angry distance. He crouched, waiting, until the thousands watching grew tense with the moment, but Nicklaus waited until the *line* of the putt appeared, *absolutely,* in his vision, and the *feel* of the putt came, *surely,* into his hands; then he drew the putter deliberately back, and his right elbow advanced it, driving it like a piston, until the blade struck the ball, sending it directly into the hole, to tie him with Oosterhuis for the Open lead.

A low murmur of approval, thick with whispered "*r*s," rolled among the thousands of Scots.

Nicklaus and Owen avoided the Hole o' Cross Bunker on the 13th hole to score par 4s.

But Simon Owen had not come the ten thousand miles from New Zealand to go quietly. On the 14th hole, where once champions Gene Sarazen and Bobby Locke had been destroyed by still-remembered 8s, Owen chose to drive his ball between the Beardies bunkers on the left and the old stone wall and out-of-bounds on the right. His second shot, a fairway wood, nearly carried the huge 14th green, and Owen was down easily in two strokes for a birdie 4 to tie Jack, who played the 14th with a more reverent caution, accepting a par 5 as a reasonable score.

The crowds were packed so closely together around the tees and greens that thousands had resorted to the cheap periscopes permitted in Scotland; as the white periscopes bobbed and weaved in search of an unobstructed view, they looked for the world like a gigantic submarine Wolfpack out to sink the tournament.

Owen had the tee at the 15th hole, and despite the advantage of a following wind, never considered backing away from his driver. Nicklaus played the more prudent three-wood.

Sullivan dragged Morris after the two of them, as if he were a reluctant little boy truant from school.

Owen, despite his daring on his tee shot, mis-clubbed on his short second shot to the enormous 15th green and was short of the hole. Nicklaus placed his second shot safely on the green but not near enough to threaten the hole with his first putt. Jack stood on the edge of the green and watched, helplessly, as Owen struck a dangerous chip shot. It ran for fifty feet, spilling over the dips and rises of the huge green, directly into the cup for a birdie 3 and a one-stroke advantage and the Open lead.

"Oh, Jack," Sullivan said quietly, as if only she and Nicklaus were standing on the Old Course, and he could hear her regret at the unfairness of the swing of fortune, with just three holes left to play. Only the year before at Turnsberry, Watson had chipped in for birdie on the 15th hole on the last round to take that British Open title from Nicklaus.

After today's round was finished, Nicklaus told Tom Rowe and an eavesdropping Morris: "I looked at that 15th flag flapping in the wind, and I thought, *Here we go again.* Then I said to myself: *He's going to have to earn it.*"

Sullivan pushed Morris onto the bed of the old railroad track that had once run into St. Andrews and now marked out-of-bounds all the way to the 16th green, 382 yards in the distance.

Owen was a man by fate possessed. Against all caution, he took up his driver and smashed the ball directly ahead, between the out-of-bounds on the right and the three bunkers making up the Principal's Nose on the left, leaving himself not twenty-five yards to land the shot on safe ground, which he did, the ball rolling within a hundred yards of the pin.

Nicklaus was unmoved. He played his tee shot carefully to the left, a full thirty yards behind the drive of Simon Owen. Jack stared at the far green as if to memorize its distance, tested the wind at his back with a toss of grass in the air, then hovered a nine-iron over his ball, and with a short, seamless swing, sent it flying to an abrupt stop, six feet from the 16th pin.

Owen sped to his own ball and his simple wedge to equal the stroke of Nicklaus. The instant the ball left Owen's club, Morris, through his binoculars, could see that it was struck too firmly, its flight too aggressive. Owen's approach shot could not hold the raised green and rolled down into a dangerous little swale.

Morris kept his glasses on Owen and could see the new tension in his face. He took much longer to choose his club, walking up the incline to the green and back down twice, suspended as he was between his twenty-seven-year-old obscurity and a certain immortality. His pitch up the hill was limp, as with fear, leaving him a putt twice as long as Jack's, which he quickly missed, fate seeming to accelerate in the opposite direction from New Zealand.

Nicklaus stared his six-foot putt into the heart of the hole, for a two-stroke swing and the British Open lead, Oosterhuis having faltered behind them.

Sullivan snuggled against a stout young man—whom

Morris wasn't sure he could whip—to share the fellow's narrow spot above the tee to the Road Hole, the terrifying, 461-yard, par-4 17th. The young man rolled his eyes at Morris, enjoying the good luck of his proximity.

Nicklaus never considered using the driver. He'd worked it out in his head years ago. He drove the ball with his three-wood over the high trellis wall, and it split the fairway beyond his own sight. Jack declined to risk the pin with his subsequent one-iron, and flew a high two-iron safely to the front of the green, which spilled treacherously down to the Road Hole Bunker on the left and fatally down to the road and the old stone wall on the right. Nicklaus lagged a fifty-foot putt dead to the cup and a par of 4.

Owen's drive found the rough. His second shot did not find the green. And his first putt did not find the hole, for a bogey 5.

No man yet born to golf could catch Jack Nicklaus with a two-stroke lead on the easy, 72nd hole of the Old Course at St. Andrews. In minutes he was holding the Silver Claret Jug on his right shoulder and patting it with his right hand, as if burping a newborn baby. It was his third victory in the 107-year-old playing of the British Open championship. His final score: 281, to the 283 of Simon Owen, Peter Oosterhuis, Raymond Floyd, Tom Kite, and Ben Crenshaw.

Sullivan gave a great Yank cheer and stood on her tiptoes to kiss Morris, as if the two of them had orchestrated the title, quite separately from Mr. Nicklaus.

"Hey, Morris!" shouted Sullivan, over the crashing applause of the thirty thousand Scots. "We had our whack on the right guy."

Morris was in no way surprised.

The sight of Captain A.W.B. Tait, standing very

straight behind Nicklaus, as if getting his last instructions before parachuting into Normandy, brought pain to Morris's eyes . . . with the memory of the grotesquely dead Old Alec MacLaine.

• CHAPTER SEVEN •

Morris and Sullivan eased into the press tent to catch Nicklaus on Nicklaus. He was entirely himself . . . no boasting, no false humility, the old Silver Claret Jug resting on the table in front of him. He sat there, in his sweater, thirty-eight years old, winner of seventeen major championships, very simply the greatest player in the history of the game.

"I won without a putter, for most of the tournament," Jack said, in his always surprisingly high voice. "It's the best I've ever played, from tee to green, in a major tournament. It's a funny old golf course that requires careful club selection and fundamental knowledge of the hidden bunkers and pin placements."

Speaking of the shift in the wind, Jack said, "It was the same wind I saw last week . . . the same wind I saw in 1970." Nicklaus was silent for a moment, listening to his own thoughts, then said, "I feel I'm a better player now than I've ever been."

Morris whispered into Sullivan's ear, "That should terrify the professional population."

"We'll not see a greater player in this old century," Sullivan whispered back, "or the next one either, if we're still around for it."

"We'll be around," whispered Morris.

"The bookies are giving odds at twelve to one . . . *against,*" whispered Sullivan.

"What do bookies know?" whispered Morris. "We better get out of here . . . if we mean to make it up to the inspector and find his killer for him."

Across the street from the Old Course, a long line of happy punters were waiting for their payoff in front of George McCormack's betting shop. The Scots knew their golf far too well to have wasted their hard-earned wages betting on home country favorites. But most of the money had tilted toward defending champion Tom Watson, so McCormack, round and hard as a rain barrel, was smoking his cigar through the huge fingers of his huge right hand with an even huger smile on his face.

Morris was surprised that McCormack recognized him and Sullivan.

" 'Ere tae clim yer whack, arre ye?" the huge bookie said.

Sullivan smiled wickedly, showing him her marker.

"Och!" McCormack said, taking the marker and raising his large hand ever so slightly, to have the thinnest old man Morris ever saw alive take it and disappear into the shop as if he had wasted entirely away to nothing. He was back in minutes with a small cardboard box of hundred-pound notes. McCormack took it and handed it to Sullivan, making an amusing little bow, as if a rhinoceros in a black suit could make a bow, and said, "Therty thoousand poonds tae the lass." He even tipped his soft hat.

"Smart work, Sullivan," Morris said, shaking his head at the size of the bet she had won. "That's about twice what Jack himself got for beating back the best golfers in the bloody world for four days. We know who gets the dinner check tonight."

Sullivan tipped the terribly thin man a note of some consequence and handed the box to Morris. "Hold on to this. I don't like to see fellas of mine walking around broke."

"I've always wanted to be a kept man," Morris said, tucking the box under his large arm. He would do many things with Julia Sullivan, but he would never, ever bet with her on *anything.*

"Old Alec iss truly deid," McCormack said, not as a question but as a statement of fact, and the regret in his voice seemed less than real.

"Yes," Morris said.

"An' 'ow did 'e die? I've seen ye wi' the inspector," McCormack said, making it plain that Morris's closeness to New Scotland Yard was common knowledge.

"He was murdered," Morris said. He did not offer how or when.

"By the sime as did Vinson?" said McCormack, drawing his huge finger slowly across his short, thick neck.

Morris ignored the gory message of the finger . . . and the question. The inspector was right. Too many people had seen how Vinson died, and now the whole of St. Andrews knew. They would know soon enough of Old Alec's similar fate.

Morris asked, bluntly, "Did you see Old Alec last night . . . at the Bull and Bear?"

"Aye." McCormick didn't hesitate to answer. " 'E left 'is cap at my tible. I took it tae 'is hoose. Aboot ten, it were."

McCormick's wide face showed less concern than his voice. He said that Old Alec came to the door alone and took his cap with only a thank-you. McCormick insisted he did not share a drink with Old Alec; in fact did not go inside his "hoose."

The idea of a late-night trip for an abandoned cap, with no spoken exchange between the two men, seemed more than a little implausible to Morris. He wondered how it would go down with New Scotland Yard. "Was he very drunk?"

"Aye. Pissed ta the gills," McCormack said, as if it were the only way for a good Scotsman to meet his Maker.

"Would you tell me what car you drove?" asked Morris, not believing he would answer.

" 'Twas ma Rolls, laddie. Wha' di'ya think, a grand Ford?" He laughed hugely, but his dark eyes were cautious.

Morris wondered if the Ford was thrown at him to demean their own rented Ford, and how would McCormack know what rental car they were driving?

"You went straight home then?" Morris said.

McCormack grinned—Morris wasn't sure if at his amateurish questions or at the memory of the night. "Nae." He shook his dark-haired head. "Ba' to the Bull an' Bear an' drinkin' wi' the lads. It's toornament time a' the Old Course, don't ye see?"

"On the way back to town, did you pass any car you recognized?" Morris asked, since the big man had answered his first questions. Of course, McCormack knew his answers would be repeated to Inspector Emerson, which was like telling his own story twice; New Scotland Yard would be calling on him again soon enough.

McCormack looked down, as if the answer were written on the pavement. "Nae." He shook his great head.

Morris found the one-word answer unconvincing.

"Perhaps a motorcycle?" Sullivan asked, her winning smile back in place.

McCormack glanced at her too quickly, as if she had caught him in some untruth. Only then did he shake his huge head no.

Again Morris did not believe him. But why would he lie? He had explained enough to convince the inspector of his own actions on Pilmour Links Road. Why not admit it if he passed someone he knew?

"Tell me, Mr. McCormack. . . ." Morris could not imagine what Sullivan was about to ask him. "How did Old Alec get home from the Bull and Bear? He damn sure didn't walk it in an hour. Drunk or sober. It must be at least five miles to his house."

"An' d'ye e'er see a caddy na' able ta walk 'ome?" McCormack laughed until his huge frame shook in its black suit.

"The question is: What time did he leave the pub?" Sullivan said, undaunted. "You said you knocked on his door at *ten P.M.* Others say he left the pub about nine, or just before nine. No seventy-two-year-old man, knee-walking drunk, can make five miles in one hour. Not even Old Alec."

McCormack ignored her, shouting some rough Scottish cheer that Morris couldn't understand, to a winning punter, and then, without another word the iron tub of a man turned to the door of his betting shop, with the terribly thin old-timer opening the door, as if hunger were letting in gluttony to some obscene feast.

"Does McCormack look like a man who would interrupt the drinking and the singing at the Bull and Bear to return an old wool cap *in a Rolls-Royce* to an old caddy who is murdered later in the night?" Morris asked.

"Sure, and he stopped along the way to start a new religion," Sullivan said.

"Odd, how he didn't answer your question. If Old Alec left the pub around nine . . . how did he get home, drunk as a coot, if he answered McCormack's knock on his door at ten P.M.? It's a helluva question. Who gave him a ride? Our killer?"

"It's possible. And if the old man was that drunk, maybe the killer helped him inside his house."

"Carrying a garrote in his hip pocket?" said Morris, skepticism overtaking his optimism.

"That's a problem," agreed Sullivan. "Do you think McCormack might have gone to see Old Alec to test his long knowledge of the Open leaders—their strengths, their weaknesses—and the weather Old Alec expected, to help him decide what bets to lay off more heavily in Edinburgh?"

"Good thinking. But why would McCormack lie about it and say he went to return an old cap?"

"Oh, he returned the cap," Sullivan said. "And the boys at the Bull and Bear will swear to it. Remember, Captain Tait was there, and he said Old Alec left his cap on the table. He *didn't* say that McCormack left the bar to return it. And Tait didn't know exactly what time Old Alec himself left, but thought it was not later than nine P.M. I'm betting our bookie, McCormack, wanted to see Old Alec *alone*. For some reason. And maybe he killed him. He's big enough to drown the Loch Ness Monster. God knows why he would kill Old Alec."

"Because Old Alec knew *he* had killed Barry Vinson?" speculated Morris, who thought about that a minute. "But Old Alec would have paid him to do the job."

"We believe that. We don't know that. And maybe we have two killers on our hands."

Morris had considered it. But he hadn't said it aloud. "That's twice as logical and twice as illogical. So Old Alec did kill Vinson. We can buy that. But why would anyone kill Old Alec for killing the Ugly American? Tell me that."

He answered his own question: "Maybe someone tried to blackmail him and wound up killing him?" He thought again. "But Old Alec was a simple caddy and a poor man, however famous among golfers. And the room in his house didn't look like the scene of an open assault. Was Old Alec surprised, not challenged?"

"What if George McCormack knows a great deal more about what happened than he admits? What if McCormack is holding what he knows over the head of the killer?"

"Jesus, the whole town didn't conspire to kill the two of them," Morris said, but admitted; "It's very possible our bookie knows more than he's telling . . . for whatever reason."

"I'm as puzzled as you, Morris. And besides, I only tell fortunes of living boy golfers," Sullivan said, patting her winnings in the box he held.

"Wait'll I tell Jack how much you won. He'll make you buy the fuel for his jet ride home."

"He can't catch me. He knows who has the fastest jet plane," Sullivan said, shaking her small pilot's fist.

"Let's ease over and see who comes out of the Royal and Ancient clubhouse," Morris said. "Then we'll look up the Inspector."

He could have sent word to Captain Tait and gotten an invitation for himself to come inside. Morris preferred to wait. Already the tall cranes in the distance that had held the TV cameras were being cranked down, as if huge eagles' nests were being lowered to the links. The thirty thousand watchers of the game had gone to their cars, their buses, their pubs, their hotels, their homes. Only the squadron of commercial tents were festive with the sounds of unseen people; drunk with energy and fatigue, raising glasses, courting favored customers who played the hour of their indulgence for all they could, a few of them savoring shots that would not die in their memories. The bright ropes along the fairways stretched forlornly over the tilting links as if some low beast had escaped their frail confinement and was loose in the gorse and heather. The westward wind blew over the grounds, leaving no trace of the great human tension that had possessed the very air, as it had done for five hundred years.

"What are you thinking?" asked Sullivan, leaning against him, feeling the absence once again of a great tournament gone into time.

Morris fixed his thoughts of the scene in his memory. And looking past Sullivan, he said, "I see a man we want to talk with."

Gerald Balfour-Melville Dougall was stepping out of the R&A clubhouse; a strongly built man, tugging on his full beard, his wide chest threatening the seams of his member's jacket.

Morris did not hesitate to intercept him while he waited for his automobile to be brought around. Dougall did not offer to shake hands. Sullivan chose to watch them from a discreet distance.

"Rather awkward time to bother you," Morris said, "but it was terrible what happened to Old Alec."

Dougall affected being in a great hurry, looking past Morris to see if his car was on the way, saying only, "Aye, aye," as if it were a matter of small concern to him.

"Did you see Old Alec last night in the Bull and Bear?" Morris asked bluntly.

Now Dougall looked squarely at him, as if he'd just materialized in his shoes. "And wha' possible business is that of yours?" he asked, his voice still more of the British public schools than of Scotland. "You may know an inspector, but tha' doesna' make you one. Put tha' in your book."

"Old Alec was a friend of mine," said Morris, pleased that his friendship with Inspector Emerson had not escaped anybody in St. Andrews, including almost certainly the killer. "I heard you were in the Bull and Bear last night, and I thought you might have spoken to him."

Dougall sucked in his breath, as if deciding whether to strike Morris in the face. Morris, leaning on his cane, smiled at the prospect. Dougall, looking around him, seeing two elderly members coming out the clubhouse door, made a deliberate decision . . . to change his attitude entirely, or at least to fake changing it. He even made a false stab at a smile. ''I dinna see Old Alec. The pub was loud, a goddamn ceilidh. Couldna' hear yourself think.''

''It must have been a temptation to leave early,'' Morris said. ''I saw you and your Pin Placement Committee at work just after daylight.''

Dougall looked at him as if he'd been spied on, caught in some subversive activity.

''I dinna drink the night away. The toornament comes first,'' the big man said piously.

''Which of the *lads* that you mentioned to me,'' Morris said, changing the subject, ''tipped you off about the deepened grooves in Barry Vinson's clubs?''

Dougall was caught off balance. He'd been girding himself for questions about last night in the pub and about Old Alec. ''I niver said such a thing,'' he lied.

''Now, why would you lie to me about a thing like that?'' Morris said, leaning on his cane into the man's face, no more Mr. Good-Guy.

Dougall began to push past him to get to his black Jaguar sedan, which had pulled to a stop in front of the clubhouse.

''Would the young woman you were with last night remember Old Alec, do you think?'' Morris looked directly down into the big man's eyes, not missing the slight flinch, or the hatred in his dark pupils.

Dougall made no attempt to answer, as he slid in behind the wheel without tipping the valet and gunned the big engine. It might have been a weapon, firing muted shots back at Morris.

"I don't think Mr. Dougall is going to have us over for cocktails and dinner," said Sullivan, having overheard most of their conversation. The two elderly members, neither of which Morris recognized, were smiling to themselves at what they'd heard of the exchange.

Morris caught Sullivan up on their entire conversation. "He blinked when I asked which of the lads told him about the grooves in Vinson's clubs. Then he *denied* having said it. Denied it . . . *knowing* that he said it to *me,* and that I am quoting him in a book I'm writing about the tournament. Why would he do a stupid thing like that?"

"You caught him off guard," Sullivan said. "He was afraid."

"Of what?" Morris said.

"Of the man who killed Vinson and Old Alec?"

"Why?"

"He knows more about what happened than makes him comfortable?"

"Why not go to the police?"

"He's terrified?" said Sullivan, again more as a question than an answer.

"He looks like a rich man more used to putting the fear of God into other men . . . rather than being afraid," Morris said.

"Yes," agreed Sullivan. "Still, he lied to you, Morris. Knowing that you *knew* he was lying. That's not a logical response. That's a panicky response. Tell me, do you know any likely gent, flush with his winnings, who might buy a lady in Scotland a drink?"

"Indeed," Morris said, "there is such a gent. He works cheap." He patted her great winnings, still under his large arm. "Then we'll look up the inspector."

Morris guided Sullivan through their hotel door into Ma Bell's Tavern.

''Who is this . . . drinking at our bar?'' Morris said.

The tall man, who was tall even sitting down, jumped ever so slightly, as if he'd been surprised in some illicit assignation. Warren Lightfoot, the USGA president, got to his feet to shake their hands, speaking only with his actions and saving his words as if they had separate value back in New England.

The young bartender was alert, and two new Scotches appeared while they were still shaking hands.

''To Nicklaus,'' said Morris, lifting his glass.

''The greatest ever to have played the game of golf,'' said Sullivan, lifting her own.

''Yes,'' said Lightfoot, his own glass in the air.

Morris replayed aloud Nicklaus's great birdie on No. 16 and his even greater par on the terrifying Road Hole, No. 17. Lightfoot nodded his thin head, husbanding his words, even his facial expressions, as if they were rationed in New England.

''Did you know Old Alec MacLaine?'' Morris asked suddenly.

''Yes,'' Lightfoot said. ''A lovely man. Terrible thing, Morris.''

''Killing Barry Vinson was felony enough,'' Morris said. ''But killing Old Alec was a crime against Scotland. It makes no sense. I understand he was in the Bull and Bear last night. . . .''

''And so was I,'' admitted Lightfoot, looking down, checking the time on his watch in spite of himself.

''You were talking to a young Scotsman,'' Morris said, not hiding his information or his curiosity.

''Yes,'' admitted Lightfoot, looking more than a little apprehensive. ''His name is Thirlwell. Jack Thirlwell. He was parking cars at the Old Course Hotel the night Vinson was killed. The young man noticed Vinson's green Jaguar sitting out front, but well past the entrance to the hotel. He swears it wasn't left with him . . . or the other lads working the cars. And then it was gone. Late. Near eleven P.M. He said he did not get a good look at the man who drove it away. But he swore the man was *old,* white-haired."

A lot of swearing, thought Morris, who had never heard Lightfoot say so many uninterrupted words in a row. "The inspector's men must've missed this Thirlwell," he said. "How did you come to meet the young man last night in the pub?"

"I recognized him," said Lightfoot. "And asked him to have a drink on me. He was most accommodating."

Morris was about to ask if he himself had been drinking alone at the Bull and Bear . . . when an attractive woman in her early middle years, with very short, dark hair, stopped at the end of the bar, obviously looking for someone, then raising her hand at recognizing the USGA president.

Lightfoot stood, much embarrassed. Morris was certain he had not known that the two of them were staying at the St. Andrews Golf Hotel when he agreed to meet the woman here. Lightfoot introduced them to Pamela Houston, an employee with the Royal and Ancient, one of the everyday keepers of the flame of golf. She, herself, was in no way embarrassed, and was effusive in her praise of Morris's golf writings over the years, even asking them to join her and Lightfoot for dinner.

"We can't," said Sullivan, quickly looking at her watch. "In fact, we've got to drink and run."

Much relief appeared on the thin face of Warren Lightfoot.

Morris opened the hotel's front door for Sullivan, both of them pausing on the high steps, looking down on the North Sea, cold-silver in the moonlight. "Do you think our man Lightfoot could be stepping out on Mrs. Lightfoot?"

"I think our man is thinking about it," Sullivan said

with a wicked grin. "Then again, it might be as innocent as dinner for two." There was no innocence in Julia Sullivan's amused eyes.

"I was about to ask him if he was drinking alone last night at the Bull and Bear before recognizing the young man, Thirlwell."

"I have an idea the answer is sitting in the bar beside him," Sullivan said.

"We can ask Captain Tait," said Morris, wincing at the idea of prying into the New Englander's private life. "Let's find the inspector."

They didn't have to find him. His driver was double-parking in the street below them.

Morris poled his way with his cane down the sheer steps, intercepting Emerson as he closed the door to the car.

"Let's walk down to the Chariots of Fire pub," Morris said. "An old friend is already inside here, drinking with a lady friend."

The inspector stuck his head back inside the car to tell his driver where he'd be.

Emerson nodded to Morris, but gave Sullivan a brief, half-hug, all animosity vanished in the chilly night air.

"It's been some day, Inspector," Morris said. "But at least one golfer flies home happy."

Emerson, who loved the tournament as much as any man and hadn't missed seeing an Open in twenty years until this one, questioned Morris about Nicklaus's winning play. Morris was happy to again re-create the last nine holes, as the three of them slowly walked the long block to the Chariots of Fire pub. Emerson could only shake his head at the great tenacity and intelligence of Nicklaus.

"I wish I managed my own investigations half as well," said the inspector, holding the door open to the pub, which was shockingly empty, as the great body of spectators, punters, hangers-on, and true lovers of golf seemed to have vanished from the streets and pubs as quickly as they had vanished from the now-dark and abandoned fairways of the Old Course.

After their drinks were brought out, and they had raised a toast to the Open champion, the inspector did not wait for their questions. "I met with the widow, Agatha Burns," he said. "You both would like her. An appealing and formidable woman. She made it very clear, without embarrassment, that she spent last night with Captain Tait."

"Shocking," Sullivan said with a smile.

"What time did she get to his flat?" asked Morris.

"That's a bit of a problem. She's up from London, and she left her hotel just before eleven P.M.," Emerson said.

"That confirms what Captain Tait told us," Morris said. "If the two of them wanted to lie, it would have been very easy to insist she came to his flat much earlier."

"True."

"Not to say that Barry Vinson wouldn't have been in harm's way if he'd run into the captain in a darkened graveyard," Morris said. "But Tait says he loved Old Alec, and I do not doubt him." Morris waited a beat. "But then, men have destroyed those they loved before. But unless Julia Sullivan is willing to bet cash that the captain did it . . . I find it impossible to believe."

Sullivan shook her head with finality.

"Careful with the word *impossible,*" the inspector said. "Good men have been hanged on every continent to the amazement of their own wives and children."

"Too true," admitted Morris. "What did you make of the midnight pilgrimage of the young Paul Mason?"

"I thank you for sending him to me," the inspector said. "I don't think he could have guessed, from his conversation with me, that I wasn't looking for him. I'm inclined to believe him . . . though it's a terrific coincidence, his losing his way in little St. Andrews and winding up on Pilmour Links Road in the middle of the night."

"Where Old Alec MacLaine was just then being murdered," Morris said. "God, I've always distrusted coincidence. Even if the kid says he was only down the road a half mile before he turned back into the city."

"I spoke with the other caddies staying at his hotel. . . . Caught them before they left town," Emerson said. "One of them was still in the hotel bar last night when Mason came stumbling in. The two of them drank a beer. Mason actually described to him how he'd been lost out Pilmour Links Road. The caddy, who is from Spain and who agreed to a taped deposition, said Mason was 'obviously tired and somewhat embarrassed,' but was 'in no way frightened or upset,' and had no blood on his clothes. He said Mason talked mostly about who might win the tournament the next day and how he was trying to locate Sharon Kirkcaldy. The Spaniard said that Mason *knew last night* that she was the granddaughter of Old Alec, though Mason insisted to him—and still insists—he had no idea where she lived."

"Do you believe him?" asked Morris.

Emerson made a wet circle on the table with the bottom of his glass. "I also distrust coincidence. But I have to say yes. I think the young man is telling the truth, as improbable as it might be."

"But you asked him not to leave the city?"

"Yes."

"But nearly all the players and other caddies are leaving Scotland," Morris said, "not to say thousands of spectators. How the hell can you hope to finish your investigation?"

The inspector shook his head helplessly. "We can't

keep thirty thousand people indefinitely in St. Andrews. I've asked Mr. Lightfoot and Sir Arthur Maxwell and young Mason not to leave town. Most of the other people close to Old Alec live here. And we can always extradite a suspect if it should come to that."

"We haven't run into Sir Arthur today," Morris said.

"I spoke with him at some length," the inspector said. "He was moved to tears that Old Alec had been killed. Again, Maxwell was alone in his hotel room last night. He did place several phone calls to London, but the last of them was made just after nine P.M. He admitted there had been quite an increase in demand for the Barry Vinson line of clothing since news of his murder. He thought it rather ghoulish but didn't deny that he welcomed the business."

"Sir Arthur must have been the only grown man in St. Andrews *not* drinking last night in the Bull and Bear," said Morris.

"Young Mason told us he saw a Bentley and a couple of Jaguars on Pilmour Links Road . . . and *one Citroën*," Sullivan said.

The inspector nodded yes.

"Do you know of any locals who drive a Citroën?" she asked.

"We're checking it," Emerson said. "It will take a while. Automobile records aren't as automated in Scotland as in America. There were spectators from all over Europe at the tournament. The Citroën could have come from anywhere. Of course, Mason didn't catch the license number, or even for certain the color of the car."

"Did he tell you about seeing a motorcycle . . . going maybe a hundred miles an hour?" asked Morris.

"Yes. I would say it was almost surely local," the inspector said. "Not so easy to pack a week's clothes for a golf tournament onto a motorcycle. I don't say it hasn't been done. *Everything* you can imagine has been done.

But it's not likely. And there are a surprising number of motorcycles in Scotland. They are cheaper to operate than automobiles. And a great deal more dangerous," he added.

"We can tell you of one young man in Scotland who owns a motorcycle," Morris said. "A local caddy, Peter Caldwell." Morris reminded him that Caldwell, whom he himself had never met, had recently been suspended from the Old Course for cheating during a big money match between four R&A members. Morris said that Captain Tait had made it clear that none of the members was involved in the cheating . . . only the caddy, Caldwell, who apparently had a side bet of his own and who nudged the ball in the "ruif." Morris said, "I expect Old Alec would have killed Caldwell for such a violation of the spirit of the game."

Inspector Emerson made a note to find Peter Caldwell immediately.

Morris re-created their conversation with George McCormack, the bookie, beginning with Sullivan's grand winnings.

"Congratulations," the inspector said to Sullivan, smiling, and momentarily slipping several days of tension from his thin shoulders. "But, of course, that makes the two of you highly suspect in the killing of Barry Vinson . . . *who was leading the tournament at the time of his death.*" His smile was genuine.

"Well, no Americans are without modest flaws," agreed Sullivan. "But I would never kill a man that good-looking, even a total bastard."

Morris could only shake his head and tell of McCormack's unlikely story of leaving the drinking and the singing, and no doubt the gambling, at the Bull and Bear to deliver an old wool cap to Old Alec MacLaine in the middle of the bloody night . . . without speaking a word . . . or entering the house . . . or having a nightcap with the old man the same night he was murdered in his own house.

"A rather astonishing story . . . to be invented," said Emerson, making another note in his pad to call on the punter McCormack.

Morris remembered that McCormack said he drove to Old Alec's in his Rolls-Royce. There was no Rolls among the cars that Paul Mason remembered seeing that night on Pilmour Links Road.

Morris said, "Captain Tait told us earlier that he had been sitting at the same long table with Old Alec, that McCormack was picking up more than his share of beers for the lot of them in the Bull and Bear. And that Old Alec had left his cap on the table . . . probably no later than nine P.M., though Tait isn't sure when Old Alec left the pub. Tait did *not* say that McCormack also left to take the cap back to Old Alec."

The inspector made another note to himself.

Morris held up his glass for a refill. "McCormack was remarkably forthcoming, considering we aren't police. But it didn't escape him that we had been seen in the occasional company of Scotland Yard."

"Little did he know how lucky we are not to be under house arrest," Sullivan said, and laughed, holding up her own empty glass. She told of her theory that with so much money at risk, and a great deal of it on defending champion Tom Watson, McCormack might have visited with Old Alec to get his idea of which golfer's game and nerves and intelligence fit the Old Course best for the final round . . . and what weather he expected. Information he could use in deciding what bets to lay off in Edinburgh.

"Good thinking . . . but why wouldn't McCormack offer that logical explanation for visiting Old Alec?" the inspector said.

Sullivan could only shake her head. "Maybe he

doesn't want you to believe he ever entered Old Alec's house for any reason . . . most especially murder. Maybe he doesn't want it known that he relies on certain locals, including caddies, in setting his odds and laying off bets when they grow too large. It's certain he wanted to be alone with Old Alec for some reason, other than returning his wool cap. And maybe it was to kill him."

"But why?" asked Morris. "Why? That is the operative question. Who would kill Old Alec? And for what reason? And what the hell does his murder have to do with the murder of Barry Vinson? Inspector, Sullivan raised the possibility we might have two killers on our hands."

Emerson agreed that Old Alec might surely have been moved to kill Vinson. But he also raised the essential question: Why would a second murderer kill Old Alec? And how did he manage to kill him in the same way, with the same weapon? "I can tell you," the inspector said, "there is no doubt Old Alec was killed with the *same garrote.* Vinson's dried blood is still on the wire and the two handles, which are covered over with Old Alec's own blood."

"Godamighty," Morris said.

"Old Alec was killed in the *barn,* not the house. We are sure of it. There was a helluva struggle in the dark. It's choreographed in the dust and cobwebs, though any once-clear footprints have been obviously swept away all through the house and barn. But we found plenty of blood on the filthy floor, though it had been smeared with a rag we didn't find. The killer, or killers, *dragged* Old Alec to the front room of the house, dragging thirteen stones of dead weight out of the barn, across the bare ground, and into the house. If not *killers,* our killer is plenty fit. So take care, Morris." The inspector also looked across at Sullivan until she nodded that she would be careful.

Morris said, "No wonder the front room didn't look as if a fight to the death had occurred there. The killer must've turned over the one chair to distract us. Why? Granted, he had to be in a panic and not thinking clearly. The police were bound to find the blood in the barn. Why were they in the barn . . . in the dead of night?"

"We've got enough questions to sink Scotland," the inspector said.

"What else did your people find in Old Alec's house and barn?" asked Morris.

"Great God, the dust and dirt!" Emerson said. "The place hadn't been swept since the Kaiser started the Great War. Old Alec's wife had been long dead, and he wouldn't let his own daughters or granddaughter touch a thing. The old barn doesn't even have electric lights. He used kerosene lamps. The house and barn are filled with old, unclean furniture, molding golf bags, some valuable feathery balls, curling posters, old ruined clubs, old trunks of cheap, unframed prints, and crap that hadn't been touched in decades, *if in this century.* It would be easier to clean up the entire London Underground than that old barn." The inspector could only shake his head at the unclean catastrophe.

"If you don't mind, Sullivan and I would like to look the house and barn over," said Morris. "It might remind us of her place in Colorado."

Sullivan reached in her glass and hit him with slivers of ice, which were more precious in a St. Andrews pub than eagle putts on the Old Course.

Inspector Emerson nodded his okay for them to explore Old Alec's stone digs.

"How is his granddaughter Sharon?" Morris asked, saving a sliver of ice off his face for his own glass.

"A gutsy young woman, you Yanks would say. She's doing remarkably well . . . much better than her mother, who is still too grief-stricken to make much sense,'' the inspector said. ''I think the murder of her grandfather has taken her mind off her own terrible experience with Barry Vinson. Oh, she will be a long time getting entirely over it. But she is a pluckly young lady. Like the rest of us, she cannot imagine anyone hating, or fearing, or killing her grandfather . . . for any reason.''

''When will the funeral be?'' asked Sullivan.

The inspector shook his head. ''I'm not releasing the body. Not until we have all the results in from the forensic tests.''

''Any surprises so far . . . other than two victims on the same wire?'' Morris asked indelicately.

''We found another feathery—*in Old Alec's throat,* just as we suspected.'' Emerson again sounded more angry at the obscenity of the act than at the murder itself. ''The old man, unlike Vinson, *was already dead* when the ball was stuck in the back of his throat. The wire strangled him. There's no question about that. And as Captain Tait suspected, he was garroted from behind. No question about that, either.''

Morris shared the inspector's anger. ''So the ball was just stuck in his throat for effect? Where would the killer get a second rare feathery? And why would he waste so valuable a collectible to make a macabre point?''

The inspector was again reduced to shaking his head. ''There were several lying around Old Alec's house. Christ, there may be a splinter off the true cross in the house or the barn.''

''Or the killer used the ball to make us think the same man murdered them both . . . in the same manner,'' Morris said.

''Or if he's terribly subtle, make us think the opposite,'' the inspector said. ''The killer—assuming there was one killer—must have been a rather large man to be able to drag the dead body from the barn, and a rather tall one, judging from the angle the wire cut into Old

Alec's neck. Old Alec was nearly six feet tall. The wire twisted somewhat downward, to the killer's hands, as it naturally would, but the killer was likely as tall as the victim, or taller. Our forensic people agree on that. Whoever killed him must have wrapped himself in a raincoat, if he wasn't badly bloodied. And he had better burn the raincoat, the clothes, and the shoes. There is no way he could have escaped the layers of dust and fibers as large as seagulls in the barn and the house, not to mention the bare dirt in the yard between the two buildings. Whoever killed him smudged his footprints in the dust on the floor of the house and barn, apparently using a towel or some sort of heavy cloth he didn't leave behind. We don't have a clear footprint that we can say with any confidence was the killer's."

The inspector hushed, exhausted with words and the questions they raised.

Morris told him of Warren Lightfoot's conversation last night in the Bull and Bear with the young valet at the Old Course Hotel. "The boy, named Thirlwell, said that Vinson's green Jaguar had been driven away from the hotel around one A.M. the night Vinson was killed. He did not recognize the driver, but *swore* he was an old man with white hair."

The inspector said his people had been looking for Thirlwell, who'd been off work, supposedly ill, but had not been in his one-room flat. They would pick him up tomorrow, if they had to empty every flat in St. Andrews. The inspector had not known that Lightfoot was in the Bull and Bear last night. Morris did not tell him the good president was dining at the moment with a woman friend from the R&A. That was a private matter, having nothing to do with murder, unless Mrs. Lightfoot got wind of it over in New England.

"One thing's certain," said Morris. "Someone had to give Old Alec a ride home last night. McCormack said he knocked on his door at ten P.M. Old Alec apparently left the bar, smashed to the gills, according to McCormack and Tait, no later than nine P.M., and not much before nine. He had a five-mile walk home. He could have walked it sober easily, but not by ten P.M. And truly drunk? Five miles? He couldn't have walked much more than halfway home in an hour. And most citizens of St. Andrews—and certainly most everybody last night in the Bull and Bear—knew Old Alec. Someone had to give him a lift home. Unless McCormack is lying about the time . . . or the whole deal."

"If someone did pick him up . . . and then killed him . . . who answered the door for McCormack at ten P.M.?" asked Sullivan.

"And maybe McCormack gave him the lift . . . into the next world," Morris said.

"But why?" Sullivan said.

"That seems to be the operative question," said the inspector, exhausted with the day's events.

• CHAPTER EIGHT •

It was not easy to understand Sullivan. She was speaking with her head under the pillow. If she couldn't see the sunlight, it couldn't be morning.

"What?" Morris said. "You sound like the gears groaning in a 1937 International pickup truck." He lifted the pillow.

Sullivan's eyes squeezed shut. "I can't believe God meant to have daylight fifteen straight hours."

"Is that what you were doing under there, questioning God?" said Morris.

"We have an understanding. He runs things, but I have bitching privileges. No, I was saying I promised to fly Sharon Kirkcaldy to London. I think I'll do it today. Her grandfather can't be buried until the inspector releases the body. What the child doesn't need more of is consecutive sadness."

"Do you think she's up to it, after what happened to her?"

"She looks so fragile. But she's strong. It's her mother who's taken to bed."

"What about her mother? Can she stay alone?"

"She has a sister who's come over from Edinburgh. And nobody can stay hysterical for two straight days. Sharon needs a day to forget *everything.* And she's never been to London. And I promised her." Sullivan sat up—

as if in penance for her sins, thought Morris . . . *no, sitting up would hardly pay the tariff.*

Sullivan threw her pillow at him. "What are you smiling about, John Morris?"

He caught the pillow square in the face. "You. I was thinking of your sins."

"Of the flesh, I hope."

It must not be as early as all that, thought Morris, always amazed how strong in the hands and arms this slender woman could be. But then, he was putting up very little resistance.

Sullivan skipped breakfast, which was an enormous indoor upset. "I won't eat until we land in London," she said. Morris made the decision to stay in St. Andrews and see what trouble he could stir up, if any, for the local assassin; he rolled away in the bed, well acquainted with "Hurricane Sullivan" once she'd made up her mind to do a thing. She made one phone call, but not to Sharon Kirkcaldy; in fact, she gave Sharon no warning whatsoever, but simply drove the small Ford to her house next to Old Alec's.

When Sharon answered the door, dressed all in black—slight, pale, and beautiful under her short, curling flow of red hair—Sullivan took her by the hand and led her to her own room in the old stone house, pausing only to speak to her aunt and to her mother still lying in her bed trying to summon up further tears to weep for her dead father.

"Young woman, we are spending the day and a fair portion of the night in London," said Sullivan, pawing through her closet, accepting no objections, tossing on the bed a simple blue skirt and white blouse and green sweater and flats for walking. "There is no mourning in London. It's not allowed. Plenty of time for that when you get back to St. Andrews."

Sullivan looked directly into her blue eyes. "Are you up to it?"

Sharon Kirkcaldy stood straight as the thin spires over St. Andrews. "Aye. Ma life is ma oon. Nae mon can rob it frae me."

"No, indeed," said Sullivan, hugging her around her thin, strong shoulders.

Sharon sat excitedly in the small Ford as they crossed the high, frightful bridge over the shimmering Firth of Forth and turned into the busy Edinburgh Airport, snaking their way to the hangar for private planes. Sharon not only had never been to London, she had never stood this close to an airplane in her young life.

"Miss Sullivan, who di'ye say wa' flyin' us?" asked Sharon, standing light-headed in the suddenly bright sun shining on the silver wings of the Learjet.

Sullivan pointed a long, slim finger at herself and watched the blush of embarrassment—or was it fear?—pass over the pale face of Sharon Kirkcaldy, until both of them were laughing.

"Would you like a Coke?" Paul Mason, looking too young in his short haircut to be a college sophomore, was waiting inside the sleek Learjet with a napkin over one arm, for all the world like an apprentice steward on a flight by a third-world airline. Sharon, surprised, took the red-and-white can before she recognized his face . . . or *thought* she recognized his face, but she obviously couldn't remember from where.

Sullivan introduced him as a "lad from that Atlanta *trade school,* Georgia Tech. You two, I believe, once met at the Bull and Bear." No avoiding that encounter . . . might as well meet it head-on, she thought.

The memory came back to Sharon, who bit her lower lip at the raw scene between Barry Vinson, whom she closed her eyes to forget, and this young man, who had been extremely polite to her in the Bull and Bear.

"Aye, I rimember ye bein' fired. An' beca' o' maself," she all but whispered, stepping back as if to leave the plane, seemingly light enough in her blouse and skirt to float to the tarmac.

"No, no, no," said Mason, careful not to touch her, or even to stand too near. "Sooner or later he fired everybody. Couldn't be helped. It's in the past. Let's go to London. I've never been there, except to change planes."

Sullivan had warned him that young Sharon Kirkcaldy had loved her grandfather and that she'd had a terrible time of it, and that he must give her all the gentleness and room in the world, or she would throw his Georgia Tech ass off the plane herself, in midair. Mason had all but dropped to his knees on the other end of the telephone, swearing by his mother's name to be better than good.

Sullivan did not tell him what Barry Vinson had done to the girl, and she did not mean to let the two of them out of her sight in London. But she also knew that Old Man Time ticked on and maybe the boy would never set foot again in Scotland. In an instant she had fancied him for the girl, though it was the worst possible circumstances for them to meet under, and probably they would hate each other. So be it, thought Sullivan. John Morris had laughed for years at her self-appointed role of matchmaker . . . but the two of them were godparents now to how bloody many kids?

Neither Mason nor Kirkcaldy understood why she was suddenly smiling.

Sullivan introduced the two of them to her young copilot, Jack Wilson, who was all business as usual, his only thoughts being to get in enough flying hours to earn his commercial license. He'd filed the flight plan to

Gatwick Airport in London, with the flyby over St. Andrews that Sullivan had requested.

"Would you like to sit in the jump seat and look over our shoulders as we take off?" Sullivan asked Sharon, who strapped herself in, looking with amazement at the complicated dials and switches in the cockpit. Sullivan was pleased to see that Sharon was amazed but not afraid as she leaned between the pilots.

Sullivan looked back to young Mason, to be sure he also was strapped in. He waved, content to watch the girl, ignoring the activity of the airport out the window.

Sullivan explained each action to Sharon as she started the two engines, then got clearance from the tower for takeoff. She had to repeat herself several times, as her Colorado accent was unknown in Edinburgh. Copilot Jack Wilson watched, envious of the takeoff. Sullivan was sure he would have been more than a little competition for Paul Mason, but he was married, and she did not let him forget it.

The twin engines wound themselves into a high whine that Sullivan loved, and they were off. Sharon Kirkcaldy gave a burst of applause that might have cheered an eagle putt on the Old Course.

Sullivan tipped the wings so that Kirkcaldy and Mason behind her could look down on the great bridge over the Firth of Forth, whose wide waters spilled away to the sea. She kept the plane at the low altitude they had been cleared for in the brief flight to St. Andrews, which was already visible below them, the small medieval city clinging to the edge of the North Sea, with the low spires of the churches and the ruins of the cathedral and The Castle below reaching up to them, as they had for five hundred years. The Old Course made a green sea of its own, spilling into the very heart of the city.

"Ma hoose, ma hoose!" Sharon said as Sullivan pointed the left wing of the plane along Pilmour Links

Road. "It's a miracle!" She marveled at the gray and green beauty of the city.

"Yes," Sullivan said, "that's exactly what it is, a miracle." She circled the city twice more, passing over the Firth of Tay and the small village of Carnoustie and its own great golf course opposite St. Andrews, finally turning the plane over to Wilson, whose young hands ached to fly it to London. He'd been promised he could make the landing.

Sullivan eased out of the pilot's seat and moved with Sharon into the passenger compartment, where Paul Mason was pleased to welcome them. Sharon leaned her red hair against the small, cool window and pointed out the great castle in Edinburgh to Mason. In her wonderful Scottish brogue, she described to him the Lake Country below and Keswick, where she had once spent the night and visited the grave of Wordsworth and his wife, Mary, in nearby Grasmere; she knew several of the lakes and mountains by name and was so excited to see them from the sky that she had forgotten, for the moment, her pain.

They flew on, past the sprawl of Birmingham, over the tame river Avon winding through Stradford-upon-Avon, and above the Cotswolds, until Mason recognized the legendary spires of Oxford. Sullivan left them, smiling at their easy familiarity, then settled into the pilot's seat, saying to herself: *Now, what do you know about man and woman, John Morris?*

Wilson made a Class-A landing, despite the confusion of planes above Gatwick. Sullivan gave him permission to fly over to Ireland, so long as he was back at Gatwick by ten P.M.

An old, black, high-roofed taxicab took them through a sea of traffic straight to Parliament Square, stopping near the slouching figure of Churchill, leaning on his cane while the Western world leaned on the power of his sentences—in lieu of artillery—to stop the Nazi advance through Europe. Sharon Kirkcaldy needed two sets of eyes to take in all of London. Paul Mason put his own at her disposal.

Sullivan wanted them to see Westminster Abbey while they were fresh with energy. The ancient cathedral shone with its own vigor, having had a thousand years of soot and dirt sandblasted off its great stone exterior. She hung carefully back while the two of them wandered through Poet's Corner and among the tombs of kings and queens. She dropped money in the poor box, asking only for a bit of luck for them all.

The three of them realized they were starved at the same instant. Sullivan led them along the Embankment to Savoy Street and the still-posh Savoy Hotel, next to the Savoy Theatre, which she explained was the first building in London to have electric lights. *John Morris would be impressed,* she said to herself. She ordered a massive late breakfast for the three of them. Sharon was struck dumb by the grand appointments of the hotel and the strict formality of its staff. The thin Mason ate as if it were the last meal ever to be served in London. Sullivan herself had only three helpings of bacon and eggs.

After a walk down the Strand to settle their breakfast, around the separate "island churches" of St. Clement Dane and St. Mary-le-Strand, Sullivan engaged a smallish boat at Westminster Pier to tour them down the river as far as the Isle of Dogs and the formal buildings of Greenwich, and then up the river as far as Battersea Bridge, where Turner painted his great sunsets on the Thames. Parliament, the Tower of London, Big Ben, Somerset House, Tower Bridge, and the other great old bridges passed over their heads, while the West India Docks, the stark, concrete National Theatre, the massive Bankside Power Station, the entire city of London crowded over the tidal river that passed through it all like a stream of time with the three of them cast away upon it.

Sullivan was pleased to see that Sharon directed most of her awe of the great city toward Mason, who could not have been more carefully attentive, considering he was a Georgia Tech man. Morris, speaking from the experience of having grown up in Atlanta, often misquoted Dr. Johnson: "Much can be made of a Tech man, if you catch him early."

When they both asked what she was laughing at, Sullivan told them. Mason, flattered to be teased, explained to Sharon that many American colleges had been jealous of Georgia Tech since the legendary football days of Coach Bobby Dodd. In any event, the idea of American football proved too complicated to explain in a country that had invented a very different sport ages ago under the same name.

The small boat docked; the old, skinny pilot had not spoken one syllable.

"Let's hit the marketplace before we do another old building," Sullivan said irreverently. She led the way up the Strand to Bedford Street and Covent Garden. Sharon loved the old floor the glassblowers stood on, the wine bars, the everywhere shops. Sullivan pointed out No. 8 Russell Street, now a coffee shop, where Boswell first met Dr. Johnson. *John Morris, the Johnson freak, must be grinning up in St. Andrews,* thought Sullivan.

Sharon flitted from shop to shop like a hungry bee in a field of wildflowers, lifting this bracelet, trying on that floppy hat, and nearly falling down with laughter at how she looked in a cracked, warped mirror. Paul paraded around with a variety of walking canes, blowing up his cheeks, imitating the large Morris with his limp until Sullivan joined Sharon in a duet of laughter. They turned into the Central Market, with its high, arching iron-and-glass roof, looking for the world like a nineteenth-century train station, but with shops at every level.

Sharon lovingly admired an expensive red skirt with pleats, which Sullivan quickly folded over to the young clerk, ignoring all protestations from Sharon and paying for it with a tiny portion of her golf winnings.

"Now help me find just the right thing for our Mr. Mason," Sullivan said, setting Sharon off in a frenzy of shopping, her blue skirt sailing over the gardens until she found an antique poster in the London Transport Museum, a print actually, of an underground train—quite handsome, if a bit pricey. "Jist the thing for a' enginiir," said Sharon, pleased to hear *him* protesting the expense.

"Mr. Nicklaus has already paid for everything," said Sullivan, hinting of her winnings, which were already famous in St. Andrews.

Of course, they were hungry again, and popped into a café that had once been a bookstore, and ate enough for six people.

"We'll just do the big moments in the National Gallery," said Sullivan, refusing to let herself look at her watch and the day vanishing under them. She led the way to the darkened corner of the da Vinci Cartoon, which had been a draft of a painting Leonardo never finished, but he managed astonishing faces on the women. "Our boy da Vinci didn't complete a lot of what he started," Sullivan said, "but he had a sure hand with the brush, woulda been a helluva putter."

The two kids snickered into their hands so as not to break the silence in the tiny room, which could only be described as *imitation holy.* Outside was the full-blown religious thing, a huge finished painting of an angel. The legend on the wall insisted that da Vinci painted at least some of the angel and certainly her face. She looked as if she might open her wings and fly off the wall that very minute, her face by da Vinci more innocent than the Queen's swans on the river Thames.

Sullivan flew them out of the building and over to the Portrait Gallery, her favorite museum in all of London, and led them up the stairs in a fury to the first painting bought for the museum: *of Shakespeare himself,* the only known work painted from life, a handsome man with a high forehead and large, dark eyes, and a gold earring in his left ear. None of them would risk a spoken word in front of the best-spoken poet of them all.

They came down the stairs, looking but not tarrying through the grand aristocracy of the old Empire, and took a turn through the contemporary photographic gallery on the first floor, with its emphasis on generals and actors and politicians. "One might just use any one of the three nouns for them all," Sullivan said.

Sharon worshiped at the great face of Laurence Olivier.

"Enough culture," Sullivan said. "I need a beer." They took the underground to Charing Cross Road and popped into the first pub they found.

Back on the street, Mason watched in both directions when they crossed at each intersection, not trusting the lights and being certain that Sharon would step into the path of a speeding taxi, as if she had never crossed the street alone in her life. Sullivan was amused to see it. That old dark magic was alive for another generation, and what was a modest thing like an ocean to tame it?

They got off the crowded train at Knightsbridge Station. Sullivan led the way up Brompton Road, stopping in front of the massive terra-cotta home of Harrods, the world's largest department store, with a modest staff of *five thousand.* Sullivan stood, as always, in amazement: "I don't think it's what Henry Harrod had in mind when he opened his grocer's shop here in 1849. Let's stick our noses inside and see what the gang has got for sale.''

Only everything. Sullivan bought them each a kelly-green scarf to remember the day by . . . *and maybe to remember one another by,* she thought sneakily.

''Let's get out of here; the world is waiting outside,'' said Sullivan, who hiked them along to Shepherd's Market, a fun, twisting little alley of shops right out of Dickens. She turned into the Old Newspaper and Ephemera Shop at 37 Kinnerton Street. The delightful gentleman who owned it, an ex-solicitor, remembered her and asked about John Morris. She was pleased to tell him that Morris was well ''and shockingly sober in Scotland.'' Sullivan remembered the owner had been a boy messenger for the London Fire Service during the terrible days of the blitz, when many of the boys were killed running messages between stations. ''It was better to be out and doing something than waiting for the bombs to kill you in your cellar,'' he said.

Sullivan could not bear to leave unbought an original issue of *The Rambler* by Dr. Johnson. Morris wouldn't be able to eat for reading it. ''Are you game to hike to Speaker's Corner in Hyde Park?'' she asked.

''Sure,'' said Sharon, her frailness belying her stamina.

''How about you, Georgia Tech?''

''The Ramplin' Wreck is ready.''

A wild, shouting Communist, the next-to-the-last of the species, finished a too-serious harangue against *the ghastly capitalistic state* to a modicum of applause.

Sullivan, before she gave it one thought, stepped up to the speaker's stand, maybe just to see the open mouths of Sharon and Paul.

''I've been in your country nearly two weeks,'' said Sullivan, amazed at what words were coming out of her mouth. ''I think that qualifies me to stand for Parliament." Quite a nice round of laughter from the clutch of spectators at the corner of the park . . . and especially at the prospect of a Yank . . . and a comely woman Yank, at that. "What a country! You have golf, you have ten grand pubs for every church—and you are not short of churches. You have a Queen Mother. May she live forever!" Solid cheers. "But one more museum, lads, and you'll sink the island." A ripple of laughter. Then Sullivan was serious. "But don't go and sell the river that runs through your city and saves us all from Time itself." An old man took off his hat: "Well said, my lady." Sullivan saluted him and leaned into the mike before leaving: "Do please lend us the English language. I'm afraid we haven't used it for centuries." And she was off the stage to a rather splendid round of shouts and applause, led by the Scottish lass, Kirkcaldy, and the Tech apprentice engineer, Mason.

Sharon ran and hugged her, as if she'd saved civilization. "Brave work tha'," she said, kissing Sullivan on the cheek, almost bringing tears to Sullivan's eyes for the daughter she never had.

The Learjet was waiting at the airport. Jack Wilson had been to Dublin and back, putting himself two countries and two landings nearer to his commercial license. Sullivan wound up the engines. As much as she loved to fly in the daylight, she loved twice as much to fly in the night. Gatwick and all the million lights of London fell below them. She banked the slim jet for Scotland, missing John Morris for the tenth time that day. A bare half hour out, she left the controls to Wilson and eased back to the passenger compartment. The two of them were dead asleep, Sharon's hair a quiet flame on Paul's firm shoulder.

* * *

Morris had started the day pleased to be alone. It lasted halfway through breakfast, when he looked up and there was nobody with beautiful light brown hair and blue eyes and arms as slim as a young girl's to harass him about the fifth piece of toast he had just eaten. Nothing to do but eat a sixth piece, and what was one more stick of bacon to a hungry man?

He pushed open the hotel door to look down on the North Sea, which rolled onto the shore as it had for a hundred thousand years.

Walking all alone up The Scores, as if abandoned by the tournament he'd been covering, came Tom Rowe, looking in his coat and tie like the *Times'* own man of golf, which he'd been for twenty-five years.

"Arre ye lost, laddie?" asked Morris, in his best imitation Scottish tongue.

"Only for these first forty-seven years of my life," Rowe said. "What's new with Scotland Yard?"

The two of them leaned on the eight hundred-year-old wall and looked down on the wide beach and the calm sea lapping silently against it.

Morris caught him up on what he and Sullivan had learned and now wondered about.

Morris would have bet a lot that the old caddy had killed Vinson, until he himself was killed. And for what reason? Why was he killed in his barn and dragged to his living quarters? Rowe did not change expressions, weighing these questions.

Morris continued, saying that once again Sir Arthur Maxwell claimed to have been in his room alone the night of a murder.

And, finally, Captain A.W.B. Tait had spent the night with his widow friend Agatha Burns, but she didn't get to his flat until eleven P.M. Tait, of course, had passed the early evening at the Bull and Bear, at the same long table with Old Alec and the punter McCormack.

"Now, what's complicated about all that?" said Rowe, spitting over the old wall, fracturing his image of London elegance.

"Kiss my ass, Rowe," said Morris, his own spittle landing some dozen yards farther out toward the sea than his London counterpart's.

"Anyway," Rowe said, "the *Times* is bored with the St. Andrews murders. The Open is over and off the telly—and, Morris, *there's been a 'gangster slaying' in London, four police officers found murdered in the same squad car.* A couple of two-day-old killings in St. Andrews—of a nasty Yank and an old Scot—are pretty tame stuff to that. These days you have to be caught in royalty's knickers to make the front page of the *Times* two days running."

"My God, you're sure they haven't moved London to America?" Morris said. "Have they arrested anybody?"

"They don't have a clue," Rowe said. "I say, where's Sullivan?" he asked suddenly, as if she had just vanished.

"She's flown Sharon Kirkcaldy and Paul Mason to London. I hope the two of them are in good health. A day in London with Sullivan will take a week off your life. Oh, she's matchmaker No. 1 and 2, Sullivan is."

"Does he know what happened to the girl?" asked Rowe.

"No. But he will be on his best behavior, not to worry about that. If he frightens the girl, Sullivan will break both of his arms. She thinks Sharon has had enough sadness for one week, and she fancies the two of them together. You wouldn't want to bet against Sullivan. Ask McCormack."

Rowe suddenly pushed himself away from the old wall. "Jesus, we both know someone who drives a Citroën. I've even seen him park it here this week in St. Andrews."

"Who?"

"Who else? Sir Arthur Maxwell."

"Let's run him down." Morris looked at his watch. "He's not an early riser. He's likely in bed at the Old Course Hotel. The inspector asked him not to leave town."

Sir Arthur was having breakfast in his room. He looked powerful enough in his dress shirt, without a tie, to have been the heavyweight boxing champ of Cambridge. Maxwell dabbed a touch of marmalade off his neat mustache. Without the mustache, he would never have passed for forty years old. "Of course I drive a Citroën. I've had it for years," Maxwell said. "Why do you ask?"

"Were you driving it two nights ago, when Old Alec was killed?" asked Morris.

Maxwell thought. "Yes. I drove it to the R&A. I left early. Back to the hotel. And back to work. By ten P.M. Why, gentlemen?"

"I think we'd better let Inspector Emerson tell you," Morris said enigmatically.

"Look, why knock on my door and ask about my automobile, and not tell me what the hell's the point?"

"Did you drive it on Pilmour Links Road?" asked Morris.

Maxwell thought another minute. "I'm not sure. I took a spin around the town. That road leads out by the Old Course, doesn't it? I might've been on it. I'm not sure. Why?"

"Old Alec lived out Pilmour Links Road," Morris said. He did not say Paul Mason had seen a Citroën on that road that night. "You didn't, by chance, give Old Alec a ride home, did you?"

"No," Maxwell said. "I would've, if I had seen him. Maybe he would still be alive if I had. I think I'd better call the inspector."

Morris nodded that it would be a good idea.

"Somebody saw a Citroën," speculated Maxwell.

Morris's face offered no expression.

Rowe risked a question into the silence: "How are things going in your business since Vinson was killed?"

Maxwell shook his head. "You could not believe it. Vinson's line of clothes, always popular, have caught fire. Kids who've never stepped on a golf course want his logo on a shirt. He's become a sort of icon. In America. In Europe. Even Asia. It's rather creepy. But it's saving my goddamned company."

"No way you could have predicted that result," Morris said. "But you'd better alert the inspector, just the same."

"Since when has the criminal set been required to furnish evidence against itself?" said Maxwell with a touch of a smile, despite the darkness of the subject.

"Best way to stay clear of Scotland Yard is to conceal nothing that can help them," Morris said. "As soon as they catch the murderer, we can all go home."

"That's fine for everybody . . . *but the murderer,*" said Maxwell, a broader smile on his lips. He was full of questions about the killing of Old Alec, which Morris chose not to answer.

Morris suddenly asked, "Sir Arthur, do you smoke?"

Maxwell was a bit taken aback. "Not really," he said. "I quit the daily habit years ago. Sometimes I—what do you Yanks say?—'bum' a cigarette, especially at parties. But two in a row these days would burn a hole in my throat."

Exiting the hotel, Morris confronted the valet, Jack Thirlwell, who was back at work parking cars. For a five-pound note Thirwell told Morris and Rowe that his *illness*—causing him to miss work the last two days—had been, in fact, the return of his girlfriend from a job in

London, her welcome home requiring two full days and nights of celebration.

"Ah, youth," said Morris, wondering if Sullivan would settle for a handshake after her one-day trip to the same city; somehow he didn't think so. Thirlwell could add nothing more to his earlier description of *an old man with white hair . . . an old man whose face he didn't see, who drove away in Barry Vinson's green Jaguar about one A.M. the night he was killed.* Thirlwell had spent half the night telling the story, and retelling it, to Inspector Emerson. Not likely he would remember anything he hadn't told the inspector.

"Was the old man you saw smoking?" asked Morris.

Thirlwell thought. "Aye, 'e might o' been. I canna be sure." He closed his eyes. "Damn, I think 'e were smokin'."

Morris did not say that the USGA president, Warren Lightfoot, had seen the same car being driven away at the same time, one A.M., and though Lightfoot did not see the driver's face, or even his white hair, he was certain he saw a *lighted cigarette.* And Barry Vinson did not smoke or allow anyone to smoke in his presence, not to mention his car. The inspector, under siege from every side, had simply forgotten to ask Thirlwell about the possibility of a lighted cigarette in Vinson's car.

Morris waited until Rowe's snappy BMW was pulling away from the hotel. "Who smokes, Tom, among the suspects? Captain Tait?"

"Sometimes a cigar. Not often," Rowe said.

"Of course, the driver could have been smoking a cigar as well as a cigarette. A cigar would have made a bigger ember. It would have been easier to see. Maxwell admitted he sometimes bums a cigarette and smokes it . . . especially at a party. Though he says he *quit* the daily habit some years ago. Do you believe him?"

"I can't ever remember seeing him smoke, even at parties," Rowe said.

"What about the self-appointed Big Noise in the R&A, Gerald Balfour-Mellville Dougall?"

"Never saw him smoking, except through his ears when he was playing the big man . . . as in attacking the grooves in Barry Vinson's clubs," Rowe said.

"How about Lightfoot?" asked Morris.

"Oh, he smokes. Long filter tips," Rowe said. "He seems careful not to do it at dinner, or in a crowd."

"You're right. In fact, I remember seeing him with a lighted cigarette many times on the golf course," said Morris. "And our punter McCormack, when he paid off Sullivan's marker . . . What was he doing? He was *smoking a big cigar.* It fit right between his big fingers and right between his big teeth, inside his big mouth. Shit, does every soul in Scotland smoke?"

"Just about," Rowe said. "They drink plenty of booze. They golf every chance they get. They only eat fried foods and never vegetables. They smoke cigarettes, pipes, cigars. They chase the lassies until they're too old to catch them. Then they take on a load of religion. It's no wonder they all die young, and Scotland is so happy a country."

"I wonder about the caddy Caldwell and his motorcycle. Do you suppose he smokes?" asked Morris.

"I have no idea. But if he's a young man, he wouldn't have white hair, now, would he? In fact, none of the men we've mentioned have white hair . . . present company excepted," said Rowe, touching his own prematurely graying hair.

"You bastard, I remember when you used to smoke like a hundred-dollar Ford," Morris said.

"Of course you do. You were the man always borrowing cigarettes you never returned, mind you?"

"Oh, no, not me," said Morris, suddenly feeling the

urge for a cigarette for the first time in years. "And where were you, Rowe, when death came to the golfer and the caddy?"

Tom Rowe turned, suddenly serious. "Whacking away at my word processor. I can show you the exact times I filed copy . . . follow-up stuff to each day's tournament play."

Morris enjoyed his discomfort. "Is it possible your stuff bored any readers to death?"

"Oh, no. They are a stout group, toughened no doubt over the years by the frightfully dull fare on the Associated Press wire."

"Och!" Morris said, and laughed. He considered what Warren Lightfoot had told him. "Lightfoot didn't see any *white hair* on the driver of the Jaguar at one A.M. But he did see the lighted cigarette. Maybe Thirlwell imagined the white hair."

"I don't know. He seemed more sure of the white hair than the cigarette," Rowe said. "I'm late with a follow-up. Let me know what you hear, old man."

Morris looked at his watch. If he played his cards right, the inspector might pick up lunch. When Julia Sullivan wasn't around, Morris's only appetite was for food. Now, if he could just sell that idea to her. . . .

Inspector Emerson would, indeed, spring for lunch. He winced at having forgotten to ask the valet, Thirlwell, if the white-haired man he saw driving Vinson's Jaguar was smoking. The inspector was pleased to get the informed opinions of Morris and Tom Rowe, as to which men among the suspects did smoke, or had once smoked. Emerson himself had seen Gerald Dougall smoking a cigar early last night at the R&A. No, the inspector hadn't yet turned up the caddy Caldwell. But it was just a matter of time. His own mother was looking for him now among his cronies, none of whom, according to her, were up to any good.

"Tom Rowe told me about the four London police found murdered in one squad car," Morris said. "What in hell happened?"

"Assassinations," Inspector Emerson said. "Plain and not so simple. Could have been a drug deal. The city has gone berserk. There's not been anything like it in this century. Even in New York it would be a scandal."

"Are they calling you back to London?"

"No," Emerson said. "But several of the men sent to help me have been recalled." He sounded somewhat relieved to see them go. "They have scores of inspectors working on it. They don't need me. And I've made precious little progress here."

"How were the four men killed?" Morris asked.

"One of them was a young woman," Emerson said. "You can imagine the outrage. Shot. They were each bound and shot in the back of the head."

"My God," Morris said. "What are these grand old islands coming to? Murder in Scotland. Massacre in London." Morris explained that Sullivan had flown to London with Sharon Kirkcaldy and young Paul Mason. But they would be back tonight. Morris suddenly couldn't wait to see her. It was foolish to think of their running into police murderers in one day among the innocent millions of London, but he couldn't help the unease in the pit of his stomach.

The inspector said, "I spoke this morning with Old Alec's daughter, Anne Kirkcaldy, who, as you know, has taken to her bed. She told me that her daughter, Sharon, had flown off to London. She said it as if she herself had been cruelly abandoned, though her sister from Edinburgh was in the house. Frankly, she couldn't tell us a thing."

"Both houses and the barn have thick stone walls,"

Morris said. "You could shoot a cannon in one and not hear it in the others. What do you forensic people make of the murder scene?"

"Old Alec was legally drunk, twice over," the inspector said. "He didn't put up much resistance. No bruises on his knuckles, no flesh under his fingernails. One odd thing: Old Alec's house and barn, as I told you, are a jumble of old golf junk that hasn't been dusted in decades, if ever. Some of it may be valuable. Much of it's broken, handles have rotted off the clubs, there are even some old sketches and cheap prints in the wooden boxes under ruined dust cloths."

The inspector swallowed a bite of sausage. "There are plenty of antique balls in the boxes, even rare featheries, which I know have substantial value, and I can tell you the feathery ball found stuck in Old Alec's throat *came from his own barn.* The same dirt and fibers clung to the ball that cling to everything in his house and barn. Also, there is no doubt that the ball that strangled Barry Vinson *also came from Old Alec's house or barn.* The dirt and fibers match, absolutely. Now, tell me what that means," Emerson said.

Morris thought about it. "Somebody had access to Old Alec's place . . . not once, but *twice.* Both balls could have been taken at the same time, before Vinson was killed. Or the balls could have been stolen, separately, for each murder. Or *one killer* could have used the ball found in Vinson's throat, and a *second killer* could have improvised, using a ball on Old Alec that he found in the barn, to imitate the ball *he knew* was found in Vinson's throat."

"Very good, Morris," the inspector said.

"So you don't rule out separate killers," Morris said.

The inspector shook his head. "Nor do I rule them in. It's a dilemma."

"When did people stop killing each other, essentially, for money?" Morris said.

"They haven't. Money, or one of the lesser motives: power, lust, hatred, envy, the grand old *verities,*" the inspector said.

"But here we have two entirely opposite men as victims," Morris said. "One young, one old; one rich, one poor; one American, one Scotsman; one barbarian, one gentleman; one hated, one well loved. What one man would kill the two of them . . . and for what reason?"

Morris thought a minute. "Take, as an example, money. Was anything stolen from Old Alec's house and barn, or from Vinson's person?"

"Remember," the inspector said, "there were *five thousand pounds* intact in Vinson's wallet. Robbery was no motive, unless something frightened the killer away before he could take the money. Of course, we haven't revealed the money was untouched. If anything is missing from Old Alec's, we couldn't determine it. And actually, it would have been impossible to loot the place without disturbing generations of dust. Believe me, the dirt and dust were for the most part intact before we went through the house and barn. Though some of the boxes had been opened, nothing seemed to be missing. Did you go by and look the place over?"

"Not yet," Morris said. "Sullivan up and flew to London. I'd like to have her with me when I do go through Old Alec's place. She sees things I could trip over and never know were there." Morris told him of the morning visit he and Tom Rowe had with Sir Arthur Maxwell. And that Maxwell drove a Citroën and might have been on Pilmour Links Road the night Old Alec was killed. Maxwell, of course, said he had been at the R&A clubhouse, but had left early and was in his room by ten P.M.

"I have an appointment with him after lunch," Emerson said. "He told me the two of you came to see him, and that he had better talk with me. He didn't say about what."

The inspector said that none of Old Alec's cronies in the Bull and Bear had admitted to giving him a ride home, certainly not George McCormack, who stuck to his story of driving the five miles to the old caddy's house to return his old wool hat . . . and of leaving immediately to return to the Bull and Bear. None of Old Alec's neighbors admitted to having given him a ride home, or having seen him walking on Pilmour Links Road. Nor had any of them seen McCormack's big Rolls-Royce parked in front of Old Alec's house, but since the turnaround was dark and never lighted, a bull elephant might hide in it.

Emerson did not hesitate to give Morris the address of the one-room flat where Peter Caldwell lived. It was just up The Scores from Morris's hotel. The police were looking everywhere for Caldwell, but they could use another pair of eyes.

Morris thanked him for the beer and the meal on Scotland Yard. He walked back to the Old Course, where the temporary bleachers had already been taken down and the 18th green again rested anonymously as it had for centuries.

Morris walked on behind the R&A clubhouse to the caddy yard beyond the small starter's box, where a bureaucratic little man with a tight mustache ruled, without compassion, on who could and who could not tee off that day on the Old Course. If your name did not appear on *his* list, you could not play, though you lived in Windsor Castle.

Morris walked among the licensed caddies, young and old, nodding, looking for faces he remembered, or that remembered him. He spoke with several caddies, all of whom knew Caldwell and none of whom had an ounce of use for him. An older Scot, his hair gone mostly gray and his faced burned raw by the wind, sought him out. Morris knew him as a man who had once caddied for the great Peter Thomason, though he could not remember the caddy's name.

"Aye, Morris, the Open's done, 'ave ye moved tae Scotland?" The caddy smiled, giving his name as Tweddell. His hand was as hard as a stone. They spoke of the just-completed Open, and Tweddell remarked on the greatness of Nicklaus, but did not find him so fine "a striker o' the ba' as Thomason."

Morris chose not to debate the point, and worked around to asking if Tweddell knew the suspended caddy, Caldwell. The old caddy spit and said that he did but would just as soon not set eyes on him again. He knew the police had been asking about Caldwell, but he didn't know why. And they hadn't asked *him*.

Tweddell said that he himself was from Carnoustie, across the Firth of Tay. And the young scoundrel, Caldwell, had a " 'alf-brither livin' thair . . . nime o' Niel Blyth . . . an' jus' above a drunkard 'isself, but na' ah villain." It seemed Blyth helped mow the grass at the great old Carnoustie Golf Course, "when 'e shewed up sober." Tweddell warned that the half brothers might just as likely be killing one another as helping one another, but neither of them would be keen on helping the police. Tweddell, speaking as though for all the caddies, said, "Tha' mon 'oo killed Ol' Alec deseruvs ta droown innis oon blood."

Morris rang up Tom Rowe, who agreed to lend him his BMW for the afternoon, so long as he "did not drive it while sober."

Morris was not one to love driving an automobile, his stiff left knee growing ever stiffer, but the BMW was like a colt let out to pasture, and he did enjoy pushing it into the countryside among the low hills of grazing sheep, and whipping it over the long bridge across the Firth of Tay to Dundee, a town rather dusty with raw business, and letting it have its head on the flat, straight road to Carnoustie.

Morris coasted into the small, poor village, which had always reminded him of the lesser, poorer mill villages of his youth in his native Georgia. The silent street among the low houses dead-ended into the Carnoustie Golf Course, which had sprawled on the Angus Coast since the sixteenth century; though always in the shadow of the Old Course across the bay in St. Andrews, a town grown prosperous while Carnoustie's perpetual drabness was relieved only by its obsession with golf and by the very greatness of its course.

Morris stood alongside the bumpy practice green while three small boys, perhaps age eleven, chased their old balls with their older putters. And maybe among them was another Tommy Armour of Edinburgh, who had won the first British Open ever played at Carnoustie, in 1931; shooting, Morris knew from history, a remarkable 71 on the last day, over the 7,200-yard course on which no man, at that time, had ever broken 70.

A huge feeling of grand-old-times-gone-forever rose up in Morris; he remembered the year 1953, when as a rookie reporter he followed the implacable Ben Hogan through his only British Open, as *he* became the first man ever to break 70 at Carnoustie and did it on the last day of the tournament, which he, of course, won.

Morris remembered that Hogan did not admire the course, the first ten holes of which were designed by Allan Robertson of St. Andrews in 1839, the last eight holes being added by Old Tom Morris himself in 1867. Despite its history, Hogan despised Carnoustie's puttylike greens and ragged tees of that era, which did not include a watering system. But ironically, by his ingenious play, Hogan added immeasurably to the glory and mystique of Carnoustie.

Morris had watched Hogan rehearse for five of the ten days he practiced at Carnoustie. Limping around the course on his bad legs, injured seven years before in a terrible, near-fatal automobile accident, Hogan, to the astonishment of the Scots, had taken the course apart, as if it were a specimen under a microscope. To this day Morris himself had never seen any other golfer walk a course *backward,* from each green to each tee, as Hogan plotted his strategy for each shot of the tournament. He put together a plan to attack the course that was still described, stroke by stroke, in the old town. And one of the men still obsessed by those four immaculate rounds of golf, Morris knew, was Captain Tom Micklem, if he was still alive—and surely he was, if he, indeed, meant to live forever.

Morris asked the three young boys where he might find his old friend. They looked up from their putting and pointed him to the low, humble brick home of the Carnoustie Golf Club, just across the narrow road from the course itself. Morris tipped the three of them enough to buy each a sleeve of new balls at the pro shop, to which they fled so swiftly that their abandoned putters still leaned in midair.

Old Tom Micklem sat alone in the dark, square room, opposite a short rum and a long beer, the three of them unspeaking equals at the table. Morris slipped quietly over and took a seat opposite him, to the astonishment—sudden, and then joyful—of the small old man, whose every hair in his beard and on his head was now gray, as if he had turned entirely gray in the last season of his life.

"John Morris, ye divil," the former captain of the Carnoustie Golf Club said, taking Morris's big hand in both of his own small ones and shaking it fiercely, as if they had agreed on a course of action to change the fate of nations. Tom Micklem asked immediately of Sullivan and frowned his displeasure that she had chosen to visit *heathen London* and not *Godly Carnoustie.* "Na' so oftin do I kiss ah grand, beautifool woman oon the lips," he said, sipping his rum in regret.

"Don't hand me that, Tom Micklem," Morris said. "I've seen the beauties of Scotland fighting to hug your neck, and Sullivan ahead of 'em all."

They talked "gowf." The Open. The greatness of Nicklaus. The murder of Barry Vinson. And finally, the killing of Old Alec, longtime friend of Tom Micklem, who did not try to hide the tears in his eyes, already blurry with age.

Morris then told him he was looking for one Niel Blyth, half brother of Peter Caldwell. Captain Micklem scowled at both names. He said that Blyth ran one of the aging mowing machines on the Carnoustie course, and kept the job mainly because the local members loved his old mother, whose dead husband had been a poor but well-respected member of the town and a splendid golfer to challenge the best of St. Andrews. The captain said young Blyth worked well enough during the week, but on weekends would fall into his whisky in Dundee and not sober up until Tuesday. He admitted there was no other harm in the young man. But that his half brother was another matter, and he was no longer allowed to caddy on the Carnoustie course: "A cheeter, don't ye see?" the old man said scornfully.

Tom Micklem turned up one glass and then the other, relishing with his tongue on his lips the opposite tastes of rum and beer. He offered to take Morris on his private electric cart, the only one in Carnoustie, to catch Niel Blyth on his mower.

"Take me first by the tee at No. 6," Morris said, "so I can imagine again the two great drives struck by Hogan." And the aspect of the year 1953 set the old man off, and he replayed Hogan's entire last round of 68 as he teetered to his cart, which sagged on its tires, seemingly as old as the old man driving it, and set off across the rising, pitching links of Carnoustie.

Tom Micklem turned the cart toward the No. 6 tee and then drove behind it into grass that was no longer mown. The tee had been moved up on the par 5 hole a good thirty yards from Hogan's time. Morris knew that the hole was now played from the old length only once a year, a round of golf in Hogan's honor, in fact, all the tees being moved back to where they were when he dominated the course in 1953, and rare was the lad who could break 80 from those tees.

Morris stepped out of the cart to see down the terrifying length of the 6th hole. A barbed wire fence ran along the left edge of the fairway all the way to the green. Any tee shot that passed over it and landed in the pasture was out-of-bounds. Morris had seen Jack Nicklaus suffer such a penalty in 1968, costing him two strokes, the margin by which Gary Player finished ahead of him before winning the British Open in a play-off. Morris had heard Jack say several times that it was the one shot of his career he would most love to hit again.

Crossing the 6th fairway and running down the right side was Jockie's Burn, ready to swallow any pushed shot. And in the center of the fairway were two huge bunkers, from which it was impossible to reach the green. There was a bare twenty yards separating the bunkers and the out-of-bounds fence on the left. From where Morris stood, the distance between the fence and the bunkers looked more like five yards.

The first two days of the 1953 British Open, Hogan had played the 6th hole conventionally, laying up to the right side of the bunkers and accepting par as a legitimate score as he positioned himself for a decisive run for the championship. On the third and fourth rounds, *played on the same day,* Hogan abandoned his storied caution, aiming his patented fade off the 6th tee far out-of-bounds over the heads of grazing cattle, and fading it back into play between the fence and the two bunkers.

Morris, leaning on his cane all these years later, could almost see the ball hanging in the air. Hogan then nailed a four-wood to the green and two-putted for a birdie in each of those two closing rounds to win the Open by an awesome *four shots* over Frank Stranahan, Dai Rees, Antonio Cerda, and fellow immortal Peter Thomason.

Morris knew that no Open competitor had risked such a tee shot on the No. 6 hole since that day. Hogan had sailed on an ocean liner back to America to a ticker-tape parade in New York City that rivaled the one given Bobby Jones the year he won the British Open and Amateur and the still-unequaled Grand Slam of Golf. Hogan never again played in Great Britain.

The silence that Morris heard, standing on the old 6th tee, seemed to him to measure the still-great absence of Hogan.

By all that was ironic, Niel Blyth, far in the distance, was riding an aging mowing machine on the 6th green.

He was a thin, tubercular lad with bad teeth, looking twice as old as his thirty-two years. He got down from his mower to shake hands with Morris, apprehension in his very blue eyes, as if he feared some new reprimand for the sorry execution of his life.

Morris identified himself as an American golf writer. Blyth was impressed into deeper silence. In Carnoustie no man was considered to be a serious writer who did *not* write golf.

"I don't know if you realize it," Morris said, "but Scotland Yard wants to question your half brother, Peter Caldwell."

Blyth looked behind him, as if about to leap on his mower and make his escape.

"If I could speak to him, I think I could convince him it's in his best interest to contact Inspector Emerson in St. Andrews. Believe me, they'll find him soon enough." Morris was careful not to openly accuse Blyth of hiding him.

"Best heer the mon oot," Tom Micklem said, sitting like Time itself in his old electric cart.

Blyth looked back again at his ancient mowing machine, this time as if *it* were accusing him of misconduct.

"Finish your mowing," Morris said, "and join us for a sandwich in the Carnoustie Golf Club."

Blyth squinted as if in mortal pain from indecision, then nodded his thin head, stood for a minute as if he might speak, and turned and climbed silently on his mower, which growled in its gears as it started its timeless pattern over the 6th green.

"Will he come, do you think?" asked Morris.

"Aye," Captain Micklem said, turning his own ancient cart toward the clubhouse.

"Take us by the Spectacles," said Morris, remembering the sight of wee Gary Player in 1968, dressed entirely in black, as if to confront his own doom, standing over his ball in the 14th fairway and looking at the giant twin bunkers up ahead: the *Spectacles* that the hole was named after. Player swung his three-wood into the ball and stepped quickly forward with his right foot, as was his style. The ball climbed into the prevailing wind and cleared the Spectacles by an eyelash, bounding forward and onto the 14th green, stopping not more than three feet from the cup for a tap-in eagle and, ultimately, the championship.

Neither Morris nor Tom Micklem felt the need to speak as they looked down the now-empty fairway as if into the past.

The old man nudged the old cart forward to the 16th tee. A wind off the Firth of Tay blew ever-stiffer into their faces. It might have been 1975, the year Tom Watson won the Open at Carnoustie, ending his reputation forever as a choker in major championships. Watson conquered Carnoustie, but he never mastered the 235-yard, par-3 16th hole, bogeying it all five days, including the play-off. And he did not claim the title until he defeated Australian Jack Newton in the last eighteen-hole play-off in British Open history. Young Newton missed a ten-foot putt on the 18th green to lose by one stroke.

Fate followed each player off that 18th green, but in opposite directions. Watson went on to win four more British Open titles, two Masters, and a U.S. Open in the next decade. Newton played to modest success in the following years, but in 1983 he accidentally walked into the propeller of a small private airplane at the Sydney Airport and lost his right arm, and with it, his career as a golfer. However, his voice and face became popular on Australian television describing the world's great matches to its golf-loving audience.

Tom Micklem eased the cart up the par-4 17th hole, whose fairway is crossed three times by Barry Burn and on which Nicklaus deposited a 350-yard drive in 1968, which Morris still found hard to believe, looking at the distance that shot had carried.

And now the old man guided the cart down the 18th fairway, surely the most difficult closing hole on any course that ever held the British Open, with deep bunkers down the right side of the hole, and out-of-bounds down the left side, and Barry Burn snaking down *both sides* and crossing one last, hellish time in front of the 18th green.

"Do you think Peter Caldwell capable of murder?" asked Morris.

"Aye. An' any other mon," Tom Micklem said. "But 'e's a nasty one, na' ta be trusted."

Morris walked across the small, dark entrance of the Carnoustie Golf Club and looked again in the aging trophy case at the duplicate of the Silver Claret Jug that Hogan had seen fit to donate to the humble club and its world-class golf course. Tom Micklem stood over it as proud as if his own name were engraved on it.

Within an hour, Niel Blyth stepped hesitantly inside the golf club where he had never set foot in his life. The few faces in the dark room turned toward him, more surprised than antagonistic.

Morris pushed back a chair for the thin young man, who sat as if fearing an inquisition. He nodded that he would like a lager and would join them in a ham sandwich, and still he hadn't spoken.

Morris held his questions until Blyth's full glass was brought by a man as old as Tom Micklem and set down on the old wooden table, which rocked on its uneven legs. The very air in the small room seemed to have aged in the dark.

"To Carnoustie and to Ben Hogan," said Morris, raising his own glass. The young man seemed glad to drink to that, even smiling with his bad teeth.

They welcomed their ham sandwiches on thick rye bread, baked locally.

After the young man had finished his sandwich, Morris said, "I would like to speak with Peter before I go back to St. Andrews. Do you think he will see me?"

Blyth opened his mouth twice before saying "Aye," as if the lone word had to be coached aloud.

Morris, pleased and rather surprised, said, "Could I see him right away?"

The young man nodded, now looking around the darkened room as if for an exit. Morris was certain he had called his brother from the lone pay phone outside the golf shop.

"Is Peter afraid?" asked Morris.

" 'E's scairt plinty," Blyth said in a rough whisper, in what for him was a spoken essay.

Morris asked if Scotland Yard had called on Blyth, and he only nodded *yes* but did not speak, as if he feared being overheard.

Morris did not ask another question, not wanting to spook the young man or, through him, his half brother.

Tom Micklem would not hear of Morris's paying for the drinks and sandwiches. And when the three of them stood, the old man hugged Morris, careless of the curious eyes in the room. "An' tha's for the fair lass Julia Sullivan," he said. "God bless 'er."

Morris did not expect to ever see Captain Tom Micklem alive again, his beloved Carnoustie not scheduled to host the British Open for the rest of the century. There were tears in both men's eyes, to the obvious surprise of young Blyth.

The dim sunlight seemed bold as fate when they stepped out of the dark clubhouse. "Will you ride with me?" asked Morris of Blyth, doubting the young man could afford his own automobile.

Blyth nodded, following him to the silver BMW, which shone in the noonday light. Blyth was pleased to sink into the leather seat and run his hand over the slick, futuristic dashboard.

"It belongs to Tom Rowe, who writes about golf for the *Times*," Morris said.

Blyth nodded and seemed to think such an automobile was appropriate for a golf writer, far above his own station on the ancient mowing machine.

Morris cranked the BMW and looked to Blyth for direction.

"Towarrd Dundee," said Blyth, sitting back as if to be chauffeured there.

Morris, of course, knew Dundee was only ten miles from Carnoustie. And that Caldwell was likely hiding in the town. But not three miles out of Carnoustie, Blyth tapped his arm and pointed toward a small, unpaved road leading off to the north. "Turn here," Blyth said.

Morris slowed and turned, then drove over a small rise, and there amongst several shrub trees sat a young man on his motorcycle, as if waiting for one unsaid word to send him speeding off.

Morris got out of the BMW, moving slowly and carefully so as not to spook him. He stopped a good six feet from the rider he took to be Peter Caldwell, who wore a brown leather jacket and short boots but no helmet. His brown hair moved in the stiff breeze, even with the motorcycle silent on its wheels. His blue eyes, which danced with distrust, resembled his half brother's, but his upper body was thicker, more muscular.

Morris addressed the young man as "Peter" and identified himself. Caldwell did not acknowledge his own name and offered no hint of recognition of Morris, though he must have seen him around St. Andrews before the thousands of spectators landed in the small town.

"You know Scotland Yard is looking for you," said Morris, and, not waiting even for a nod, added, "and they will find you, Peter. Don't doubt that."

Caldwell's blue eyes offered only a certain coldness.

"They want to question you about Old Alec," Morris said. "They want to know when you last saw him."

Caldwell blinked in spite of himself at the name *Old Alec.*

"When *did* you see him last?" asked Morris. He did not ask Caldwell if he rode his motorcycle a hundred-miles-an-hour out Pilmour Links Road the night of the murder. That was the inspector's question.

Caldwell turned the handle of his motorcycle, as if he were about to fire it into life. "I niver kilt 'im," he said, his voice sounding oddly younger than he looked, and he couldn't have been older than twenty-one.

"Do you know who did?" asked Morris directly.

Caldwell spit, maybe to fill the silence. Then he shook his head, but not convincingly.

"Why are you hiding from the police?" asked Morris.

Caldwell looked at him as if he'd asked a stupid question.

"Are you running from someone else?" asked Morris.

"I'm na' afraid o' naething," said Caldwell, but he sat poised on his seat as if already in full flight.

"Inspector James Emerson is a man you can talk to," Morris said. "I've known him many years. He loves golf. Never misses a British Open . . . until this one."

Morris waited out the silence as Caldwell chose not to reply. "I know you've been suspended from caddying at the Old Course . . . for cheating," said Morris, risking the young man's anger. "Do you fear some member there . . . who killed Old Alec, and maybe Barry Vinson too?"

Again Peter Caldwell looked at him with surprise, as if he should know better. *Know what?* thought Morris. "Why did you agree to see me?" Morris asked, frankly. "What did you want to find out? I'll tell you if I can."

" 'Ave they caught the mon 'oo killed Old Alec?" asked Caldwell.

"No," Morris said. "Do you think the police want you as a witness? Is that what you fear?"

"I havena' seen yer killer," said Caldwell, but he spit again rather than look at Morris.

"Did you ever meet Barry Vinson?" Morris asked.

The boy only shook his head, more in exasperation than denial. Morris was not sure if he meant he'd never known him or never killed him.

"What can I tell Inspector Emerson for you?" asked Morris.

"Naethin'," said Caldwell, spitting again, but looking more frightened, to Morris, than hostile.

"Scotland is small enough," Morris said. "You can't hide forever. Or are you waiting until they *catch* the killer?"

Caldwell did not spit or nod or shake his head. Morris took his silence to mean he'd guessed his intention exactly.

"The inspector can offer you all the protection you need," Morris said.

Now Caldwell spit again and did fire up his motorcycle, which roared into life as if in denial of Morris's promise, though the boy nodded his head once, meaning Morris knew not what. Caldwell eased the motorcycle forward just slowly enough for his half brother to jump up behind him and was off down the narrow dirt road in a dusty fury. Morris climbed in the BMW, pulling his stiff leg after him, and wheeled the car around and reached the paved road in time to see the two of them in the distance, the motorcycle hurtling toward Dundee on the narrow, dead-straight road. Morris guessed they were vanishing at a hundred miles an hour.

• CHAPTER NINE •

Morris patted the BMW as if it were an obedient animal, and dropped off the keys with the hotel clerk. Tom Rowe had left word that he was lunching at the Royal and Ancient clubhouse.

Morris walked through the quiet streets of St. Andrews, congenially abandoned by the tournament's masses. Still, he met the occasional, anonymous foursome, carrying their clubs over their shoulders, come from six thousand miles to try their luck on the Old Course, the same as Nicklaus.

Inspector Emerson, his eyes raw from exhaustion, was eating a late sandwich at his temporary desk.

Morris told him first of his trip to Carnoustie, delaying any reference to the half brothers. He described standing on the No. 6 hole and remembering Hogan's two great tee shots of 1953, which the inspector as a very young man had also seen struck. Morris steeled himself for Emerson's wrath at not being told *in advance* of his true intentions in driving to Carnoustie. He cut to the end of his narrative and described Peter Caldwell on his motorcycle and the enigmatic nod he had made when Morris guaranteed him the inspector's protection if he would meet him in St. Andrews.

"*Guaranteed* him, did you?" Emerson slapped his open palm on his desk.

Morris nodded.

"I'll *guarantee* him a cell for his natural life if he had *anything* to do with killing those two men." The inspector's curiosity got the best of his anger. "Do you think he will come?"

"I don't know. Maybe."

Emerson's anger gave way to self-contempt. "*You* found him by yourself in a few hours, and I've had *four men* all over Dundee and *one man* in Carnoustie, since we discovered Caldwell had a half brother living there." Emerson shook his head in disgust. "I doubt if among them they could have found the Firth of Tay."

Morris did not envy those men's next conversation with the inspector, not realizing he was about to hear one end of that very dialogue.

"It was a fluke," Morris said. "I happen to be old friends with Captain Tom Micklem."

"The captain's still alive?" Emerson smiled in spite of himself.

"Oh, yes. And as old as Time and drinking his rum and beer. Just sitting in his old electric cart, he carried a lot of weight with the half brother, Niel Blyth, though he said very little." Morris described the sequence of events in Carnoustie that led him to Blyth and then to his half brother, Peter Caldwell.

Emerson nodded, anger lingering in his eyes.

Morris described Caldwell and handed over the license number of his black Harley-Davidson motorcycle.

"Well, goddamn, did you fingerprint him?" asked the inspector, who had to smile to keep from cursing his own men.

"I got the feeling the kid knows *something* that makes him truly afraid of *somebody.*" He repeated the one question that Caldwell had asked: *Had they caught the man who killed Old Alec?*

Morris also quoted the boy as saying that he "*havena' seen yer killer.*" Morris recalled that the boy spit rather than look at him when he said it, and that he was less than convincing. He also described Caldwell's shaking his head, more in exasperation than denial, when he asked him if he'd ever met Barry Vinson.

"The kid seemed to think it was a dumb question," Morris said. "I got the feeling he didn't understand my *combined* interest in Barry Vinson and Old Alec, as if the two of them hadn't been murdered in the same week in the same town during the same tournament by the very same garrote."

"You got the impression from Caldwell that the two of them were killed for different reasons . . . or by different people?" asked Inspector Emerson.

"I'm not sure. But he didn't seem defensive about the death of Vinson. And he only asked if you had caught *the man who killed Old Alec.* He didn't mention Vinson's killer."

"Odd. You last saw the two brothers disappearing up the road to Dundee at a high rate of speed?"

"Like they were shot out of a gun."

The inspector picked up the phone and dialed the number of a Dundee hotel. One of his men obviously answered the phone. The inspector did not edit his anger for Morris's ears. He wanted to know how the hell they planned to find Peter Caldwell "sitting in a goddamned hotel room." He gave them the information Morris had given him. "I want both brothers here, if you have to bring the goddamn populations of Dundee and Carnoustie with them," said the inspector, not listening to any excuses as he hung up the telephone.

Morris let him sizzle for a minute, then asked what information he had on the four policemen found murdered in London.

"All I know is what you can hear on the television, the four of them shot in the head wearing their own handcuffs. *Splendid police work,*" he said cruelly. "Of course, the only thing I've done better in Scotland is not be killed in my own automobile. But then, I can't get close enough to the killer to be shot by him. Why didn't you tell me you hoped to find Caldwell in Carnoustie?"

"I went over on a wild hunch," Morris said, "as much to see the old golf course and Captain Micklem as anything else." He was not lying about that, but he was careful not to involve the caddy at the Old Course who had tipped him off that Caldwell had a half brother in Carnoustie.

"Just *guessed* he had a half brother in Carnoustie," said Emerson, as if reading his thoughts in midair.

"No. I knew that much."

"And so did we, of course, days ago," admitted the inspector. He looked at his watch. "I'm interviewing the members again at the R&A, those who live here and those I've asked not to leave town. I'm starting over. As if I hadn't asked them a goddamned question. Listen, thanks for the tip on Caldwell. I'll let you know if he shows up. We'll find him if he doesn't. But keep us in mind if you get a second *hunch.*"

Morris nodded unconvincingly.

A late afternoon nap was the only possible antidote for a small city whose population did not, at the moment, include Julia Sullivan.

Something was smothering him. Morris tried to rise up in his dream but was trapped. And then he knew too well the mouth that was against his own.

Came her voice, reciting into the dark: "*Among many fanciful Parallels which Men of more Imagination than Experience have drawn between the natural and moral State of the World, it has been observed that Happiness as well as Virtue consists in Mediocrity; that it is necessary even to him who has no other Care than to pass through the present State with Ease and Safety to avoid every Extreme; and that the middle Path is the Road of Security, on either side of which, are the Pitfalls of Vice, and the Precipices of Ruin."*

Morris could not stop laughing, even with her squashing the breath out of him with her body.

"The Rambler. *Number 38. To be continued on Tuesdays and Saturdays."*

"The hell you say? Where did you get that? I've got to see it." Morris tried to switch on the lamp, but she had unplugged it.

"Oh, no," said Sullivan, trapping his hand. "It's late. No time for reading tonight." She took him through every step and bite of their trip to London, from da Vinci, to Shakespeare, to Harrods, to their old solicitor friend at the Old Newspaper and Ephemera Shop, to Speaker's Corner. . . .

"You've got to be goddamn kidding me, you got up and *spoke . . . without me there*?" He said the last plaintively, as if she and the whole world had passed him by.

She quoted him her entire speech. "I just opened my mouth and couldn't believe what was coming out," she said, laughing at the spectacle of herself following the last of the outraged communists to the stand.

"Oh, I can believe most anything coming out of your mouth," said Morris, who couldn't find it in the dark.

"I didn't tell you about the huge breakfast at the Savoy Hotel," she said, dodging him.

"What is this, some new kind of torture?" said Morris, suddenly lying back, starving in the darkened bedroom.

"It's legal. I checked with the Geneva Convention," said Sullivan, herself hungry to taste him again. "I did bring you a snack." She reached behind her and handed him a sack of pastries to die for.

"So how did Sharon Kirkcaldy respond?" asked Morris, between swallows of pastry.

Sullivan was happy to describe the young girl trying on funny hats in Covent Garden and laughing at herself, and the young Paul Mason guiding her across each intersection as if she were of the Royal family and had never before been afoot in London. Sullivan described how her hair was a dark flame on the boy's shoulder on the flight home.

"Maybe she will have a terrible relapse one day over what happened to her and to her grandfather," Sullivan said, "and maybe it will even be best if she does. But she will have this good day to remember."

"I'm sorry I missed it," Morris said seriously.

"Oh, you were there," Sullivan said. "I could remember you at every spot we stopped. Especially when *I* picked up the check."

"You are altogether shameless, Sullivan," said Morris, catching her hand.

"At least," said Sullivan, slipping under the light sheet, careless of the moist crumbs on her bare stomach.

When he had his breath, Morris told her of his trip to Carnoustie. And his visit with the inspector.

"What did you think of this Peter Caldwell?" she asked, propping up on one elbow.

"He looked dangerous enough on his motorcycle, burning the road to Dundee at about a hundred miles an hour."

"Did he come by to see the inspector?"

"I don't know. Emerson hasn't called. But then, maybe he called *earlier* and I was *too occupied* to hear the phone ring." He added the last with fraudulent wickedness.

"*Too occupied to hear the phone,*" said Sullivan, digging her fingers into his flesh, "*in your fantasy.* When I climbed into this bed you were out like a light, John Morris. The girls from the Folies-Bergère could have danced through the room, and you'd have still been snoring."

"Oh, yes?"

"Oh, yes. *Oh, yes!*" Sullivan said, unable to stop giggling.

It was still dark in the room when the phone did ring.

"Oh, shit," said Morris, falling out of sleep, fumbling for the receiver. He knew that nothing good had ever been said over the telephone in the last hour before daylight.

Morris guided the small Ford out of St. Andrews, toward Newport-on-Tay, across the bridge from Dundee.

"Was it an accident?" asked Sullivan, leaning back in her seat, refusing to open her eyes as the sun came obscenely up.

"I don't know," Morris said. "I don't know if the inspector knows. It wouldn't take much to destroy a motorcycle going at the speed of sound."

There was little traffic on the narrow road this early in the morning.

"I don't see how the Scots live in all this daylight," groaned Sullivan, her eyes still closed but the sun leaking through her lids.

Morris could see the police barrier set out up ahead, where the road made a serious bend toward them and St. Andrews. Any traffic was being slowed and moved to the far side of the road from the clutch of police cars and the ambulance, all flashing their yellow warnings like grotesque lightning bugs. Morris eased the Ford well off the road.

Inspector Emerson waved them through the police barrier.

"Not a sight I would ask a man to," Emerson said, for the world like Dr. Johnson himself. "But the boy was carrying no identification. Just the license number of his motorcycle. I need to know if this *is* Peter Caldwell . . . or maybe his half brother. We've only found the one body." He waved toward the single tire track that tore down the high grass and passed through a five-foot-high metal fence twenty yards off the road.

"You sure you want to see this?" said Morris, touching Sullivan's arm.

Her eyes were now wide open. "I've come this far. I'm game," said Sullivan, who had seen two awful private plane crashes at the Denver airport.

Emerson told them to walk directly behind him, well away from the path of the motorcycle, which cut through the high, wet grass like the frozen wake of a motorboat.

The motorcycle was twisted into a metal pretzel, with both wheels missing. One boot was tangled in the steel and from the blood on the leather, Morris was sure the foot was still in it. He was surprised when the inspector walked past the motorcycle and then the torso, sprawled in the grass as lifeless as a straw man in a brown leather jacket. Finally, the inspector stopped several steps from an object in the grass.

"Jesus Christ!" Morris said.

"Yes," the inspector said.

The face on the head was remarkably intact and the one eye Morris could see was open.

"That's Peter Caldwell," said Morris, his voice as thin as air.

"*. . . A pale horse: and his name that sat on him was Death,*" quoted Sullivan, as amazed as she was shocked at the round horror of the boy's head.

The inspector led them back to the narrow road. Early morning traffic was stacking up a bit, as drivers leaned out of their vehicles, hungering for the aspect of a bloody crash but puzzled at the absence of a wrecked automobile.

"What happened to him?" Morris asked.

"Good question," Inspector Emerson said. "Obviously his motorcycle left the road at a tremendous rate of speed. But it was still upright until he hit the metal fence. There aren't a thousand yards of metal fence in Scotland, and he hits one straight-on at God knows what speed. It took his head off as cleanly as a guillotine."

"What time do you think it happened?" Morris asked.

"Had to be late last night. Dr. Calvin Stewart hasn't gotten here yet. We had some trouble rounding him up. But we know the kid hasn't been dead that long. An old man, homeless, hiking along the road, found him. The old man didn't have a watch. But near as we can figure, it was about four A.M. The old man said the engine on the motorcycle was still warm to his touch. The sight of the body made him ill, or more ill than he already was. Luckily he didn't stumble on the head. He flagged down a truck that nearly ran him over. We've taken him to the hospital."

"Was it an accident?" Morris asked skeptically.

"Come look at the one skid mark," the inspector said. He led them up the pavement about twenty-five yards. And stopped short of a square area of the road that had been sealed off from traffic.

There was not much to see. Just the one short skid mark, not more than three feet long, obviously made by one small tire, the rubber angling toward the shoulder of the road like the path of an ill-hit golf ball starting its fade toward a lateral hazard. *Some hazard, the metal fence,* Morris thought. *How did Caesar say he wanted to die? 'Suddenly.'*

"No doubt it's a tire of a motorcycle," the inspector said. "If you get down on your hands and knees you can see a small abrasion on what's left of the rear fender of the motorcycle . . . *as if it were struck from behind.*''

''Godamighty, can you imagine the speeds they were going,'' Morris said, ''and the boy's terror at being bumped?''

''He didn't panic; you have to credit him for that. He kept it upright through the grass until he hit the fence,'' the inspector said.

''*The rest is silence,*'' quoted Sullivan. *Maybe it's standing on an island of dead poets that's dragging up all these quotations,* she thought, *anything not to think about the boy's head lying in the grass.*

''It was no slow automobile that hit him, if indeed one hit him,'' Morris said. ''Nothing could have overtaken him that wasn't fast and gunning for him. The driver picked the perfect turn in the road to nudge him.''

''It's still possible it was an accident,'' the inspector said. ''He could have been racing with some drunken buddy, who didn't see the curve coming up in the road and didn't slow down and hit him before he knew it.''

''Do you believe that's what happened?'' Morris asked.

''No.''

''Somebody knew Caldwell was hiding in Dundee. Somebody knew, or feared, he was coming to see you in St. Andrews. That *somebody* waited for him in Dundee and followed him across the bridge over the Firth of Tay and ran him down in the dark.'' Morris listened to himself thinking aloud.

''The boy must have feared somebody, as well as the police,'' Sullivan said, ''or why would he be riding to St. Andrews at four o'clock in the morning?''

''He was plenty afraid,'' Morris said. ''What would the contact have done to the bumper of the car that hit him?''

''Hard to say. Not that much contact was made. And it

wouldn't take much at that speed,'' the inspector said. ''It might not even have dented the automobile's bumper. There would likely be traces of black paint, but they could be removed.''

''The height and angle of the contact would tell you something about the car that hit the fender of the motorcycle,'' Morris said.

''Oh, yes. You would have to estimate the speeds they were traveling and what that might do to the height of certain automobiles that lower themselves the faster they go. It should tell us a good deal. We are alerting every body shop within a hundred miles. It wouldn't be a good time to have your front bumper straightened in Scotland. Though I don't think the damage will be apparent to the naked eye. We will check the automobiles of our friends in the Royal and Ancient Golf Club and those of all the men who were hanging out in the Bull and Bear the night Old Alec was killed. That will put the wind up the natives and visitors alike.''

''What do you think Peter Caldwell knew that got him killed?'' Sullivan asked.

Both men tilted their heads as they considered it.

''I believe he knew *why* Old Alec was killed,'' Morris said. ''He may have known, or suspected, *who* killed him. He may have even *been there or done it himself.*''

Inspector Emerson nodded tentatively, not in agreement but not in disagreement. ''We've taken Caldwell's one-room apartment in St. Andrews into tiny pieces, and we don't know anything except he was a sloppy boarder. We have two men in Carnoustie waiting for his half brother to come home. He lives, as you may know, with his old mother, God rest her. Maybe his half brother, or even his mother, can tell us something.''

Morris remembered the dull eyes of Niel Blyth, pale candles to the electric eyes of Peter Caldwell. He didn't imagine that Caldwell had told his half brother very much. He hoped he was dead wrong.

The ghastly sight in the grass would stay with Morris and Sullivan the rest of their lives. But it did not stymie their appetites for breakfast.

"One more scone, Sullivan, and you will sink and drown in the tub," Morris said.

"I would have to drown in installments in our tub. I'm not sure there's room to sink both of my feet at the same time."

"You have a point there." Morris nudged her long, slim shoe with his own wide one.

"The Little Old Lady Who Lived in a Shoe could have let apartments in that shoe of yours," Sullivan said, biting carefully into a fifth scone.

"I keep trying not to remember the boy's boot and what was still inside it," said Morris, wincing.

Sullivan swallowed her fifth scone and winced as well.

"I guess the thing I really try not to think about is my trip to Carnoustie. Did I spook somebody else when I spooked the kid? If I'd stayed in my room would he still be alive?"

Sullivan tapped him seriously on the back of his wide hand. "He was already afraid, Morris. He was already in hiding. The police would have smoked him out sooner or later. But I'm betting whoever killed him would have found him first."

"I'm trying to tell myself that," Morris said.

Sullivan pushed her chair back gently, as if she'd eaten the daintiest of meals. "Let's go look through Old Alec's house and barn," she said. "Maybe the police were looking for all the wrong things. What could be there to kill a man for?"

"Good question. I wanted to go by yesterday. But I

waited for you.'' He left unsaid, *and went to Carnoustie instead.*

''You've never gotten the hang of gloomy guilt, Morris. And it's too late to take up the habit now,'' said Sullivan, guessing his thoughts.

Morris had to smile at himself. But if he closed his eyes, he knew he'd see a path through wet weeds that looked like the frozen wake of a motorboat.

A young policeman was waiting at the door to Old Alec's stone house to let them in.

''I don't blame Old Alec for keeping it so dark in here,'' said Sullivan, squinting at the dim light in the low living room. ''There's fifteen hours of daylight outside, enough to drive a man blind.''

Only the body and the smooth-handled garrote had been taken away. Nothing else had been touched. The one straight-backed chair was still overturned and an outline of a body was drawn on the stone floor where Old Alec's had lain. One naked bulb hung down to illuminate the dark scene.

''Why? Why move him in here?'' Morris asked aloud, as if his own subconscious might answer.

''Because the killer didn't want the police to look too hard at something in the barn,'' Sullivan said.

''Possibly.'' He saluted Sullivan with a raised trigger finger.

Morris had borrowed a flashlight from their hotel and was shining it around the room, stopping at each of the few separate objects. A parson's bench, a couple of chairs, and, unexpectedly, floor-to-ceiling bookshelves sagging with many old volumes, which were covered with dust.

''Who would have thought of Old Alec as a reader?'' said Sullivan, lifting a large book that carried the title *A History of Golf in Britain.* She handed it to Morris, who turned to the copyright page. He knew the book and, in fact, had a copy in his own library. This one was a first edition, published by Cassell and Company in 1952. It was signed by *each* of the six authors: Bernard Darwin, Henry Cotton, Henry Longhurst, Leonard Crawley, Enid Wilson, and Lord Barbazon of Tara. Morris recognized Darwin's shaky handwriting: *To Old Alec, and to the memory of his father and his grandfather.*

Sullivan, looking over his shoulder, said, "Could Bernard Darwin have known Old Alec's *grandfather*?"

"Oh, yes," Morris said. "Darwin's chapter in this book begins in 1884."

It was obvious the book had been read and read again, but its pages had been well protected, despite the dust on the leather binding.

Morris lifted up a slim volume that proved to be *A History of Golf* by Robert Browning, another first edition, and another book he himself owned. This copy was also signed by the author, whom Morris had met in his old age. Browning had edited *Golfing* magazine from 1910 to 1955. And he had signed the copy to *Old Alec and the MacLaines' grand tradition of golf.*

Murder receded into time as Morris turned to a favorite paragraph of the introduction and read it to Sullivan:

> "It is impossible for me to acknowledge the sources of all the items of useful information which have come to me—often in the most unexpected way. For instance, when the British forces in France were gradually assembling for the final advance in the late summer of 1918, the Commanding Officer of one of the battalions of the famous Fifty-first Scottish Division on its way up to the line turned his horse aside to make some casual inquiry from a young subaltern in temporary command of a battery in position near the road. The familiar query regard-

ing my occupation in civil life led to the discovery of a mutual interest in golf, and I learned that I was talking to the son of that Captain J. C. Stewart of Fasnacloich who in partnership with George Glennie won the first championship ever played. I think Colonel Stewart was rather pleased to find that I was familiar with that stage of golf history. But here was a direct link with the start of championship golf in 1857—and who would have thought to find it in the battlefront of the Somme?"

Morris said, "How many hundreds of thousands were about to crawl to their deaths . . . and a colonel and a subaltern have a moment to spend for the love of the game of golf."

"I don't think the killer of Old Alec would want to run into the ghost of Robert Browning," said Sullivan, who also remembered the old gentleman and his contemporary, Bernard Darwin. It was as if she and Morris were linked to the golden age of golf by having known these men from the nineteenth century.

The third volume Morris picked up was Robert Clark's *Golf: A Royal and Ancient Game,* published in 1875. It was carefully signed to *My good friend, Alec MacLaine.* Morris said, "The book had to belong to Old Alec's grandfather. I know he caddied here before our own Civil War."

All of the books on the sagging shelves were of golf, and all of them *first editions,* and all of them signed, including Bobby Jones's own *Golf Is My Game.* They made a wonderfully rare and valuable collection of books, fit for the British Museum.

Morris opened each book until, high on the top shelf, he came upon an old, cracked leather binding that was not a book at all, but what he quickly understood to be a sort of journal. Entered on separate lines—going back to

1855—were identifications of objects: golf clubs, an ever-growing list of them up into the twentieth century; club-making equipment from the early nineteenth century; early golf bags; caps, jackets, shoes, club neck ties, trophies; vintage balls seemingly of every variety, including wooden balls dating back as far as the seventeeth century; ball-making equipment; and lists of artwork, sketches, portraits, the names of some of the artists known to the great museums of the world.

Each entry was dated and included a name of who had owned it, or made it, or used it, or found it, or won it, or worn it, or sketched it, or painted it. In many places a sentence or two described in greater detail the club or ball or portrait and how it came into the possession of the three diarists, each of whom shared the name Alec MacLaine, and each of whose handwriting was quite distinctive. The entry at the top of the last page was: *Wedge, A. Palmer, American, a' St. Andrews, '70 . . . 'E said, for olde times.* The number *651* was written by that entry, and the numbers ran backward to the first entry: *Play-club, twin o' Cosser's. Gie o' Admiral Bethune, '55.*

Sullivan looked up from an old Scottish book she was reading. "Why are you so quiet all of a sudden?"

Morris, stunned, showed her the journal and explained how the entries were made and the simple numbering system identifying each entry.

"I recently saw Admiral Bethune's name," said Morris, pointing to the spidery first entry in the journal, which had survived on good rag paper.

"Of course you did," Sullivan said skeptically. "I think he piped us on board his battleship."

"I'm serious. The museum in the South Room of the Royal and Ancient clubhouse . . . that's where I saw his name. The room is practically dedicated to him. The old Admiral Bethune was the force behind the R&A

starting a golf museum in the middle 1860s. But that was *ten years after this first entry* in the MacLaines' journal. I wonder if the admiral got his inspiration for collecting the early artifacts of golf from our caddy here, the first Alec MacLaine?''

"But what does it mean: *Play-club, twin o' Cosser's*?''

"I did a magazine piece once from here in St. Andrews for *Sports Illustrated* . . . on the historic artifacts of golf. I believe that the oldest existing club in Great Britain is the Play-club in the R&A museum, made by Samuel Cosser in the middle of the eighteenth century. If Old Alec had a *twin* to that club out in the barn, it would be worth a bloody fortune.''

"Do you think Old Alec left over six hundred golf collectibles in his barn?''

"Yes.''

"They would be invaluable!''

"Yes.''

"Invaluable enough to kill for.''

"Yes.''

"John Morris, you have never been so positive that many times in a row since I first taught you what golf was all about.''

"No.'' He closed the journal in his large hands. "Do you imagine someone has backed a truck up here in the night and hauled this *invaluable* stuff away?''

"Not likely, not with a police seal on every door,'' said Sullivan.

"And it would be impossible to authenticate it without admitting you had killed Old Alec MacLaine. Let's see for ourselves what's in the barn.''

They walked out the back door of the old croft house. The young officer had already unlocked the barn door and was standing outside enjoying the rare sunshine.

Morris switched on his flashlight and coughed just at

the sight of the dust settled over every shape and form in the long, high room. The police had cordoned off a rectangle in the center of the barn where Old Alec had been garroted before being dragged into the front room of the house.

There was the making of a great spiral of dust and smeared blood on the stone floor where Morris was sure at least *three men* had struggled. All footprints had been clumsily swept away, as a man might rake a sand bunker while leaving it.

"Let's stop standing here," Sullivan said. "Let's see the collection for ourselves."

There was no electric light in the old stone barn, which had no windows and was as dark as a coal mine. Morris shined his flashlight over the wooden boxes scattered over the floor and the chaos of objects leaning against the walls, all of them covered in a ghostly film of cobwebs and dust. They found two oil lanterns in good repair and matches to light them.

Morris passed the journal and one of the lanterns to Sullivan, who held it up like Diogenes looking for the last honest man.

Morris held up his own lantern and said in pale jest: "Alms for the poor."

"But we are looking for the *riches* of the North," Sullivan said.

"God knows where a man would have lain down a golf club in 1855."

"I know one thing, it hasn't been dusted since," said Sullivan, unable to cover her mouth before a gigantic sneeze came.

Morris poled his way among the huge old wooden boxes, whose lids had been raised in this century only by police looking for they-had-no-idea-what since Old Alec was killed. *And maybe by the killer,* he thought.

Morris didn't stop until he reached the farthest wall in

the barn. It might have been a movie set from the 1930s for the filming of *The Mummy's Hand.*

"What the hell," said Morris, lifting up an object leaning against the center of the wall. It was white with cobwebs and dust, but it was definitely a golf club, a wooden golf club, both handle and head. "I need a rag," Morris said.

"I've got a couple of handkerchiefs." Sullivan held the journal between her knees and pulled the handkerchiefs out of her shoulder bag.

Morris dusted only the bottom of the shaft and the head of the club, raising a cloud of dust that set Sullivan again to sneezing. Fixed around the neck of the wooden club, which was obviously a putter and as beautiful as a piece of sculpture, was a leather strap, all but rotted through. Faintly inked, or dyed, into the leather was a number: *7,* made in the old way, with a slash, making it resemble a reverse F.

"Wait, wait, wait," said Sullivan, setting her lantern on an old chair and turning to the first page of the journal. Morris watched as she pointed to entry No. 7: *Putter, McEwan, gie H. Philp, '55.*

"Oh, shit!" Morris said. "Hugh Philp was the R&A's official club maker from the early decades of the nineteenth century until just before our Civil War. He must have given the first Alec MacLaine this putter not long before he died. Great God, it's worth a seat on the New York Stock Exchange."

Sullivan made as if tucking it under her arm. "Take me to Wall Street."

Morris counted six objects along the wall to his left. The club he lifted was definitely too long to be a putter. It was all of a piece, from wooden handle to wooden head, with the number *1* inked or dyed into the leather thong around its neck.

Morris couldn't even whistle. He tested the perfect

balance of Samuel Cosser's eighteenth-century Play-club, careful not to stress its long dried-out and brittle wooden shaft. In his hands rested one of the two oldest golf clubs known to time.

"Japanese collectors would give half the Rising Sun for this club," Morris said.

Sullivan slid her fingers over the smooth head of it, and was again reminded of a fine sculpture.

"We might as well be standing in King Tut's tomb," Morris said, holding the lantern high over his head.

They were giggling like children as they found a box of priceless *elm* golf balls in shockingly perfect condition, brought over by the Dutch in maybe the *sixteenth century* and lost and found for generations by players and caddies along the links of St. Andrews. The cool balls felt like wooden diamonds in Morris's big hand.

They found dozens of rare feathery balls—stuffed with goose feathers—and a complete set of equipment to make them, given to the first MacLaine by *Old Tom Morris* himself. Golf had gone to the gutta-percha ball in the 1850s and gradually wiped out the cottage industry of the handmade feathery. There was an entire box of the first rubber-core balls, introduced to the game in 1901 to replace the gutta-percha ball. Not one of the rubber-core balls had ever been struck.

Morris loved the feel of a Willie Achterlonie–made wooden niblick, Achterloinie having been the club-making disciple of Hugh Philp.

Moving along the wall, they found a small wooden box that held three wool caps from the Triumvirate: J. H. Taylor, James Braid, and Harry Vardon, who ruled British golf from 1894 to 1914. And there was a wooden-shafted club from each man that had been given to the second Alec MacLaine in the year 1899.

There were additional artifacts from the modern greats of the game: a sand iron from Walter Hagen as concave as a shallow bucket; Bobby Jones had given Old Alec's father a set of three neckties he wore in winning the British Open and the British Amateur during the year of his Grand Slam, 1930.

Old Alec had carried on the family tradition of collecting during the years of Henry Cotton and Peter Thomason and Palmer and Nicklaus and Player and Miller and Trevino and Watson. All of them had given clubs or balls or shoes or old bags or signed programs or hats or gloves to the amazing collection.

Morris and Sullivan were too exhausted to stand, and the dust was too thick over everything to offer a seat.

They got their breaths and opened several of the long wooden boxes until they came to one with two layers of sheetlike material covering the contents. Under the covering were sketches and portraits and landscapes by Sir Francis Grant and by John Rhind; there was a portrait of Old Tom Morris by Sir George Reid that John Morris had never seen the likes of; and a finished portrait of the first true golf professional, Allan Robertson, by an artist Morris did not recognize; and there was a painting of the Old Stone Bridge over Swilcan Burn done in the eighteenth century; and more than one cityscape of St. Andrews and renderings of the Royal and Ancient clubhouse by painters whose signatures were too faint to read in the dim light. There were many rough sketches of the R&A members and club makers and leading players of the nineteenth century.

"Let's get out of here," Morris said. "I don't trust my greedy self. I'll be hiding sketches down my trousers."

"You could take them all," said Sullivan, laughing, avoiding the tip of his cane.

They blew out their lanterns and blinked at the sunshine shattering over the world. The young policeman locked the door behind them.

Morris led the way back into the main room of Old Alec's house and was about to put the MacLaines' journal back on the top bookshelf, when it occurred to him to check the very last entry, though he didn't expect anything more startling than they had already discovered. He was dead wrong.

The young officer was glad to reopen the barn door. And it took Morris and Sullivan only a few minutes to find the last artifact saved by the MacLaine clan.

• CHAPTER TEN •

Morris opened the MacLaines' journal on the desk of Inspector Emerson. He kept his voice exactly level, offering no hint of accusation as to the failure of the police search of Old Alec's house and barn. He explained that the journal was a family record of now-priceless golf artifacts collected since 1855. He turned to the last entry, dated July 14, which spoke for itself: *Putter. B. Vinson, Yank, '78, w. Open a' Royal Birkdale, '76. Deid, July 13, '78. 'Welcome to your gory bed.'*

"I'm sure that last line is from Robbie Burns," Morris said to fill the silence. "I don't know from which poem."

Emerson opened his mouth but still could not speak. It was as if his voice box had failed in his throat.

Morris explained that simple curiosity and love of golfing lore, and not an inspired intuition, provoked him and Sullivan to turn through Old Alec's signed first editions, until he came on the family journal resting in the dust among the other old volumes on the top row of the bookshelf.

Morris leaned against the inspector's desk and flipped through the pages of the journal, pointing to many of its more than six hundred entries since 1855. He described how he and Sullivan took it into the old barn and traced the artifacts back to the first entry: a twin of the oldest known surviving golf club, *made by Samuel Cosser in the 18th century.* Morris stopped talking when he sensed that the inspector had recovered his composure.

"You two were right all along," Emerson said. "Old Alec did kill Barry Vinson." His face was as empty of animation as his voice, like a man found guilty of apathy at the Last Judgment.

"We were right only because we learned Old Alec's granddaughter had been raped," Morris said. "And you were also right: we had no intention of ever accusing Old Alec of murder, and if we'd told you what we'd learned, the old man would still be alive."

"Yes," Sullivan said defiantly, "to never step on the grass at the Old Course again. I think he'd choose to be where he is over dying in a jail cell. Count me out of the group apology."

"Good ol' Sullivan, always more honest than I am," Morris said.

"You both embarrass me with your insight and your understanding," said Emerson, no hint of the old anger in his flat voice.

"Then tell me why Old Alec's murder baffles us just as much as it does you," Morris said, "and why he was killed with the same goddamn garrote that killed Vinson. It makes not one drop of sense."

"Oh, yes, it does," said Sullivan, tapping the MacLaines' journal. "You couldn't buy these artifacts and signed first editions and signed sketches and portraits and landscape paintings *for several hundred thousand dollars.* You couldn't buy them for *any price,* for Old Alec's barn *is the only place in the world where they exist.* Lady MacBeth herself would come down from her castle to kill for such a treasure."

"Agreed," Morris said. "But nobody has come down to claim the treasure, least of all the killer."

"Old Alec hasn't been buried yet," Sullivan said. "And his estate is months from being settled."

"True." Morris turned to the inspector. "Do any of our *friendly suspects* admit to being on the road to Dundee in the late hours when Peter Caldwell was killed?"

Emerson shook his head. "Tait, Dougall, Maxwell, McCormack, Lightfoot, the kid Paul Mason, even our friend Tom Rowe, insist they were in their beds fast asleep. And I can't prove differently. We are working our way through the entire local R&A membership. But if any one of them admits to being on the high road to Dundee when Caldwell was killed, I'll hand in my inspector's credentials." He paused. "Well, they may take them from me soon enough."

Morris ignored his self-pity. "Have they caught the cop killers in London?"

The inspector shook his head.

"I imagine Scotland Yard has heat enough in its own kitchen not to set fire to you in St. Andrews," said Morris. "There's no doubt Caldwell's motorcycle was struck?"

"No doubt. Our forensic team has made a case for deliberate murder. It would only take a light nudge to send the motorcycle out of control. And there is not one hint of an automobile skid mark. The driver of the car never attempted to miss him."

"What kind of car?" Morris asked.

"A bit of uncertainty there," the inspector said. "But the front bumper was traveling very low to the ground. Certain large automobiles sink quite low at such high speeds. . . ."

"Including the Citroën," Morris said. "It's famous for it. Or infamous, as the case may be. Have you located many of them in Scotland?"

"More than you would imagine. But if it had plates from London, or anywhere outside Scotland, we'd have no way of tracing it here. Our people are stopping or inspecting every Citroën they see or know of. No luck so far. The automobile we are looking for suffered no serious damage to its front bumper, nothing you could notice without a close examination.''

''Only Sir Arthur of our *friendly suspects* drives a Citroën, I take it?''

''Yes. So far as we know,'' the inspector said. ''It will take time to visit every house of every R&A member, but we are working on it. We've checked all the public garages and parking lots in St. Andrews. Tell me, Morris, who knew the depth and value of the MacLaine collection?''

Not waiting for an answer, he continued, ''I'm embarrassed again to say I walked through the old barn with a flashlight, breathing dust and cobwebs, and all I saw were some valuable old balls and wooden-shafted clubs I figured to be worth maybe a hundred pounds apiece, and old sketches and portraits I barely glanced at in the dusty goddamn trunks and took to be cheap prints. It never occurred to me that golfers and club makers and even artists had made serious gifts over the last century to their favorite caddies, gifts that time has made priceless. Or the caddies were clever enough to salvage or buy many of the objects when they had little value. I am supposed to be an inspector and a lover of the game of golf, and I'm a pretty sorry specimen of both.''

Again Morris did not speak to his self-pity. ''Captain Tait knew something of Old Alec's collection. He mentioned it while showing me about the South Room museum in the R&A clubhouse. He said Old Alec wouldn't discuss selling his collection of artifacts 'from the old days at St. Andrews,' or even let anyone see it except a few caddy friends, who wouldn't discuss what they'd seen. Tait had been sure Old Alec would have a good collection of 'antique golf balls.' ''

Morris said, ''I expect the captain will be as astonished as any of us at the depth and value of the

MacLaine collection." Something else that had been said, somewhere, by somebody, hung on the edge of Morris's recollection, but he couldn't wrap his memory around it.

"Oh, yes, true to the journal, we found Barry Vinson's putter," Morris said. "Goddamn if Old Alec didn't steal it out of his hotel room, apparently when he went there to take any evidence of what had happened to his granddaughter. He knew Vinson was plenty *deid.* Because he'd just killed him. Why risk taking his putter? Well, it was historic enough, having been used to win the bloody Open. And maybe he wanted the world to eventually know what happened to Barry Vinson after he himself was dead. I do not think Old Alec counted on dying himself so soon."

Inspector Emerson stood, unable to keep sitting. "He killed the man. Took his putter. *And wrote it down.* And *I* couldn't connect him to the killing. I should do like you Yanks and pave over my office at Scotland Yard and make a shopping mall. Not to confuse the Yard with my own amateur bumbling."

Morris continued to ignore his self-flagellation. "The truth is, we still can't *prove* that Old Alec killed Vinson. He dated the entry in his journal *July fourteenth.* By that day the world knew Vinson was dead."

Morris rapped the journal with his knuckles. "We can't even *prove* he stole the man's putter. Vinson might have given it to him, for all we can document. Although that is a lunatic thought—a golfer leading the British Open *giving* his putter to a local caddy after the first round. And it is the same putter he was using. I know it, a mallet-headed putter by Ray Cook. It has Vinson's *name* engraved on the handle. But no one *saw* Old Alec take the putter. No one can even swear they saw him enter or leave the hotel the night Vinson was killed. And certainly no one has come forward to swear he saw Old Alec in the graveyard the night Vinson was killed."

Inspector Emerson sat back down, resting his chin on his fists. "You are exactly right. We can't prove a goddamn thing against Old Alec MacLaine."

"Maybe not, but you can convince the people at Scotland Yard of what happened to Vinson," Morris said.

"Lovely," the inspector said. "We just can't convince the people of Scotland and America of what happened to him. Or what we *believe* happened to him."

Sullivan asked, "Will you release the existence of the journal and the golf artifacts in Old Alec's barn, including Vinson's putter?"

"The fact of his journal, yes—maybe we can smoke out anyone who would kill for such a collection. But no mention of Vinson or his putter," Emerson said. "Let whoever killed Old Alec think we are convinced the same man killed Vinson."

The inspector passed a list of suspects to his acting secretary and quickly had one of them, Captain A.W.B. Tait, on the telephone. Tait was obviously agreeing to come to the police station.

"Please stay," the inspector said to Morris and Sullivan. "I want to ask the captain about Old Alec's golf collection in your presence. And get your reaction to his answers."

Within just a few minutes Captain Tait stepped through the door. His rugged, wind-blown face broke into a smile at seeing the three of them.

Inspector Emerson did not waste an informal sentence, asking: "What do you know about the golf artifacts in Old Alec MacLaine's barn?"

Tait, having just taken a seat, looked up in surprise at the question. He took a minute to answer, looking to Morris once as if for help.

"I luffed Ol' Alec's faathir. A gran' ol' man, as were

'is oon faathir afore 'im.'' Tait might have been stalling to gather an answer to the question he hadn't anticipated. He finally told the inspector how Old Alec's father once donated to the R&A a golf club that had been owned by J. O. Fairlie, a wonderful player in the mid-nineteenth century. In fact, in the summer of 1860, it was Fairlie who won the golfing medals at St. Andrews, Prestwick, and North Berwick, and it was Fairlie who suggested that a subscription be opened to offer a medal for what became the Open Championship on October 17, 1860.

Tait was warming to his subject and might have been giving a history lesson. The inspector let him ramble. Tait said that Old Alec's father, knowing that the R&A desired but did not own a club used by Fairlie, one day in the 1930s handed such a club to the captain of the R&A and said he would be pleased to have it added to the museum collection.

Tait said that he and other R&A members had long wanted to go inside Old Alec's barn and see what other golfing artifacts he and his father and his grandfather before him had collected. Tait said that Old Alec always put them off, saying, *''One day ye ma' ken ma poor gowf clubs an' ba's, but na' taeday.''*

Captain Tait, mindful of a proud man's privacy, had not pressed him as the years passed. He imagined that Old Alec had a grand collection of balls, with the three generations of caddies searching in the heather and the gorse these last one hundred years. Tait guessed he might have a number of valuable clubs, seeing as his father in the thirties had owned a rare club of J. O. Fairlie's.

Tait said the R&A membership had recently discussed asking Old Alec and other St. Andrews elders to consider donating any historic balls and clubs and golfing artifacts to the proposed British Golf Museum that was to be built behind the R&A clubhouse. They were even prepared to raise a bit of money to make the giving less painful.

Morris smiled at Sullivan—a smile that said, yes, the good R&A members might raise a *modest* amount of money to buy the MacLaine collection, say, enough to purchase her own Learjet. Sullivan smiled back that it wasn't for sale.

"Captain Tait, have you ever been inside Old Alec's house or barn, for any reason?" asked Inspector Emerson.

Tait ran his hand through his steel-gray hair, as if he could touch his own memory. "Aye. I've givin' 'im a lift 'ome, don't ye see. 'Ad a whisky innis hoose. But niver been innis barn. Na' in my liff. An' tha's the truth."

"Then you wouldn't know about these six hundred golf artifacts the MacLaines collected these last one hundred years and more," said the inspector, pushing across the family journal, opened at the first page.

Captain Tait pulled on his reading glasses and coughed, even choked on the first entry: a playclub made by Samuel Cosser in the eighteenth century, twin to the oldest known surviving club in golf, which he knew rested in the museum at the Royal and Ancient clubhouse. Tait's concentration was so focused on the journal, the three of them might have vanished out of their chairs.

Inspector Emerson never took his eyes off the turning of the pages and was careful to lay his hand on the book before the captain approached the last page and the entry by Old Alec of Barry Vinson's putter, with his gory quote from Robert Burns.

"Ma God!" Tait said. "Heers the British Golf Museum in tha' ol' barn of Ol' Alec MacLaine."

"And worth a significant fortune," said the inspector.

"Aye," Captain Tait admitted.

"And who would be wanting it, in addition to the R&A and the future British Golf Museum?"

Tait did not hesitate to answer. "Any gowf collector innis senses. Ba' it belongs to Scotland, lads. An' no one else."

"In fact, it belongs to the estate of Old Alec MacLaine," Emerson said. "To his two daughters and his granddaughter. He left a will, and in it . . . everything to the three of them."

This was news to Morris and Sullivan.

Tait filled his cheeks with air, as if ready to challenge the last will and testament.

"Old Alec suggested the lot of it be offered to the R&A, but *at fair market value,*" the inspector said. "How does that sit with you?"

Tait looked at his weathered hands in his lap. "Scotland'll na' turn its back onn its gowf 'istory."

There was no more to be learned from Captain Tait. After he left the room, the inspector asked, "What do you think?"

"I think the good captain had to know Old Alec had more than a few rare golf balls and the odd club in his family collection," Morris said. "He also knew better than to put the wind up—as you English say—a Scotsman as hardheaded as Old Alec. It sounds as if the R&A was about to bring pressure on him to *give* his artifacts to the new museum, or sell it to them at bargain prices."

"Not a tactic consistent with Old Alec's last will," the inspector said.

"He was crazy proud of his granddaughter, who is going to university," said Sullivan. "If he was willing to kill for her, I doubt he would have given away her family inheritance."

Emerson nodded his agreement. "I will see the others I have sent for, alone. But I will stop by your hotel for a drink and tell you what I've learned, if anything."

Morris and Sullivan agreed, as if they were paid consultants to the Queen's own inspector.

"You like Captain Tait as much as I do," Sullivan said, "but you don't believe him either." She touched her half-pint mug to his.

"No," Morris said. "He's lived his life in St. Andrews and admits having taken Old Alec home after many a round of golf and, no doubt, drinks. And their fathers had been equally close before them. *And Tait didn't realize Old Alec kept a priceless golf collection?* No, I don't believe that. I do think Tait was shocked at just how priceless the collection turned out to be. Or he and the R&A would have offered good money for it years ago."

"Do you think Tait might have killed him over it?" asked Sullivan.

Morris thought about that. "It's possible. But it's not an action that fits the man. I think the captain would have killed him with *money,* and with a sense of his family duty *to Scotland and to golf.*"

"I agree," Sullivan said. "But just the same, we'll ask Old Alec's daughters and his granddaughter if they ever saw Captain Tait in Old Alec's house or barn."

Morris grinned. "Grown suspicious, have you? Could you be the same woman who in her youth drank with wild, random golfers on two continents?"

"Only those who reminded me of the young Paul Newman."

"Come to think of it, who could blame you for lifting a glass with guys like me and Monty?" said Morris, signaling for another beer.

Inspector Emerson had his lager in his hand before he spoke. "To Scotland," he said, raising his glass.

"Oh, yes." Morris lifted his own.

The inspector had finished his round of questioning. He said he had been most startled by the licensed booking agent, George McCormack, who had stuck his unlit cigar in his huge, round face and smacked his large hand on the MacLaines' journal and said, "Eye'll offer the grandest whack in Scotland fur tha' lot o' it."

"But you haven't seen it," Emerson had said to him quietly.

"Na. But ah kenned Old Alec an' 'is ol' daddy and 'is word iss gold," Emerson quoted the punter.

Sullivan nearly spilled her drink laughing. "McCormack wouldn't buy Ireland without seeing it and weighing it."

"He'll pay the *grandest whack in Scotland* and he's *never seen inside Old Alec's barn?"* Morris echoed, and laughed incredulously. "The man admits he took Old Alec's cap to his house the night he was killed, but he swears he's never been inside his barn?"

"So he claims. The only thing he said that I believe is that he means to make an offer for the lot of it," the inspector said.

"Good," Sullivan said. "Sharon Kirkcaldy and her mother deserve top dollar. It took those three caddies—as men and boys—a hundred and twenty-three years carrying rich men's clubs all day for a pence to put together their collection. If the Royal and Ancient want Scotland's *gowf* history to remain in Scotland, let the bastards ante up."

"Hear, hear," said Morris, ordering another round of beers.

"One man admitted to having been inside the barn," Emerson said. "Sir Arthur Maxwell."

"And . . ."

"Somehow he'd heard that Old Alec's father had been given wool caps by each of the great British golfing Triumvirate: Taylor, Vardon, and Braid," the inspector said. "Maxwell doesn't remember how he learned of this. He said it was some twenty years ago. Anyway, Old Alec admitted he had caps that each of the men had worn when he won the Open. He was agreeable to Maxwell's offering reproductions of the three caps for sale in his sporting goods line. He took Maxwell into the barn and showed him the three caps, which were, indeed, signed by the three men. Maxwell said the place even then was a cobweb nightmare, and he only remembered seeing wooden boxes on the floor and old clubs leaning around the wall. The three caps were in one of the wooden boxes."

"Did they work out a deal?" asked Sullivan.

"No. Maxwell insisted on buying and owning the three original caps for promotional purposes. Old Alec refused to let them out of his possession, even insisting they be measured and a pattern for them made there in his own house. Maxwell wouldn't agree to it. He wanted the caps more for their promotional possibilities than as profit centers. *Or so he said.* The deal never came to pass."

"What did Maxwell think of the MacLaine family collection?" Morris asked.

"He seemed as amazed as the rest of us. He couldn't take his eyes off the journal. I thought he would pull the hairs out of his military mustache. I had to be careful that he didn't see the last entry. Maxwell made it clear he would like to do business with whoever winds up owning the caps and sweaters and jackets, and especially the ties . . . custom neckties being the thing these days."

"But he wouldn't kill to get his hands on the lot of it," Morris said.

"No, I think not," the inspector said. "Not to say he is incapable of killing a man. I don't know how Sir Arthur stays so fit at his age, running a company that has flirted for some years with bankruptcy.''

''How did the president of our USGA react to the MacLaines' journal?'' Morris asked.

''Warren Lightfoot was like a tall, thin child looking through a mail-order catalog,'' the inspector said. ''He did not deny that the Cosser playclub would be the crown jewel of your own country's golf collection. He didn't seem to think it would be a problem, raising the money to buy it.''

''I see a bidding war in the making,'' said Sullivan, clapping her hands with enthusiasm.

''No doubt,'' Emerson said. ''Lightfoot admitted knowing Old Alec's father, not long before he died. He seemed terribly nervous to admit that he had bought a tie that had been worn by Bobby Jones at St. Andrews . . . from the elder MacLaine, for five hundred pounds. Lightfoot said he donated it to the USGA collection. That was twenty-five years ago. He admitted his generosity impressed the USGA. I don't imagine it damaged his rise to power within the organization.''

''No,'' Morris said.

''How much did he know about Old Alec's artifacts?'' Sullivan asked.

''He claims not much,'' the inspector said. ''Lightfoot swears he never set foot in the barn. That the old man MacLaine sold him the tie in the front room of his house, after telling him at the Bull and Bear how he came to own it. It seems he caddied for Jones in a practice round and Jones not only tipped him handsomely but took off his necktie and gave it to him as a keepsake. The old man said he hated to sell it but needed the five hundred pounds. Turned out, he needed it for his own burial.''

''Is Warren anxious to go home?'' Morris asked.

''He was when we began our conversation,'' the inspector said. ''After he learned of the MacLaine collection, he admitted he was anxious to see it.''

''I bet,'' Morris said. He knew Lightfoot had wealth enough to spend a few hundred thousand dollars for Old Alec's artifacts and never miss the money.

''Gerald Dougall was just as curious about Old Alec's artifacts as the others,'' said Emerson. ''But he wasn't quite as greedy to see inside the barn. He looked at the journal carefully enough, but only at the first few pages.''

''Then he saw the oldest, most valuable items,'' Morris said. ''We have to give him greed points for that.''

''I also spoke with Tom Rowe,'' said the inspector. ''I gave him permission to quote from certain older items in the journal . . . being careful that he did not see the last page. He is making quite a story of the collection in the *Times*. I was careful to ring the local newspaper. They are angry enough with me without my giving a huge St. Andrews story exclusively to London.''

''Was Tom shocked at the items in the journal?'' Morris asked.

''Not so shocked as you might imagine,'' Emerson said. ''He denied ever having been in Old Alec's barn, but admitted he had been in his house a number of times, having done major profiles on him and his old father before him. I get the feeling Rowe knew the family had a singular collection of golfing artifacts.''

''What did he say when you asked him directly?'' Morris asked.

''He said he was 'not surprised that three generations of caddies on the Old Course had saved a substantial golf collection,' that he was 'only surprised at the quantity and the quality of it.' ''

''He *knew*,'' Morris said. ''I'll hot-box his ass.''

''Do that,'' the inspector said. ''But don't make him angry. I'm catching heat enough.''

"Have you met with Old Alec's daughters and granddaughter?" Morris asked.

"I'm doing that in the morning," the inspector said.

"Would you mind our visiting with them after that?"

"No. But call me first. I'll tell you what I learned, if anything. And after you see them, we'll share information. Let me say *thank you,* Morris . . . and Sullivan. If I survive this case, I'll owe my pension to the two of you."

"If we don't help get you fired first," Morris said.

Morris waited until just before noon to call the inspector. He hadn't been in his office a half hour.

"What did you find out?" Morris asked.

"Nothing," said Emerson. "The St. Andrews sister, Anne Kirkcaldy, is still one spoken word from tears. Mention Old Alec and there she goes. The Edinburgh sister, Mary Whyte, is altogether another matter. She's prepared to auction off the lot of it, barn and all. I got the feeling she is more than a little unhappy that her own two sons are not mentioned in Old Alec's will, while Sharon Kirkcaldy gets a full third."

"Had either sister seen any third person in the barn in recent months or years?" Morris asked.

"No. To tell you the truth, I doubt either of them had set foot in there in twenty years."

"How about Sharon?"

"She calls her grandfather 'Pa-Pa.' "

"I know," Morris said.

"All she would say was that Pa-Pa kept the barn private. I made her nervous, no question about it. I'm not sure why. I don't usually have that effect on the very young," Emerson said.

Morris knew exactly why the inspector made her nervous. With Barry Vinson dead, the last thing she would want to be known as was a rape victim.

"We'll drop by," Morris said. "I'll holler if we learn anything."

"No need to *holler,*" said the inspector, amused at the Southernism, "just get on the *blower.*"

Morris occupied the two sisters, Anne and Mary, while Sullivan eased Sharon Kirkcaldy to her own room. Sharon was still full of her trip to London and lifted her red skirt with pleats out of her closet and pulled it on to show off its perfect fit.

"And have you heard from young Georgia Tech?" Sullivan asked.

Sharon blushed as fiery as the roots of her bright red hair.

"Called, has he?" Sullivan said.

"Aye." Sharon did not suppress her smile.

"I like Paul Mason," Sullivan said. "But he'll have plenty of competition when you get to university."

"I dinna know aboot that," said Sharon, but she was obviously pleased to be told so.

"Tell me about Pa-Pa," Sullivan said.

"Aye." Sharon sat on her bed, spreading her new skirt around her like a small sea of tranquility.

"Did you understand the value of his collection of antique golf clubs and balls, and paintings of the Old Course?"

"Aye. Pa-Pa oftin reid ta me from 'is record o' gowf," Sharon said. "The grand players o' oldin yeers 'oose clubs and caps an' trophies 'e kept in the barn. An' thair portraits. 'E luffed 'em all, Pa-Pa did."

"And you knew they were valuable?" Sullivan said.

"Aye. 'E meant to sell it awtigither for ma' education, don' ye see? An' for ma' mother and aunt. I cried for 'im ta keep 'em always. But Pa-Pa said 'e was the last o' 'is line. E' wanted the world o' gowf *tae 'ave the glory o' the past.* An' us ta be safe." Tears slipped from her eyes. But she kept her chin up to meet the world directly on.

"If he meant to sell it all, had he shown it to anyone?" Sullivan asked.

"Aye."

Sullivan waited, barely risking a breath.

"But 'e dinna like the mon. 'E told me so," Sharon said.

"Who was he?" Sullivan asked, willing her hands still in her lap.

"I dinna see 'im," Sharon said. " 'E came this winter, in the night. I only ken tha' with the mon came a lad . . . on 'is motorcycle. I 'eard it roar in ma bed. Pa-Pa did na' like the lad or the mon."

"Were they strangers?" Sullivan asked, catching her breath at the word *motorcycle.*

Sharon shook her head. "Pa-Pa said 'e niver liked 'em at all, but the mon *'ad a' ocean o' money.* After seein' 'im, Pa-Pa said 'e *wuidna' swim in tha' mon's ocean."* Sharon smiled at the memory of the expression.

"Then who did he mean to sell the collection to?" Sullivan asked. "The Royal and Ancient Golf Club?"

" 'E luffed the R&A. But 'e bilieved they 'oped ta get it all *free.* 'E meant ta get *fair market value."*

"And it's now your job, young lady, to see that you do just that," Sullivan said. "I don't think your mother or your aunt understands the value of the collection. I can get you the name of a proper expert to come up from London and appraise it."

Sharon nodded that she was very much agreeable. "After Pa-Pa is properly buried."

It was Sullivan's time to nod her agreement. "Did any R&A members recently ask Old Alec about the collection?"

Sharon shook her head. "I dinna know o' it."

"How did the man Pa-Pa never liked learn of the collection and that it might be valuable and for sale?'' Sullivan asked, the questions suddenly popping into her head.

''Tha' lad wha' came wi' 'im told 'im. I think 'e was a caddy at the Old Course. Some o' the ol' caddies know wha's in the barn. They niver tell. But I think the lad 'eard somethin'.''

''Was his name Peter Caldwell?'' Sullivan asked.

Sharon tilted her head as if the name was familiar.

''He's been suspended from caddying on the Old Course,'' Sullivan said.

''Aye. I rimember 'im. 'E also rides a motorcycle. But I canna say it was 'im.''

Sullivan did not say *and he was murdered last night on his bike.* She did not want to frighten the girl unnecessarily. Sharon would hear of Caldwell's death, but the police were calling it an *accident* for now, to let the killer take his comfort. But whoever he was, he would not dare harm Sharon Kirkcaldy. *Or God help him if he did,* Sullivan thought.

Morris stopped the small Ford on the side of Pilmour Links Road to give her a hug after she told him all she had learned from Sharon Kirkcaldy.

''Jesus, the two sisters don't know how many holes go in a golf green,'' Morris said.

''On seven greens on the Old Course, it's *two,*'' Sullivan said impishly.

''I take back the hug,'' said Morris, kissing her on the forehead like she was a wee child. ''The Edinburgh sister, Mary, is ready to auction off the barn with everything in it. The St. Andrews sister, Anne, thinks the world is trying to steal her house out from under her. I'm not surprised that Sharon understands *everything.* God bless her.''

Morris put the Ford into gear. ''The boy who came with the 'rich man' had to be Peter Caldwell. Remember,

Caldwell was sitting at the long table with Old Alec and George McCormack the night Old Alec was killed. Who do you think the 'rich man' might have been?"

"The same man who killed Peter Caldwell," Sullivan said.

"Driving a Citroën?"

"Probably."

"The inspector's men have hand-checked the public garages and parking lots and the automobiles of our *friendly suspects* in St. Andrews," Morris said. "It will take time to physically check the automobiles of *every* R&A member. But they are working on it. I have no recollection of seeing anybody we know in St. Andrews in a Citroën other than Sir Arthur Maxwell."

"Anybody rich enough to import a Citroën is also rich enough to store it out of town," Sullivan said. "Especially if he has used it to commit two felonies."

"Yes; I have a friend who parks a Learjet at the Edinburgh airport," Morris said. "We better see if she also owns a Citroën."

Sullivan ignored him. "Perhaps he keeps a lover in the Highlands . . . or maybe he has an apartment in Edinburgh . . . or London. Who knows?" Sullivan said. "It's a small country."

Inspector Emerson let his lager sit in his glass as Sullivan told him all she had learned from Sharon Kirkcaldy. He reached in his coat pocket and pulled out his inspector's credentials and pushed them in front of her. "I surrender. We are moving Scotland Yard to Colorado."

She pushed them back in his lap. "You must remember, Morris and I have been holding Sharon Kirkcaldy on our laps since she was old enough to climb up in them. She trusts us, Jim."

"I'll have to talk with her tomorrow," said Emerson.

"Promise you'll do it alone, at her house. And you won't frighten her, or mention my name," said Sullivan.

"I promise not to alarm her. And I won't mention our conversation. Oh yes, the young man, Niel Blyth, from Carnoustie turned himself in," the inspector said. "He was in a rage over his half brother's death. He believed the 'bloody police' ran his half brother down. I finally calmed him, somewhat. He says he can't think who might have wanted his brother dead. Although Caldwell did tell him he was *workin' oon a big deal, wi' 'opes o' nae mair livin' like piss-heads.* Blyth is a simple man, as you know, and a *piss-head* if one ever crawled out of a pub. But he's never been in trouble more serious than public drunkenness and a simple brawl or two." The inspector finished his beer. "Caldwell was another matter. He was suspected of helping steal golf clubs out of the backs of rental cars . . . a cottage industry in St. Andrews. A new set of American clubs, with bag, brings a thousand dollars on the black market. The local police believed Caldwell was tipping off the thieves as to which cars to hit. He was also suspected of breaking into hotel rooms. The police picked him up, but they couldn't prove anything."

"Did Blyth know Old Alec?" Morris asked.

"Yes. He'd met him several times, caddying at tournaments at Carnoustie," said the inspector. "Old Alec was known all around the Firth of Tay and the Firth of Forth, for that matter. Even Blyth speaks well of him. He can't remember his half brother ever mentioning him. I think Blyth is too simple to lie very well."

Morris nodded. "Had he recently seen a Citroën in Carnoustie?"

"*Yes.* He saw one two days ago, on the road from Dundee to Carnoustie," Emerson said. "But Blyth had caught a ride in the opposite direction during a small rainstorm and didn't really get a look at the driver. A

Citroën is a rare car here, and he remembered it. He's not absolutely sure, but he believes the car was black. Of course, he didn't look at the plates. He just assumed it was some tourist from the Continent up to see the Open at St. Andrews after playing some golf in the morning at Carnoustie.''

''Now, why would a man be driving a Citroën to Carnoustie if *not* to play golf?'' Morris said. ''There is *nowhere* for the owner of an expensive car to comfortably spend the night in Carnoustie. As you well know, that's why Carnoustie is not on the regular seven-course rotation for the British Open.''

''If the man—if it was a man—drove to Carnoustie to see Peter Caldwell two nights ago,'' said the inspector, ''I have no doubt the same man met up with him again on the road from Dundee to St. Andrews.''

''Why would a rich man do business with the likes of Peter Caldwell?'' Morris asked.

''Caldwell was a thief,'' Sullivan said. ''And he was a *positioned observer.* He learned which pricey golf clubs were being loaded into which rental cars. And which hotel rooms held wealthy golfers. And he eventually learned from other caddies, friends of Old Alec, the value of his collection of golf artifacts. And what did he do with that knowledge?'' Sullivan answered herself: *''He sold it to a rich man.''*

''And the rich man left the Bull and Bear and followed Old Alec MacLaine home, *or gave him a ride home,* and Caldwell met them there, and he and/or the rich man garroted a drunken MacLaine in his own barn,'' Morris said.

''One very rich man admits following him home,'' the inspector said. ''George McCormack. But he swears Old Alec was alive when he returned his cap and that he left him alive in his house.''

''I can see Peter Caldwell *wanting* to work for George

McCormack,'' Morris said. ''But I can't see McCormack trusting him an inch, with his money, or his punters, or certainly taking him on as a silent partner in that most dangerous gambit . . . murder. McCormack would have left them both dead.''

''And maybe he intended to,'' said Sullivan.

''And the kid got away at a hundred miles an hour up Pilmour Links Road,'' the inspector said.

''It's possible,'' said Morris, not believing it for a minute, not with the big hands hanging on the arms of George McCormack.

''The kid wanted his share out of the hide of the rich man,'' Sullivan said, ''and the rich man killed him.''

''But why kill Old Alec?'' asked Morris. ''That leaves his collectibles to be disposed of by his estate.''

''Perhaps the killer figured Old Alec's sisters would have no idea as to the value of the collection,'' Sullivan said. ''If so, he was right. He didn't figure on *you,* Morris, finding Old Alec's journal, or on his granddaughter knowing the value of the items in the barn.'' Sullivan paused to think. ''It would also take a reckless killer to step over the body and make a bid for the artifacts. I think a man who can afford to drive a Citroën *as a second car* would have a better sense of self-preservation.''

Morris said, ''Maybe the kid, who knows breaking and entering, *found the garrote* in the barn. And they confronted Old Alec with it. To *make* him sell his artifacts at a bargain price. And Old Alec said he didn't give a goddamn what they told the police and went into a drunken rage and *they had to kill him.*''

''I like that better,'' said Sullivan. ''Maybe the Citroën driver struggled with Old Alec. . . . You can see there was one helluva struggle in the dark in the barn, and even drunk Old Alec would have been a handful. . . . Jesus, I can hear them fighting for their lives in there . . . and the kid comes up behind Old Alec and *garrotes him* before the rich man knows what's happened and it's too damn late to undo anything. And the kid runs for his motorcycle, leaving the older man, who is in a panic, to drag the body into the house. That's what he did, *drag* it. He didn't carry it."

"Blackmail gone sour," the inspector said, "and gone doubly sour when Caldwell demands money to keep quiet, knowing he could make a deal with the courts by giving them the rich man, the same as would happen in your own country. But the man in the Citroën was judge and jury on the midnight road from Dundee. Congratulations all around. Now, whom do we arrest?"

"Now's when we dial Scotland Yard," Morris said.

"Scotland Yard is going to bed. I will see you two tomorrow."

Before the first light, Morris came awake. He smiled at the gentle snoring of Julia Sullivan. He knew exactly what he meant to do.

At breakfast, working on her fourth scone, Sullivan looked up suspiciously. "Why are you so damn quiet, John Morris?"

"I'm apprehensive," he said, not smiling.

Sullivan dropped her scone on her plate. "You know something I don't."

"No."

"You remember something I don't," Sullivan said.

"Maybe." He looked at his watch. "I'm waiting to give Tom Rowe time to wake up."

"And?"

"I'm going to ask him to invite me into the Royal and Ancient clubhouse," said Morris. "Tom is a member, like Bernard Darwin before him. In another two hundred years, Sullivan, they will probably welcome a beautiful woman like you for a cup of tea in their male-infested clubhouse."

"I think I'll hang out with a younger set, thank you. Why don't you ask Captain Tait to invite you there?" Sullivan looked at her own watch. "You know him—he was up hours ago."

"I'd rather not," Morris said.

"You still haven't answered my question: *What do you remember that I don't?*" Sullivan asked.

Morris told her what he hoped to find, and she did remember the incident. "But it won't prove anything, Morris."

"No. But I'm curious as to where it might lead us."

"Call Tom Rowe now," Sullivan said. "England's premiere golf writer ought not to be asleep with the sun up in Scotland."

Rowe was, indeed, up and dressed. He immediately agreed to meet Morris at the R&A clubhouse for morning tea. "Who is it you want to see?" he asked.

"Not *who, what,*" said Morris. "I'll tell you when I get there. I hear you were surprised at the richness of Old Alec's family golf collection?"

"Good Lord, yes," Rowe said. "I was not surprised. I was *amazed.* So were my editors. All St. Andrews needs to start the British Golf Museum is the contents of Old Alec's barn."

"A treasure to kill for," Morris said.

"Is that a statement, or an accusation?" asked Rowe.

"I'll see you in a few minutes, old man. I'll bring the handcuffs," said Morris.

Tom Rowe looked rather splendid in his coat and tie and jaunty Hogan cap. "Morris, what the hell do you want to see that you haven't seen before in this ancient fortress of a clubhouse?"

"I'm interested in the members' tradition of recording their bets," Morris said.

"Oh, yes." Rowe seemed somehow relieved. "It will

make a nice bit of eccentric relief in your book: John Whyte-Melville of Strathkinness *betting his life* against Sir David Moncrieffe in 1820 . . . agreeing that the man who died *last* must give the R&A a Silver Putter as a standing trophy, on which the arms of the two families must be engraved. Sir David was the survivor and the donor. You can see the Silver Putter and the silver balls attached to it that were won over the years at club meetings. Is that what you are looking for, that sort of thing?''

Morris ignored the question. ''Are bets among members still recorded?''

''Oh, yes. Not by everyone, just those of us hidebound by tradition,'' said Rowe, puzzled again over what Morris was after.

''I'd like to see the members' bets of recent months.''

''Certainly,'' Rowe said. ''Do you mind my asking what particular bet you are interested in?''

Morris again ignored the question for the moment. ''What happens if a match can't be played, or if some argument comes up over local rules—and that seems rather absurd here in the house of the Royal and Ancient rules of golf—or if one party is caught *cheating*?''

Rowe had led them into a small room and stopped before a large ledger. He looked back at Morris with some alarm. ''Oh, the bets are often canceled if someone is ill, or called out of town, or business presses—a great variety of reasons. And you couldn't believe the arguments over the rules that go on among this membership, with some of our amateur historians citing rules interpretations of two hundred years ago. You said *cheating,* Morris. Anyone found cheating is dismissed from the club and from the company of golfers. It is a very, very rare thing.''

''Among *caddies*?'' Morris asked.

Rowe paused while opening the ledger. ''And now I

know what specific bet concerns you, Morris. And maybe I know why you asked *me* to find it for you. Of course, I was in the foursome when young Peter Caldwell was found cheating and suspended from the Old Course. *Suspended* is a euphemistic way of saying *barred for life.*''

Morris could not have been more surprised that Tom Rowe had been a party to that particular bet. Rowe traveled the golfing world for the *Times,* but he was most often found in London. The odds were very much against his being in St. Andrews for any one local golf match between members. It was obvious to Morris that Rowe credited him with information about the bet that he did not have.

Rowe flipped back several pages into the ledger. He pointed to a date three months before. Morris bent forward. Lines had been drawn through the date, as well as the names of the foursome and the bet.

''The bet, of course, was canceled on the spot,'' Rowe said.

Morris could easily read through the thin lines of cancellation: ''Apr. 23, 1978. T. Rowe & A.W.B. Tait vs. J. Craufurd & G. Dougall, best ball, for £500.''

''Let's have a cup of tea,'' said Rowe, not avoiding his eyes.

After the tea had been poured, Morris said, ''Rather swift company you keep, Thomas, playing for five hundred pounds a whack.''

''A bit rich for my blood,'' Rowe admitted. ''Perhaps you don't realize it, Morris, but I do not find it necessary to live on my salary from the *Times.* Thank God,'' he added.

''If I had known it, I would have picked up far fewer bar tabs over the years,'' Morris said.

"You have picked up *few enough,*" Rowe said, and laughed, more his old, natural self.

Morris asked, "Did you mention anything about the bet, or about Caldwell's being banned for life from caddying at the Old Course, when you filed your story on his death? Or did you file anything on it?"

"I did file a brief news report," said Rowe. "I pointed out that the police had been looking for him as some kind of material witness in the murders. I did not include the match or the bet, but I did say that Caldwell had been banned from the Old Course. The police are calling his death an *accident.* Are they concealing something?"

"Maybe," Morris said. He didn't offer to explain. "How did your golf bet come about?"

"You've had your own run-ins, Morris, with Gerald Balfour-Melville Dougall?"

Morris nodded.

"He is a man with an inexhaustible supply of his own opinion," said Rowe, "which he inflicts on the membership at every opportunity. James Craufurd III is a harmless enough older golfer, with an excellent short game. Dougall considers our friend Captain A.W.B. Tait to be an obstacle to his personal ambition; as you know, he lusts after the captaincy of the R&A, which he will assume over Tait's dead body. Dougall also takes exception with nearly every word *I* write in the *Times,* which he also despises as 'a great voice of English propaganda,' which, of course, it often is."

Rowe replenished the tea in their cups. "Dougall was arguing with Tait over the upcoming placement of the pins for the Open. Every Dougall argument sooner or later degenerates into a personal attack. And somewhere among the hot words and the late-night whisky, Dougall said he could take old James Craufurd and *beat the life* out of Tait and *yours truly* on the Old Course. I don't know how my name got into the bargain, except Dougall despises me almost as much as he despises the captain."

Rowe swirled the tea in his cup. "Captain Tait called me and asked if I would join him against the two of them for five hundred pounds. That he would arrange the time and the match to suit me. I said you bet your sweet ass I would, though Dougall hits a powerful drive and Craufurd knows every blade of grass on the Old Course."

"How did the match go?" Morris asked.

"We had the buggers one down coming into the 15th hole," Rowe said. "Dougall launched a tremendous drive, only he pulled it left into the high rough short of Elysian Fields. His caddy, young Caldwell, walking up ahead, found the ball in a *decidedly advantageous* lie, and Dougall played his fairway wood very near to the green for a real chance at a birdie four. It happened that another member, playing up No. 4, had pulled his own tee shot wildly left into the same rough. He came over to Captain Tait and advised him that as he himself turned around, this way and that, looking for his own lost ball, he saw Caldwell kick a ball out of the rough."

Rowe finished his tea and set down his cup. "Caldwell, of course, denied it. But it was not a lucky day for Mr. Caldwell. The member reporting him is a presiding bishop of Scotland, a man whose honor has never been called into question. I prefer not to use his name, although it would be easy enough to determine. Over Dougall's objection, Caldwell was dismissed from the course, and our four-ball match and bet were canceled on the spot. I have my suspicions, but there was no evidence that Dougall was in league with Caldwell, so the matter was dropped. Is that what you wanted to know, Morris?"

"Exactly," Morris said. He thought: *If a rich man would hire a caddy to cheat for a five-hundred pound bet, what would he do for a golf treasure worth hundreds of thousands?* A memory that had eluded Morris suddenly flooded into his mind: Gerald Dougall saying to him, the day after Barry Vinson was murdered, *I've collected many clubs, but na' a dishonest one.*

"So which of us is guilty of the murders of Peter Caldwell, Old Alec MacLaine, and Barry Vinson?" Rowe asked.

"No one of you," Morris said with no explanation, least of all that *three* separate men very likely killed the lot of them.

Rowe squinted in obvious confusion.

"How did Caldwell happen to be caddying for Dougall and Craufurd?" Morris asked. "I assume he was doubling on both bags?"

"He was. Come to think of it, he often caddied for Dougall," Rowe said. "Do you imagine that Caldwell might have done other, darker things for Dougall?"

Darker than you might imagine, Morris thought but did not say.

"You don't consider Captain Tait and myself to be capable of *darker* obsessions?" Rowe asked.

Morris actually grinned. "I wouldn't bet five hundred pounds that you two ornery bastards couldn't swim the Firth of Tay. But if you two were going to kill someone, I believe either of you would be man enough to do it yourself." *And maybe they had, however unlikely,* Morris thought.

"But you weren't entirely sure that Peter Caldwell hadn't caddied and cheated *for us,*" said Rowe.

"No," admitted Morris. "In fact, I had no idea *you* were a party to the bet. I had a hunch Captain Tait might have been in the foursome. I'm aware of the animosity between him and Dougall."

"Tell me more, Morris," Rowe said. "What do you think Caldwell was involved in? Or Gerald Dougall?"

"Not yet. Let me ask you not to say anything about our conversation to anybody, even to the captain. I'll let you know where it leads, if anywhere," said Morris.

"Done," Rowe said.

• CHAPTER ELEVEN •

Sullivan was sitting on the high steps to the St. Andrews Golf Hotel, looking over the North Sea.

"Sit down, John Morris, and tell me everything," she said.

"Are you prepared to get me back up?" he asked, leaning on his cane.

"I'll just roll you down the steps." She patted the step she was sitting on.

Morris lowered his considerable bulk, stretching out his stiff left leg and told her of the April 23 golf match for five hundred pounds and of Peter Caldwell's cheating for Gerald Dougall.

"It doesn't bother you that Tom Rowe and Captain Tait were in the foursome?" she asked.

"Yes," Morris admitted. "You know how much I distrust coincidence. And the captain and Rowe are plenty strong-willed enough to kill a man that *had to be killed.* But why would they hire Caldwell to cheat *against* them? And both men loved Old Alec. And neither man needs money. Or so I understand."

"I remember James Craufurd III," Sullivan said. "The old man can barely kill a half-pint in a long evening. Let's not dodge the obvious, Morris. Caldwell was caddying and cheating for Dougall, and he was very likely working for him and *maybe killing for him.*"

"I can see Dougall lusting after Old Alec's artifacts,"

said Morris. "I can see him trying to steal them with a low-ball offer . . . even trying to steal them *outright.* But would he have the guts to kill him?"

"He might have the guts to hire Peter Caldwell to kill him," Sullivan said. "And make it look like he was killed by the same man who killed Barry Vinson, even to stuffing a feathery ball in his throat. Then Dougall buys the golf collection from the widow for a fraction of what it's worth. Dougall couldn't have known that Old Alec had taught his granddaughter the value of the collection . . . and even left a journal describing it."

"Dougall is plenty arrogant, but too smart to be in the barn when Old Alec was killed," Morris said.

"Something went badly wrong," Sullivan agreed. "Somebody gave Old Alec, drunk as a loon, a ride home from the Bull and Bear. Maybe it was Gerald Dougall. George McCormack brings his cap out to him but doesn't go in the house . . . he says. Why does he take the trouble? Maybe the greediest punter in Scotland has a soft spot for the old man. Maybe *he* wanted to buy Old Alec's collection, or steal it from him. And maybe *he* killed him with those huge hands of his."

Sullivan shifted her position on the steps as if shifting herself back to her original argument. "But sticking to our story: Caldwell leaves the Bull and Bear and shows up at Old Alec's on his motorcycle; we know from Sharon Kirkcaldy that someone had been there before *on a motorcycle* in the company of a *rich man,* and we can be pretty sure it was Caldwell and maybe it was Dougall. And maybe Dougall made one last offer to Old Alec for his artifacts, knowing he was three sheets to the wind. But even drunk, Old Alec wouldn't do business with him. Maybe Dougall formulated an instant *final solution* to the problem: Kill Old Alec *the same way Barry Vinson was murdered.* And let the police suspect the same killer . . . with his own bloody garrote left around Old Alec's neck."

"I like it," Morris said. "I think." He told her of remembering what Dougall had said to him before the Open began, that he had collected *many clubs, but na' a dishonest one.* "Never trust a man who first tells you how honest he is," Morris said. "But I keep wondering if Dougall had the nerve to kill Old Alec. I can see him running down Peter Caldwell with an automobile. Dougall, burly as he is, strikes me as more the bully than the bare-hands killer. I could be very wrong. Old Alec is *very dead,* and by his own garrote. Maybe Gerald Dougall is more greedy and more murderous than I imagined."

"Or maybe *something went terribly wrong* in the barn. And Caldwell killed him before Dougall could stop him."

Morris thought about that. "Caldwell might have been desperate enough and clever enough to kill him on the spot, with Dougall *there,* compromising them both. And giving Caldwell a hammer over the rich man's head."

"Whoever killed him, or helped kill him, or paid to have him killed, or watched while he was being killed, or all of the above, was driving a French Citroën," Sullivan said. "You can lay odds on that with Mr. George McCormack, boy punter."

"I doubt he would get up early in the morning to make another bet with you." Again Morris looked at his watch. "How would you like an early drink at the Bull and Bear?"

"Oh, yes. With whom?"

"With Issette and her *boy* bartenders."

"It's early," Sullivan said, "but then, this is Scotland. All you need to sustain life is a sheep on the hill, a ball on the tee, and a lager in the glass."

"Oh, no, Robbie Burns always added a mournful song to a 'fair maid.' "

"Well, lead the way for the maid." Sullivan took his large hand and leveraged him to his feet.

"If a rich man drove a Citroën to two killings . . . and the Citroën wasn't licensed in *his* name . . . whose name would it be licensed in?" Morris asked, poling himself along with his cane.

"Not his wife's," Sullivan said immediately. "She would park it in his own garage—couldn't have that. Not in any of his family's name; in fact, too close for comfort. It wouldn't be a stolen Citroën, that would complicate matters and be too dangerous. It's easy, Morris. *It would be driven by his mistress who lives nearby, who else?*"

"I'll stand you the first half-pint," he said, his big arm around her slim shoulders. "You capture Issette. I'll have a go with whichever bartender is drawing the beer."

"Do you remember what I asked you when we were trying to find out the identity of the young red-haired girl in the Bull and Bear? And we had no way of knowing it was Sharon Kirkcaldy?"

"What did you ask me?"

"I asked if you could believe that 'two lecherous old bartenders, and a table of sun-ruined caddies, wouldn't know a beautiful, red-haired dolly bird' when she stepped in the pub? I was right. They all knew her and denied it to the floor. It was Issette who told us Sharon's name."

"You think all of them also know what young woman was in the Bull and Bear with Gerald Dougall the night Old Alec was killed?"

"You are a quick one," Sullivan said. "Captain Tait saw them but said he didn't recognize the woman."

"Do you believe *him*?"

"Maybe. But there's bound to be 'honor among Scotsmen,' and that sort of tripe, even among Scotsmen who despise one another, when it comes to lovers outside of marriage."

"She might have been his daughter," Morris said.

Sullivan looked at him with grand disbelief.

"No, I think not."

"Whoever she was . . . why would a man bring a lover to a pub the night *he meant to kill* one of the other customers?" Sullivan asked.

"Not likely," Morris admitted. "But then, she'd be excellent cover, if you will excuse the pun."

"How would she get home, if he drove *her* Citroën?"

"Maybe she went with him and was sitting in the Citroën while Old Alec was being murdered? There's a thought."

When they reached the Bull and Bear, Morris did not sit down but headed straight for the old bartender, Laidlay, who grunted a good morning.

Meanwhile, Sullivan stepped around to the small room in the back where Issette kept the books of the pub she had lashed herself to all of these years.

Morris offered no small talk. "Two half-pints of the bitter, Mr. Laidlay. The other day you wouldn't tell me the name of the red-haired Sharon Kirkcaldy, who you've known since she was a tyke, and who I've loved since she was the size of the mug in your hand. Now try telling me the name of the young lass who was sitting with Gerald Dougall the night Old Alec was killed." Morris slapped his money on the bar like a dare.

Old Laidlay did not look up from his artistry with the bitter. "O', ah lively one, tha'. Aboot twenty-five. Frae Edinburgh, but I've niver 'eard 'er name, Morris. An' tha's God's truth."

Laidlay would not budge from that position. He could not offer a closer description of the woman. Just that she was young and attractive, her hair wasn't short, he couldn't say what color, and she had come to the pub several times in the past year with Dougall and drank vodka and not whisky. He said the last as if it were a terrible failure of character. The other, younger bartender—not a year older than seventy-eight—would not be in until five P.M. Laidlay was sure he didn't know the young lass's name either.

Sullivan met Morris at an empty table, and she was shaking her head. "Issette could name a half dozen young things who've taken up with Dougall over the years, but not that particular one," she said. "She's only certain the young woman is not from St. Andrews. Issette doesn't care for Gerald Dougall and has long since lost interest in his miserable love life."

"Laidlay says she's from Edinburgh," Morris said. "He swears he doesn't know her name. Maybe he's even telling the truth." Morris repeated Laidlay's vague description of her and of her lamentable taste for vodka.

Morris took his half-pint over to the pay phone. Inspector Emerson was not in a happy mood. The killers of the four London police had been caught in a cocaine raid. *Clever fellows.* They'd kept one of the police officer's badges for bragging rights. Each of the four was blaming the other three for the actual killings. Now Scotland Yard had turned all of its anger and impatience on Inspector Emerson and his failed St. Andrews investigation.

"How many Citroëns have you located in Scotland?" Morris asked.

"Three hundred and two," the inspector said, as if answering a question in his university orals. "Only six of them in St. Andrews including Sir Arthur's. We've checked out the six. Nothing."

"How about Glasgow and Edinburgh?" Morris asked, as if he had equal interest in both cities.

"They are all over goddamn Glasgow," the inspector said. "Forty-three of them. And twenty-five in Edinburgh. We've called most of the owners on the phone and followed up on a dozen suspicious conversations that led nowhere."

"Could I get a list of the owners, say, starting in Edinburgh?"

"Why? What do you know?" Emerson asked, more hope in his voice than suspicion.

"I want to see if any of the names mean anything to me, or to Sullivan, or to Sharon Kirkcaldy—"

"Who trusts *you,*" the inspector interrupted. "I'll have the bloody names from Glasgow *and* Edinburgh sent to your hotel. Lots of luck. I need a couple of days to get my hands around this case, Morris. Then you'll be dialing a stranger, who won't take your calls."

Sullivan tapped the table with her mug. "What did you find out?"

"You want to go by the Edinburgh airport and pat your plane on the wing?" Morris asked. He explained about the twenty-five Citroëns registered in Edinburgh. "I doubt the young woman we're looking for is married, but you never know," he said. "The social editor of the local paper might be able to help you weed out the married owners and the old timers."

"Leave it to me. If she's in Edinburgh, I'll find her and her Citroën."

"When you find her . . ." Morris said, and went carefully over what he wanted her to say and do.

Sullivan listened, nodding. "You won't take any foolish chances yourself," she said. "If the young woman cooperates with me, you'll call the inspector."

"Oh, yes." Morris touched her hand. "You be careful. This woman might not have been waiting in the car. She might have been in the barn, *using the garrote.* I'll be making the rounds of our other *friendly suspects.* I'll try to get a tighter description as soon as possible of Dougall's girlfriend . . . from Captain Tait and the others who were in the Bull and Bear. Call me at the hotel. If I'm not in, I'll leave what descriptions I can get of her with the front desk."

Sullivan put her hands in his large coat pocket and fished out the keys to the little Ford. Morris lifted her to her feet as easily as if she were weightless and held her until she promised again to be careful.

Morris hiked over to the Old Course Hotel, whose lobby had recovered from the frenetic mobs of the Open. He nursed a beer until Sir Arthur Maxwell squinted into the dark of the bar.

"Sit down, you might sell me a new sweater," Morris said.

"Fat chance, selling a man who changes sweaters every twenty years, whether he needs a new one or not." Maxwell needed a real drink of whisky. He said he was leaving tomorrow for London, couldn't stay another day, business was suddenly thriving, how the hell could you explain it, this obsession with a dead golfer's clothes; the inspector knew he was going. All that run together in one sentence.

Morris asked if in recent months he'd seen Gerald Dougall with a tall young woman from Edinburgh, who wore her hair, probably brown, to her shoulders, who preferred to drink vodka, and who had a rather high, distinctive laugh?

Maxwell didn't have to think. "I saw him with a young woman who fits that description about two months ago. But it was in *London* . . . just outside London, actually. I ignored his table at the Roehampton

Club, though I couldn't help hearing the young woman's rather silly laugh. I think she must have been deeply into the vodka. Dougall seemed as anxious to avoid me as I him. I despise the bastard, Morris. Why are you interested in the woman?"

"Did she strike you as attractive?"

Maxwell thought a minute. "Oh, yes. Even looking at the menu with her reading glasses, she would catch your fancy. To be honest, even her laugh was more amusing than annoying. At least the old bastard Dougall is married and she doesn't have to worry about that. She can concentrate on his *money,* I hope."

"One other thing," Morris said. "Do you know if she drives a Citroën?"

Maxwell covered his mouth with his hand. "That's an odd question. I have no idea."

Morris could not read his eyes. He asked if Maxwell knew of the aborted golf match in which Peter Caldwell had kicked Dougall's ball out of the rough.

"Of course," Maxwell said. "We all love a scandal. I dare say it wasn't the millionth ball nudged in the rough on the Old Course in the last five hundred years. But the members wouldn't tolerate it in a *caddy,* of course." Maxwell was curious to know what the police had found out about Caldwell's accident. "If it was an *accident*?" he added.

Morris declined to comment and asked Maxwell if he intended to pursue a contract with Old Alec's estate, to duplicate some of his historic golf wear.

"Oh, yes," Maxwell said. "I'm finding out that the public loves the famous dead and what they wore. I won't bother the daughters, of course, with their father not yet in the ground."

Sir Arthur stood, saying he had to get back to his room and to the telephone.

"Do hang around until tomorrow," Morris said. "I hope to have some information by then."

Maxwell paused, as if incapable of movement. "What information?"

"If I knew, I'd already have it," Morris said mysteriously. "I'll give you a ring in the morning."

Maxwell was reluctant to leave but could think of no question that could keep him standing there.

Morris stood to catch the eye of Warren Lightfoot, who stumbled into the dark bar like a tall, endangered water bird on dry ground.

Lightfoot seemed oddly pleased to shake hands with an old friend and fellow American, though they had been seeing each other every day for over a week. "I love St. Andrews," the New Englander said, "but I'm needed at home."

"I can imagine," said Morris, while nursing a new bitter. Lightfoot settled on a whisky.

Morris cut to the chase. "Have you had an opportunity to actually see Old Alec's golf collection?"

"Yes. Some of it," Lightfoot said. "The inspector himself took me through the barn. And gave me a look at the journal. The collection is astonishing. The American artifacts alone could make priceless additions to our USGA museum." The laconic Lightfoot was so moved by the collection that he did not seem to realize how many words he was using up.

"How would you appraise the value of it all?" Morris asked.

"More than half a million dollars, perhaps a good bit more," said Lightfoot, having obviously given the matter some thought. "The art I saw, is alone worth half of that. There are images by significant artists that the museums have never seen. There is even a pen-and-ink sketch of the Old Course by Turner. I was not aware that he was ever at St. Andrews.''

Morris changed subjects with no hint of transition. ''You were in the Bull and Bear the night Old Alec was killed. Did you see Gerald Dougall there?''

Lightfoot, in an instant, became his old, laconic self. He only nodded yes.

''Who was he sitting with?'' Morris asked.

The USGA president measured out his words as if in fear of being misquoted on the front page of the *Times*. ''A young woman.''

''Can you describe her?''

Lightfoot turned his whisky in his hands as he thought. ''Rather tall. Long, brown hair. Young. Attractive.''

Morris waited, conserving his own words in unconscious imitation.

''Smoking a cigarette,'' said Lightfoot, having just remembered it. ''And she was carrying the largest shoulder bag I ever saw.'' The memory of the very size of it shook loose the extra words to describe it.

''Do you know if she came in a Citroën?'' Morris asked.

Lightfoot lifted his glass, concealing his mouth while he thought. ''I didn't see her arrive, or leave,'' he said.

Morris saw nervousness but no outright fear in his eyes. ''Does Dougall have a substantial golf collection of his own?'' he asked, kicking himself for not having asked it before of anybody.

''Yes,'' Lightfoot said.

''Have you seen it?''

''Yes.''

''Describe it to me,'' said Morris, willing his hands to be quiet in his lap.

''A marvelous collection of early balls, from a rare wooden ball of the eighteenth century to the feathery to the gutta-percha. A limited variety of early clubs by the great club makers, the Robertsons, the McEwens, Old Tom Morris, of course. But not to compare with the MacLaine collection and certainly not its incomparable artwork.'' Again, the idea of golfing artifacts loosened Lightfoot's vocabulary.

''Have you met Dougall's wife?'' Morris asked.

''No,'' said Lightfoot, happy again with a one-word answer.

''Did you offer to buy his collection . . . or any part of it?'' Morris could not think how the question jumped into his mouth.

Lightfoot appeared rather startled. But he answered, ''Yes.''

''What was his reaction?''

''Anger,'' said Lightfoot without having to think about it. ''He made me aware that he did not 'require any Yankee money.' I had no intention of offending him. I was only interested in the few American artifacts, including a silver bowl that had belonged to Francis Ouimet.''

''Don't suppose you considered killing him for it,'' said Morris, the black humor jumping out of his mouth, again unsummoned.

Lightfoot appeared more frightened than offended. ''Certainly not,'' he said, appalled at the idea.

''Sorry about that,'' Morris said. ''Sullivan is usually around to hit me over the head when my poor attempts at humor fall disgracefully short of the mark. She's on an errand at the moment. I'll hear from her tonight—I hope with information to sort out some of this dark business in old St. Andrews.''

''What . . .'' Lightfoot began, ''information?'' He said it like separate sentences, each of which unnerved him.

"I'm in the same boat as you. I'll have to wait until tonight and hear," Morris said.

Lightfoot risked several questions as to the type of information Sullivan was searching for, but Morris deflected them all, until the New Englander finished his second whisky and left reluctantly for his room.

George McCormack's betting shop was doing a listless business. George himself was in a back room but agreed to see Morris, even standing until Morris sat down.

Morris did not waste a sentence in small talk. "Are you prepared to bid for Old Alec's golf collection?" he asked.

"Nae mon'll bid higher," said McCormack, resting his big hands on his formidable girth.

"Not even Gerald Dougall?" Morris, again, was surprised that another of his questions had asked itself.

McCormack looked dead at him with his black eyes, giving away nothing. " 'E can bid fur 'isself wha' 'is wife doesna' spend in London shops." McCormack laughed.

"Dougall doesn't strike me as a Scotsman who would welcome an unseemly remark about his wife." The words jostled the large punter out of his laughter.

"Na 'arm intended," said McCormack, his eyes darker and deader.

"Did you see the young woman Dougall was sitting with in the Bull and Bear the night Old Alec was killed?" Morris asked, looking directly back at the Scotsman.

McCormack lied. "Nae." He shook his large head as if such a possibility was out of the question.

"Odd," Morris said. "Everybody else in the pub with a body temperature saw her. You wouldn't know the name of this girlfriend?"

McCormack did not bother to answer or even shake his head but sat in his formidable silence.

"Then you don't know if she drives a Citroën?" Morris said.

McCormack again looked directly at him with his dark eyes but said nothing.

"Well." Morris stood up. "Sullivan is out spending your shop's good money and thanks you for it. And tonight I hope to hear a bit of news from her that will help clear up what has happened here in St. Andrews." Morris turned, as if to leave.

"Here now," said McCormack, rising ponderously. "An' wha' sort o' news might tha' be?"

"What are your odds, George, on any one of us having offed the lot of them?" Morris asked. Not waiting for an answer, he added, "Maybe the odds shrink after tonight." Morris left him standing, his hands over his huge torso.

Now Morris sat at the bar of the St. Andrews Golf Hotel. He checked his watch and had another sip of lager. He hadn't been sitting thirty minutes when the familiar voice of Captain A.W.B. Tait spilled over his shoulder: "An' wha' are ye sayin', Morris, all orver toon aboot knowin' the killer?"

"Too early, Captain, try me tomorrow," Morris said. "Sit down. I'll buy you a bitter."

"Ah whisky," Tait said.

The week's wind had blown Tait's rugged old face into deeper furrows under his steel-gray hair. The brimming round glass of whisky did not soften his expression. *"'Eer's 'ealth an' prosperity . . . an them tha' doesna' drink wi' sincerity . . . may be damned fur all eternity."*

Morris drank to the unfamiliar quotation, even though it sounded very much like a threat. He offered no apologies as he repeated Tom Rowe's version of his and the captain's ill-fated golf match with Dougall and Craufurd.

"Aye," Tait said. "An' guid riddance ta the scoundrel Caldwell."

"Do you think Dougall hired him to cheat?" Morris asked.

"I canna prove it," Tait said, taking a mighty swallow of his whisky. "Na' a thing 'is ol' grandfather'd do, an' maybe na' 'im 'ither."

"Certainly not a thing that would help Dougall's ambition to captain the R&A," said Morris.

Tait shook his gray head no. "An' so na' lik'ly 'e paid the wretched Caldwell ta cheat."

"You told me Dougall was sitting in the Bull and Bear with a young woman the night Old Alec was killed," Morris said. "Can you describe her?"

Tait considered it, closing his eyes in concentration. "As tall as 'im," he said, not opening his eyes. " 'Air doon ta 'er shoulders. I canna ken the color, brown per'aps, the same as 'er eyes. 'Alf as auld as Dougall, miybe twenty-five." And that was all he could remember. He was sure he had never seen her before, with Dougall or alone.

"Do you know if she was driving a Citroën?" Morris asked.

Captain Tait's square face did not change expression. He only shook his head that he had no idea.

Morris said, "Why hasn't Dougall donated his golf collection to the proposed British Golf Museum?"

" 'E's na' ah mon to give away wha' 'e owns," Tait said, "na' wi'out ah reward."

"Could Dougall kill a man?" Morris asked, not taking his eyes off Tait's.

"Aye. A vile temper, tha' one. But na' face-to-face. A bloody coward, 'im."

"Is he the sort of man who would steal another man's collection . . . or maybe *have him killed for it*?"

"Och. Keerful o' ye accusations, 'e's ah powerful mon ta cross."

Morris said, "And you are certain you never saw the young woman with him? The bartender said she'd been in the Bull and Bear before, but that she wasn't from St. Andrews."

"I niver saw 'er b'fore in St. Andrews," Tait said. "But 'e's ah evil mon fur the dolly birds, tha' one." Tait ran his fingers through his gray hair.

Morris believed him one second and doubted him the next, but what reason would he have to lie about the girlfriend of a man he despised? He tried once more: "Dougall's seen with this *dolly bird* in St. Andrews, his hometown, and does his wife just ignore it?"

Tait waved her away with one hand, as if out of existence. "An' wha' iss it Sullivan iss toorning up, Morris?"

"Ask me tomorrow," said Morris, as he'd said all afternoon.

"An' ye warn 'er to be keerful," said Tait, raising his glass to the absent Sullivan. When the captain's glass was empty, he left for a committee meeting at the Royal and Ancient Golf Club.

Morris sat alone, thinking back through every conversation he remembered since landing in St. Andrews. The next voice behind him was not that familiar, more English than Scottish, and yet he recognized it without turning his head.

"Why are ye askin' questions about me, Morris?" Gerald Dougall asked, as he pointed the young bartender to the near bottle of Scotch whisky.

"To learn the name of the woman you were sitting with in the Bull and Bear the night Old Alec was killed," Morris said. "I'd like to ask her what time you took her home.'' Morris could only hope the burly Scotsman wouldn't guess he'd really like to know if she drove a Citroën.

Dougall took a seat next to Morris's and pulled on his dark beard. ''A comely lass,'' he admitted. ''Her name is Diane. Up from London for the Open. I dinna ken her last name myself. She joined me at my table, but wuid'na give her name. You ken how wimmen are?''

Morris did not ask him if she also joined him at his table at the Roehampton Club outside of London. The man was lying, and *knew* that Morris *knew* he was lying, and he was enjoying it.

''Do you intend to bid against George McCormack for Old Alec's golf collection?'' Morris asked.

'' 'E's a big man among the wee punters,'' Dougall said, and laughed. Then he grew very solemn. ''Do ye mean to slander me in my oon town, Mr. Morris?'' Dougall put both palms down on the bar as an open challenge.

''To slander is to 'utter defamatory statements injurious to the reputation of a person,' '' Morris quoted as best he could remember from a dictionary definition. ''The word carries with it the added meaning of being *untrue,* or *unproven,* and therefore actionable. I do not propose to say any *untrue* thing about you, *Mr.* Dougall,'' Morris said. ''Of course, you are a goddamned liar. You know the woman's true name. And she didn't just *sit* at your table, *up from London for the Open.* Not that I give a flying damn about your pathetic women friends.''

Dougall tried his fiercest glare over his dark beard.

Morris smiled over his own glass of bitter. ''Here's to wimmenfolk,'' he said, ''and to *motorcycles.*''

''Na' a wise thing to insult our oon people,'' said Dougall again. ''Thair's a monument to all o' them as died for less.''

"I expect there's room for another seven-letter name on the goddamned monument," Morris said, "though I believe hanging is out in the Empire. A pity. By tonight I'll know if any friend of yours drives a *Citroën*." Morris could have kicked himself in his considerable ass for being provoked into the angry statement.

Dougall looked at him, perhaps in alarm or perhaps it was only anger, and threw money on the bar and left without looking back.

Morris cursed himself. The man was sure to call the woman in Edinburgh and warn her off. And he'd been careful all day not to say that Sullivan was looking for her, or for anyone, in Edinburgh, or certainly for anyone who drove a Citroën. If Edinburgh was where the Citroën was parked, the killer would be plenty nervous about it. Now he'd put the wind up Dougall, and he'd have to warn Sullivan and also tell her what little additional information he'd learned about the young woman.

Morris went to his room and told the front desk clerk that he was in and expecting a phone call. There was only one chair in the room and it was too small for comfort, so he lay down on the bed and was instantly asleep.

Morris had the telephone in his hand before realizing he'd picked it up.

"Speak to me, Morris. I know you are asleep on the other end of this line," said Sullivan.

He was instantly awake. "I've complicated your job," he said, and told her about his encounter with Gerald Dougall.

"Not to worry," said Sullivan, her voice as cool as if she were visiting Edinburgh Castle for high tea. "You didn't tell him I was *here*."

"He knows you are looking for *something* or *someone,* and probably it's the owner of a Citroën," Morris said, "and that you'll pass the word to me *tonight.* I made that very clear to him and to the other players in the game. Dougall also knows *I* am looking for his girlfriend. This boy is big enough to put two and two together and get a garrote.''

Sullivan did not respond to the warning. ''I'm calling from this wonderful old wreck of a newspaper. The society editor has adopted me. She threw out four of the twenty-five Citroën owners in minutes. Old dames living on the ill-gotten goods of their happily dead husbands. As you know, twelve of the Citroëns are registered to men. My editor knows nine of them, or knows who they are and what their wives look like, not to mention their dolly birds. I called the houses of the other three men and spoke to their wives about a phoney offer we have for a half-price oil change and lube job. Damn, I'm in the wrong business, Morris. All three of them took me up on it. I even got their *ages,* which are all wrong for our woman-friend, assuming these women are lying no more than a decade or so. That leaves *nine single women* I've got to check out. I mean to do it in person.''

''You mean to do it *carefully,*'' Morris said. He then told her what additional things he'd learned about Dougall's paramour. ''She smokes cigarettes; she was carrying a shoulder bag that night the size of France; she wears glasses to read a menu; she wears her hair down to her shoulders, and it is brown, the same as her eyes; and she has a high, rather silly laugh that is more amusing than annoying.''

''No tattoos?'' said Sullivan.

''You catch the lady, and I'll inspect her.''

''Dream on.''

''Listen, call me back by ten P.M. I don't want to wait any longer than that.''

''Remember, Morris, you promised to ring the inspector as soon as we know this young woman drives a Citroën . . . if, indeed, she does.''

"Yes." Morris was careful not to say *when* he would call him.

He hung up and looked at his watch. It was three hours until ten P.M. There was only one thing to do alone in bed; he rolled back over and went straight to sleep.

Sullivan kept the Edinburgh street atlas in her lap and the great Edinburgh Castle high over the city in view, so it was impossible to get entirely lost. Even now, in the late dusk that would soon descend into darkness, the castle was lighted and easily seen. Still, she turned up dead-end streets, and missed signs and street numbers, and misjudged distances so often that she was constantly stopping and checking her map. She was only glad that John Morris was not in the small Ford harassing her about being lost. She was down to only two women who lived in Edinburgh and owned registered Citroëns. She had driven around the Scottish National Gallery of Modern Art twice and finally recognized Belford Road and made the turn onto Douglass Palmerston and, finally, onto Chester Street, where she pulled to a stop in front of a low-rise apartment house.

She checked her watch. It was ten P.M., damn late to be making a business call, and Morris would be stalking around the hotel bedroom like a rookie golfer waiting for his tee time on the final day of the Open.

Sullivan had used the same spiel in each of her seven stops. She introduced herself as an independent representative for the Citroën Corporation doing a spot check with owners to determine their level of satisfaction with the machine. She flashed an expired press card, which none of the women bothered to examine. Five of them worshiped their cars, three saying they preferred them to any man they'd ever lived with. Two of the women had experienced nothing but trouble with their Citroëns and were delighted to unload their grievances on a captive listener. Only one of the seven women had been young, and she had been a full head shorter than Sullivan herself. Which brought her to Chester Street and the name A. B. Morrow.

Sullivan drove around to the rear of the apartment house and eased through the parking lot. She slapped her steering wheel in excitement. A dark green, almost black, Citroën of recent vintage was parked in the center of the lot.

She parked and walked to the front of the Citroën. Dusk had given way to darkness, and she was unable to see the condition of the front bumper. Running her fingers lightly over it, she felt what might have been a small dent in the very bottom edge. It was impossible to judge the damage in the dark.

The woman who answered the door, reluctantly, to the third-floor apartment was not young or tall, and was not smoking a cigarette; she was attractively middle-aged, had short, blond hair, but was, indeed, peering over a pair of black granny glasses. She looked nothing like anybody's description of Gerald Dougall's woman-friend.

Sullivan made the instant decision to drop the entire charade: "Please excuse such a late knock on your door, but it's rather an emergency. I'm Julia Sullivan. Were you recently in the Bull and Bear in St. Andrews?"

"Come inside," said the woman, as if she'd been expecting her. Her two spoken words proved she'd not grown up in Scotland. She was English to the verb. Sullivan glanced apprehensively around the rather spectacular apartment, but she did not hesitate to step inside.

Morris looked at his watch for the twentieth time. It was ten fifteen. *Why didn't she bloody call?* He was worried. He consulted the long-distance operator and got through to a subeditor of the Edinburgh daily newspaper, which by the random sounds he could hear was submerged in typical newspaper chaos. He asked for the society editor and was kept on hold before a male voice finally said the society editor had gone for the night and did he want to leave word?

He felt helpless. Nothing he could do to protect Sullivan from forty-nine miles away, except call the Edinburgh police. And what could he tell them? He had no idea. Morris decided it would be better to get on with his frail plan than to go crazy waiting in the narrow bedroom.

He pulled on a sweater and picked up his cane and left a note pinned to the door, then took the narrow stairs down. As he stepped into the sitting room–lobby of the hotel, his own telephone began ringing relentlessly in the bedroom.

Morris paused on the top step of the hotel, looking at the scattered lights on the North Sea, which flickered as if small stars had shattered into the cold water. No cars moved up The Scores and every available parking spot in front of the hotel was taken.

Morris took his time, poling his way with his cane down the steep steps and turning east, careful not to look behind him. Clouds from the sea moved over the sky, and the street itself seemed to narrow in the darkness. No lights were burning in St. James Catholic Church, but University House was lit up as if for a party. He kept to a steady pace, past United College and St. Salvator's Hall, which backed up to The Scores. On his left, tumbling down to the sea, were the old, evil walls of The Castle, dark as the Bottle Dungeon underneath them.

Morris turned onto North Castle Street and slowed to an even more deliberate pace as he came to the Preservation Trust Museum. He stopped at the narrow gate in the abbey wall around the cathedral, but did not look behind him. He pushed against the gate, which was not locked, and entered the silent cathedral grounds. The ruins of the cathedral and the thin, square Tower of St. Rule rose from the dark grounds as if reaching for the vanished light.

Morris slipped through the gate and, tapping with his cane, found his way to the wide path between the centuries-old gravestones. He kept to a slow, deliberate pace, never turning his head. The wind off the sea whispered through the tall ruins as if through the masts of a stone ship. Morris stopped at the base of the slim Tower of St. Rule. In the dark he could imagine that long-ago monk carrying the bones of St. Andrew to this *farthest outpost* of the Western world. Little could St. Regulus have imagined that this sacred ground would become a sanctuary to murder and terror.

Morris pried open the door to the tower; he knew it was unlocked and would make a sharp creak. He waited to hear if the sound drew any discernible reaction behind him, still being careful not to turn his head. Hearing nothing, he closed the tower door behind him and pulled a round penlight from his trouser pocket and shined it up the ancient stairs, which spiraled overhead into the absolute darkness. Roosting pigeons cooed on the cold wind blowing down the damp stairs, sending a shiver up Morris's neck. The tap of his cane on the steps sounded a slow, steady code into the dark. He stopped every few minutes to rest, hearing only the silence and the darkness and the soft cooing of the pigeons above him.

Killing his thin light, Morris pushed open the door to the lead roof, which offered a low stone wall and no protective railing from the dark oblivion below. Pigeons rushed out of the tower, their feathery passage startling him, as if the soul of St. Regulus itself had fled some ancient captivity.

The medieval city of St. Andrews lay below him, much of it shining in the darkness, the Old Course lying like a black lake in the heart of the town, leading down to the sea that rocked everlastingly against the faint brightness of the shore. Morris could see a sprinkling of lights as far away as the hills of Fife and Dundee.

He stood, soundlessly, watching, listening to the quiet of the graveyard below him, not seeing or hearing any moving thing. He watched in the direction of the gate to the abbey wall, but could only stare into the darkness briefly until his eyes lost all focus. He would scan the scattered lights at sea, some of them rocking gradually away, and then stare back into the darkness toward the abbey gate.

Morris shielded his light around his watch: it was now 11:20 P.M. But it seemed he had been standing there a full week of nights. The wind picked up until he wished for a heavy jacket. The deep clouds parted, and the moon shone down on the graveyard, and Morris was sure he saw a figure moving away from the abbey gate, but it disappeared into the deeper shadows. His stomach tightened in an old familiar way, and he felt a rush of blood to his head, his nerves telling him it was time to flee, but he did not move. The clouds closed again over the wide sky, and the landscape receded into complete darkness.

A *sound,* muted but *sudden,* rose up from below him, distinct from the wind whistling through the cathedral ruins. Morris, who had been listening for the door to creak open to the tower, was surprised by the unexpected *bluntness* of the sound, as if the night had *grunted* at the sky. That one *grunt,* and then only stillness. And then he thought he heard a kind of whimpering, as from a small, injured animal. And then again, stillness.

Morris turned to start down the stairs when he heard the one sharp *creak* of the tower door being opened far below him. He smiled in spite of the tremors running down his spine. He'd found the one place above the entrance to the roof that gave him the most room to swing his cane, which had been born as Monty Sullivan's two-iron. After the wreck that killed Monty and ruined his own knee, Julia Sullivan had ordered the two-iron made into a cane, so that the spirit of Monty, whom they both loved, would be always with them, but never between them.

Morris squeezed the steel head of the cane, which made a fearful bludgeon. *But not so swift as a bullet,* he thought, listening to the footfalls on the stairs that the climber made no effort to soften. *But a man must stick his head out to see where to shoot,* he reasoned.

The footsteps ceased, the last of them sounding as near as the roof under Morris's own feet. Morris did not move, or speak, or make any sound, the cane resting firmly but not tightly in both of his large hands, the steel head poised behind him as if he would make a dangerous shot to a distant green. *The sonofabitch who opens the door has a steel surprise and a long fall under him.* The thought brought an unexpected smile to his face.

The man's voice when he spoke stunned Morris as surely as if he'd been shot: "Na' ta fear, John Morris. Ah'm comin' oot."

"Nae, Captain," said Morris, the words driven like nails into the dark. He could imagine the erect Captain A.W.B. Tait standing at attention at the top of the spiral stairs. Morris did not give a goddamn what he held in his hand.

Silence gathered while the captain made his decision.

"Th' bastard Dougall's lyin' doon b'low."

"Dead?" Morris asked quietly, as if they were discussing the speed of the greens on the Old Course.

"Nae. Th' Yard's welcome to 'im as 'e lies, the murderin' divil."

"It was *you* who drove Old Alec home," said Morris, the door and the dark as natural between them as if they'd been sitting at the bar in the Bull and Bear.

"Aye. I dinna know the divils were oot ta kill 'im."

"Dougall and Caldwell?"

"Aye," the captain said.

"You drove him home in a *Citroën,*" Morris said, "belonging to Dougall's lady friend."

"Nae. Th' lass kenned nathin' o' it."

Morris smiled unseen with relief, but Sullivan would be furious at being sent on a dead-end mission to Edinburgh. "Whose Citroën did you drive?" he asked.

"The widow's, an' na' 'er doin's, 'ither, Morris. She's na ah widow, but aboot ta be divorced."

Morris understood immediately; the *widow* Agatha Burns. It had been *her* Citroën. Now he was fearful again for Sullivan, if the *grass widow* was involved in the murder. The Citroën in Edinburgh would be registered in her true name. "She never occurred to me," he said, almost to himself.

"An' 'er up frae Edinburgh, and na' London, niver knowin' any o' it," said Tait, true anguish in his voice.

"*Why?*" Morris asked, finding himself believing the anguish in Tait's voice, but never relaxing his grip on the two-iron walking stick.

"Ma Jean died 'n' broke ma 'eart and ma fortune. Dougall craved ta be captain o' the R&A. 'E lusted fur Old Alec's gowf treasure, ta' gif ta the R&A fur the 'onor o' Captain. Ol' Alec dinna like 'im. Dougall swore ta pay me well fur ma 'elp 'n convincin' Ol' Alec ta sell. Ah made ma pack wi' the divil. Ol' Alec luffed me, an' it kilt 'im."

"You drove him home, and *Dougall* and *Peter Caldwell* were waiting, and he let them in because he *trusted you,* and they killed him in the barn, when he wouldn't agree to sell," Morris said.

"Aye. An' I 'ad nae idea, answerin' the call o' ma kidneys innis hoose. Ol' Alec ask'd only a fair market price. An' 'e knew the value—but na' o' the Turner paintin'."

"The Turner *sketch,*" Morris said.

"Nae. The *paintin'* o' the sketch. Dougall saw it pack'd aw'y an' 'e toorned killin' crazy. Caldwell 'elped 'im, an' Ol' Alec drunk. Dougall dinna let the paintin' oot o' 'is 'ands an' 'e 'as it 'idden innis hoose. But 'is next hoose wi' 'ave bars till 'e dies, an' 'e won't be walkin' thair. 'E 'eld it all ower ma 'ead ta ma oon grave, so' as ta steal tha' paintin' if 'e couldna' be captain o' the R&A."

Morris knew a Turner landscape of the Old Course would be worth millions, enough to push Gerald Dougall from greed to murder. How could he have missed it in the MacLaines' journal?

"You knew Old Alec killed the bastard Vinson," said Morris. "And you knew he had a garrote from the war, the same as you. And you knew where he kept it. You put the bloody garrote in Dougall's hands as *evidence,* to make Old Alec sell his collection. *You'd been in his house and barn since you were a boy,* the same as your father before you."

"Aye." The word in the dark might have been the last confession at the Cathedral of St. Andrews. "Ol' Alec tol' us ta go ta 'ell 'an ta the police, too, an' they kilt 'im innis barn."

Morris could have kicked himself for his ignorance. He'd always believed Old Alec trusted *someone* if not the killer himself, but which of the old friends and suspects had access to a Citroën? He'd never thought of the *grass widow* Burns, who was in fact about to be divorced and the car registered under her real name; God help Sullivan, if she were truly involved in the murder. But, oddly, he believed Tait that Agatha Burns knew nothing of the killing; Scotland Yard would find out soon enough.

Morris said, "I'm to believe that Dougall found a Turner *painting* worth *millions* and went *crazy on the spot.* And Caldwell helped him garrote the old man, drunk in his own barn, while you pissed your life and reputation away in the house? That's your goddamn story? Why didn't you go straight to the police?"

"An' explain 'ow ah was *thair* an' Ol' Alec *deid* and 'im like a brither to me? Wha' could ah say?" But there was little conviction in his voice.

"So *you* waited for Peter Caldwell, fearing he was turning himself in to the police, and *you* ran him down on the road to Dundee," said Morris.

"Aye!" And now it was a *boast* and not a confession.

Morris tightened his grip on the steel-headed stick. "And now Dougall lies down there in the graveyard. Not dead, you say? And John Morris *is not going to be dead beside him at the foot of the tower* and you're not planning to leave *and let Scotland Yard puzzle it all out?"*

From behind the door, in the dark, came only silence.

Julia Sullivan burned rubber over the bridge across the Firth of Forth, never lifting her foot from the accelerator until she left the four-lane highway for the winding, two-lane road to St. Andrews. Even then she banked the light Ford through the turns as if she were at the controls of her Learjet, switching off her headlights to be sure no car was coming as she took the curves from inside out. She made the city limits of the medieval town in what must have been a new nighttime land record for the forty-nine miles. She left the Ford double-parked and its engine running as she fled up the stairs to their room. There was the note stabbed to their door with John Morris's penknife and written in John Morris's hand: *Call the inspector to the Tower of St. Rule if I'm not back. P.S. I lied.*

If John Morris was not dead, she would kill him on the spot.

"D'ye na trust me, Morris?" came the voice of Captain Tait.

"I trust you to die like any natural man if you step through that door," Morris said.

"Tha' iss ma intention," said Tait softly.

Morris could imagine him holding his shoulders abruptly straight, as he must have in the plane waiting to jump over Normandy . . . *to kill Germans.* "Put your hands through the door one at time, slowly," Morris said.

It was strange to touch the naked warmth of Tait's strong hands, as if the two of them were practicing some secret ritual handshake. Morris then felt into Tait's jacket pockets and patted his chest and waist and felt no bulky weapon.

Now Tait stepped out onto the small, square lead roof like a stout shadow in the darkness, but a half-head shorter than Morris.

"What have you done with Dougall?" Morris asked.

"Broke 'is back wi' ma bare 'ands," Tait said. He listened in the dark. "I canna 'ear 'im, but 'e's alive. 'E was comin' ta kill ye an' maeself, Morris, an na' wi' 'is bare 'ands."

"He followed you here, following me?"

"Aye."

Every way the captain turned had sucked him deeper to his fate, Morris thought. He wondered who would have killed whom if Gerald Balfour-Melville Dougall had stepped onto the tower roof. *And maybe Tait means to try his bare hands on me,* thought Morris. *Well, it's a free Scotland, let him try.* For a second Morris even hoped that he would.

"Inspector Emerson will be here shortly," said Morris, and hoped that it was true. If Sullivan had found Captain Tait's innocent grass widow and learned of her Citroën, it would not have taken her long to push the Ford to St. Andrews.

"John Morris, wi' ye leef me 'ere ta die alone like a true Scotsman?"

Morris did not have to think, and chose not to answer. He switched on his penlight and found his way down the tower stairs, tapping his cane like a code on every step. Morris heard no scream, no body strike the earth through the thick stone walls. The only sound, other than the tapping of his cane, was the *crack* of the tower door when he pushed it open.

Morris stepped outside and began a wide circle of the tower. His narrow light quickly found the thick puddle of clothes that had once been a man.

Morris made his way up the wide path toward the abbey gate. His small light danced in the great darkness, settling on another pile of clothes that seemed half alive. Gerald Dougall's hands clawed at the ground, his mouth quivering but releasing only a low whine from his parched throat, his legs sprawled lifeless below him, a handgun shining on the path beyond his reach.

A car door slammed in the night outside the abbey wall.

"John Morris!" Julia Sullivan might have been rounding up a reluctant sheep dog. She saw the thin light waving like a semaphore and began running up the path between the gravestones. Now other car doors were slamming in the dark outside the abbey wall.

Inspector Emerson sat on the hotel steps like a tall, thin, aged boy come to St. Andrews to see his first Open. Sullivan huddled against Morris as the wind blew the clouds to pieces and the sun rose over the North Sea.

"Please don't kill this man in Scotland, Sullivan," the inspector said. "I've had all the holiday I can bear."

"No, I'll drop him out over the Atlantic on the way home," she said. "Now that you've seen the Turner painting, Inspector, what do you think it's worth?" she asked.

Emerson, who had stopped by the hotel as he had promised he would do, said, "It's priceless, a classic Turner with a sky over the Old Course—what do the art critics say of Turner's work—like *tinted steam*?"

"However did Old Alec's grandfather come to have it?" wondered Sullivan.

Emerson said, "In the family journal it's simply listed 'Sketch, p by Turner.' We all missed the lowercase *p*."

"Too bad that it didn't stay lost for another century," said Morris.

"I would be surprised if Old Alec ever saw it," said the inspector. "The paintings and portraits in the old wooden boxes seemed not to have been disturbed in this century—before Dougall opened the boxes up. Well, the museums and the collectors will be fighting over the Turner."

"Then I will stop worrying about the education of Sharon Kirkcaldy," Sullivan said.

The inspector, his voice all accusation, said, "Morris, you meant to lure the killer after you."

"I hoped to spook him with the idea of a found Citroën," Morris admitted. "I never dreamed Captain Tait's *widow* was the owner of the car."

"Agatha Burns *Morrow* knew nothing about the motorcycle crash," said Sullivan. "Of course, that night the captain had borrowed her Citroën. The poor woman is ill. She leaves an unfaithful husband to find out her lover is very likely a murderer. She gave you her maiden name, Inspector. Her divorce isn't final." Sullivan buried her head in Morris's sweater. "I was terrified, John

Morris . . . that you didn't know you were dealing with at least *two murderers.*"

"I had no idea," admitted Morris, "but I never doubted you would get back from Edinburgh with the true scamp."

That got him a major league smile.

"And if Dougall had come up the tower stairs with his pistol?" said the inspector.

"Close quarters up there," Morris said. "Not so easy to open the door onto the roof with a gun in one hand. I went up in the daylight to be sure . . . and to be sure the door to the tower would be unlocked."

"Yes, locks that are smashed rarely work," said Emerson, looking out to sea.

"True," Morris said innocently.

"You expected Dougall to come," Sullivan said, "or did you expect someone else?"

"I wasn't sure," Morris said. "I always thought Old Alec would have only allowed someone he trusted into his house that late at night; he would never have let anyone he didn't trust into his barn anytime. There was no sign of a forced entry to the house, and all of the death struggle was in the barn. But *who* did he trust, drunk as he was? *Who* gave him a ride home, very likely in a Citroën? And *who* killed him with his own garrote? And *who* killed Peter Caldwell, very likely in the same Citroën? It could have been any of our friends and suspects."

Morris tapped the steps with his cane. "Dougall came to the cathedral grounds because he knew if we found the Citroën, we would ultimately suspect Tait, and if we suspected Tait, we would suspect *him.* I believe he followed Tait and not me to the graveyard and meant to kill *him* and not *me.* But he should have checked on Captain A.W.B. Tait's war record on the night of the Normandy invasion before he followed him alone into a darkened graveyard.''

''Will Dougall live?'' asked Sullivan.

''It's touch and go,'' the inspector said. ''He's paralyzed, of course, and has developed a dangerous pneumonia.''

''With luck, he'll die,'' Morris said. ''One thing is certain, he will never be voted captain of the Royal and Ancient Golf Club.''

''No,'' Inspector Emerson agreed. ''I owe you two a drink . . . a career of drinks. Come seven years, Morris, will you and Sullivan be back at the Old Course for the Open?''

''Oh, yes,'' Sullivan answered for them both. ''But we won't be drinking at the Bull and Bear.''

• EPILOGUE •

Julia Sullivan walked past Martyrs' Monument to the intersection of Golf Place and Golf Links. The high, temporary bleachers obscured the 18th green in the heart of St. Andrews. She passed Old Tom Morris's Golf Shop, busy since the middle of the nineteenth century. She spotted John Morris, just off the 18th fairway, the size of two Scotsmen, leaning back on his portable seat, one leg resting on the low, white rail that defined the Old Course.

She stopped to see the great Jack Nicklaus walking to his practice drive, which had carried the Valley of Sin up onto the 18th green. Nicklaus waved to Morris and shouted some irreverence.

Sullivan caught her breath, imagining that the last seven years had never happened, and they were back at St. Andrews in 1978, and the British Open of that year had yet to be played, and Barry Vinson had yet to be murdered. She found herself so dizzy with déjà vu that she unfolded the *Times* she was carrying to be certain it was the Year of Our Lord, 1984.

Sullivan leaned down and kissed John Morris full on the lips.

"Och!" he said in his imitation Scottish accent.

"Enough!" Sullivan said, as though to the lesser gods. "I want to forget 1978."

"How did your new Gulfstream fly?" Morris asked obligingly.

"It flew so like the gods, I was afraid they'd swoop it up into the heavens."

"Disappointing, huh?"

"Have you missed me?" she asked.

"God, yes," Morris said. "None of us could sleep. Only thing to do was keep each other up—"

"All night at the Bull and Bear pub," she said.

"Where else?"

"Who have you seen?" Sullivan asked.

"Only everybody."

"Just them? Too bad."

"Morris, is this woman violating your right to privacy?"

Morris did not get up, but waved Julia Sullivan into the long, thin arms of the *Times'* own man, Tom Rowe, his longish hair gone quite gray. There was a silver sheen to Sullivan's own brown hair, which shone in the full sun of St. Andrews.

"Do we talk about 1978?" Rowe asked.

Sullivan lifted her wristwatch. "Five minutes, team. And that's it!"

"Did I see Sir Arthur Maxwell last night at a distance?" Morris asked.

"Oh, the distance of about nine lagers, Morris," said Rowe. "He's back on top of the fashion world, of course. Sold his business to a Yank entrepreneur but still runs it like the best-dressed Hound of Hell."

"Did you tell Tom that Warren Lightfoot was killed?" Sullivan asked.

"My God, when?" Rowe asked.

"Two weeks ago. In the vintage green Jaguar he gave to his wife," Morris said. "Slid into the abutment of a bridge. He was the lone passenger."

"So much for indulging a rich wife," said Rowe, then apologized. "I can't believe I said that."

"Yes, you and not John Morris," Sullivan said.

"George McCormack is waiting for you, Sullivan," Morris warned. "He wants a large piece of your worldly goods."

"I'll own that betting shop after this Open," said Sullivan, patting her purse. "No need to play the *toornament,* Morris. I've got the winner right here."

"Tell me and I can go home to London," Rowe said.

"Oh, no," said Morris. "You've got to write and drink and hurt like all the good journalists before you."

"What happened to the grass widow Agatha Burns, who fancied Captain Tait?" Sullivan asked.

"She divorced and married a rich widower in London," Rowe said. "I see her from time to time. She never speaks. And the Royal and Ancient has taken down Captain Tait's photograph. It's as if he never lived."

"There was a time he lived that the world will remember," Morris said. "No one will be forgetting the invasion of Normandy, when A.W.B. Tait was a brave man among brave men."

"And Gerald Dougall?" Sullivan asked.

"Died in prison. Two years ago. Pneumonia," Rowe said. "I understand his ex-wife—she divorced him after the trial—never went to see him once. She sold his golf artifacts to a rich American. Dougall's name is never spoken at the R&A. I forgot to tell you, Morris, Peter Caldwell's half brother still mows the greens at Carnoustie, but Old Tom Micklem died."

"I know he did," Morris said. "I had a small package in the mail. The old man left me the diary he kept as a lifetime member of Carnoustie. I'm giving it to the British Golf Museum. Tonight we'll drink to Old Tom Micklem and to Scotland."

"Agreed. At the moment I've got to write some improbable prose," said Rowe, and headed to catch Nicklaus in the press tent.

Sullivan sat on the white rail, happy to feel the sun on her face. A tiny hand moved along the low rail, the voice of a mother urging it along, and then a cyclone of red curls followed the hand. Sullivan looked up into the eyes of Sharon Kirkcaldy Mason and behind her, Georgia Tech himself, Paul Mason, still as skinny as in his days as a caddy.

Hugs and congratulations flew all around and in a very short time the mop of red curls rested in the ample lap of John Morris.

Sharon Kirkcaldy caught them up on her life. It seemed the Scottish National Gallery of Edinburgh had bought the Turner painting . . . for one-third the price offered the two daughters and granddaughter by a German collector. Old Alec MacLaine's golf artifacts now made up the heart of the new British Golf Museum at *fair market value.*

"Old Alec would be proud to see where it all rests," Sullivan said.

There was a long silence after she spoke the name Old Alec, and it was not a sad one.

The Masons lived in Atlanta and Scotland, his family's business carrying him all over Europe.

"Well, how can I marry this young woman on my lap," Morris said, "if I don't know her name?"

"Let me introduce you," Sharon said. "John Morris, Julia Sullivan, meet *Julia* MacLaine Mason."

"God help the brave men among the Scots," said Morris.